a lost souls novel

reators

Book 3

Entangled Publishing, LLC
2614 South Timberline Road
Suite 109
Fort Collins, CO 80525
Visit our website at www.entangledpublishing.com.

Edited by Stacy Abrams
Cover design by Pamela Sinclair

ISBN   978-1-50056-110-9

Manufactured in the United States of America

First Edition April 2014

To GiGi: May you always fight and rage when it is needed.

It was time to fight.

    It was time to rage.

    For the girl who lived inside of me.

Chapter 1

"Tessie? Are you hurt?"

My throat went dry as I tried to swallow the hard, knotty lump that had formed. I didn't know how to answer his question. It should have been a simple yes or no. But I couldn't speak; I could barely breathe. It wasn't the question that was impossible to answer—it was the man asking it.

My father.

He was alive.

For years and years, I'd thought the man who stood before me was dead. Taken from me by the council, an organization of men who had long ago replaced the government lost to civil war. My father had been considered a traitor, so one day chosen ones, genetically engineered superhumans who made up the council's army, came and ripped my father from my grasp. There was only one certainty about this life— all traitors, all men or women, who attempted to stand up against the all-mighty council, would die.

Or at least that's what I had thought.

I opened my mouth. Attempted to swallow again. I needed to speak. So many things to say, so many questions to ask. But all I could do was nod. My father gingerly reached for me, and I froze. I was afraid that if I touched him, my hand would go straight through, that he would be nothing but a ghost. But when my father lifted the bottom of my shirt, revealing the stab wound I'd received only a day before, he didn't disappear.

Instead, he paled. His eyes narrowed and his head gave the smallest of shakes. But he didn't disappear. He reached down and pulled something from a satchel he wore near his waist.

"I'm sorry it went down this way. I sent her to stop you. I knew I wouldn't make it in time, and I didn't want you meeting that creature without me. An army can't move as fast as a single woman—even a small army. She was one of my fastest," he explained, pouring liquid out of a bottle onto a cloth. "I thought you would see her disheveled and fragile state and take pity on her. I wanted her to slow you down. I never told her to stab you."

An army? My father had an army. And he had sent the girl to stop me? A dull heaviness overtook my head. Foggy. Disorienting. I just wanted to sit there and listen to him, to his every word. Every breath between us made it more and more certain that the man standing before me was very much alive. He pressed a wet cloth against my wound, and the fog disappeared instantly. I bit the inside of my cheek to keep from crying out. The liquid stung, shooting electricity up and down my abdomen.

My father smiled thinly. "Sorry, Tessie, I probably should have warned you that would hurt like hell. It's important to keep wounds clean. Especially in these conditions."

In these conditions. The reality overtook the dream I had nearly lost myself in. We were in the woods controlled by the Isolationists, the Middlelands—home to the men and women who sought refuge from the council of the West and government in the East. These men searched out freedom in the harsh and unforgiving territories, but it came at a price. Conditions were rough and as the new war between the east and west surged closer and closer, their home was the new battleground.

The naturals, those not created in a lab, had no part in this new war. It was fought between the council of the east and west; these governments no longer needed us when they could make a whole race of humans to follow their every command. Now, these councils would fight to see who would conquer this new world of artificial life.

The naturals had two choices: sit back and die, or fight for whatever freedom they could grasp.

My father had chosen the fighting side.

"How?"

He widened his eyes slightly. How could he not? It had been years since he had seen me as well. How strange it must have been to leave a child and find a woman in her place. I cleared my throat. "How are you here?"

The side of my father's mouth pulled up. "That's a mighty long story."

Despite the pain in my side and the way my heart pounded in disbelief that he was standing before me, I smiled. "I always liked your stories."

His eyes shifted from mine to the ground. Whatever emotion swept across them, he hid it from me. Hesitantly a hand reached up and touched my cheek. "And I promise to tell it to you one day, but these woods aren't safe, and we must be on the move."

He pulled his hand from my cheek, and I instantly wanted to clutch onto it. He was real. He was alive, and, somehow, that made everything seem all right, even if the feeling was only temporary. It dulled the pain of once again losing James, the chosen one I had fallen in love with. It quieted the fears of knowing I had no home to return to, after being banished from the Isolationists' camp. It alleviated the nauseous feeling that threatened to consume me when I thought of what fate awaited Louisa, my little sister, who now sat pregnant in a world where pregnant women had little chance of surviving.

Women. My sister could barely call herself a part of the group the council blamed for most of the world's problems. Barely fifteen, yet in some ways she had seen and felt more of what it meant to be a woman than I had at eighteen.

My father would fix it. As he had always done during my childhood.

As he began to walk away from me, he stopped and held out his hand. "Come, Tessie. It isn't safe here."

Hand and hand, we trekked to where the others waited. A rag-tag team of outcasts and survivors, and sitting amongst them, her knees cradled to her chest as she leaned against a tree, was my doomed sister. Seeing her, my father's grip tightened painfully around my fingers.

And then his hand was gone. With no words of affection or encouragement, he walked ahead of us, and I knew we were supposed to follow.

"Are you taking us to the resistance?" I called out to him as I helped my sister to her feet.

"I am the resistance," he replied without looking back.

Chapter 2

"You're out of your damn mind!" Eric screamed at my father.

I clutched onto Louisa's hand, loosening my grip when she whimpered in pain. I hadn't realized I had been holding onto her so tightly. We sat on the ground, leaning against a tree deep in the forest that was becoming a larger part of my life as time went on—uncivilized, unsafe, unpredictable. I reached up a hand, tucking Louisa's bright blond hair behind her ear. She refused to meet my eyes, only sat silently next to me, her arms wrapped protectively around her swollen abdomen.

I tried to keep from staring down at it. I was definitely no expert on babies, but I guessed she was about four months along. There was no mistaking that she was carrying a child. Her thin, frail, sickly frame announced it to the world, almost defiantly.

"We need to move out, and we need to move out now,"

my father replied sternly, ignoring Eric's protest.

"Are you okay?" a voice asked softly. I turned my head from the brewing confrontation in front of me to find Henry crouching down to my right.

All I could do was nod. I didn't know if I was okay. I didn't know if anything was okay. Every time I seemed to get a grip on the world, it moved and changed beneath my hands, becoming a place I had no hope of navigating. Only moments before I had gotten my father back. The same man who taught me the beauty of music and the endless opportunities hope offered, but this man wasn't him. It was as if the moment he saw Louisa, truly saw her, that man disappeared.

Nothing ever stayed. Nothing was permanent.

I looked over the crowd surrounding me—a collection of my past and present. My father and sister were relics of a family nearly destroyed by the council's brutality. Henry, my best friend, a symbol of my life in the compound. Lockwood and Eric, men from my life in the Isolationists' camp, men who sought freedom at any cost. Now, we were all together in the woods. Worlds colliding with unknown consequences.

Eric marched up to my father, pushing right into his face. "I don't know you, which means I don't answer to you. So, excuse me if I don't give a crap about what you have to say. I'm not going anywhere until we bury him."

History had a strange way of repeating itself. After I went on the run from the council, McNair and Eric had escorted me, Henry, and Robert through these very woods. Early in our journey, I had argued with McNair, begging him to help us go back and rescue my sister, but he always refused. He only worried about safely delivering me to his people. I was special, and it was his duty to make sure I made it back to the Isolationist community. I could do what the other women couldn't — the thing I prayed my little sister could do, too. If I chose to, I'd give birth without dying. Whatever affliction affected the women didn't affect me.

Eric didn't wait for my father to respond. Throwing his hands in the air, he stalked over to where McNair's body lay. He crumpled to his knees next to his fallen leader and began to dig with his hands.

I got Eric's need to bury his friend, but even I could partially understand my father's hesitation at staying put. We needed to move. We had already spent too much time standing in the woods, discussing our next move, less than a mile away from where I had lost James, the boy I loved. But all the warnings in the world wouldn't matter in the end. Eric didn't have any loved ones waiting for him back in the community. The closest thing he had to family was now dead, his neck effortlessly snapped by George.

George was a chosen one I had met during my days of servitude at the council's compound, Templeton. But he was nothing like the chosen one I loved. He thrived on torturing the naturals he thought were below him, and he had lured me into the woods to save my sister.

George wanted to make a trade. James for the sister he'd defiled. When James came after me, seeing my illness in one of his visions, George figured out his gift. He realized he could use James, return James to the council, and get back in with the people who created him. He had been almost excommunicated by the council, sentenced to stand guard over naturals in a compound. But now that he had James, now that he discovered James's own gift, he could gain what he had always thought was his right—power.

George. The boy who whispered in my ear that I would help him bring down the council.

Looking at Eric, the despair I felt in the deepest, darkest parts of my soul echoed in his eyes, and I knew I had to help him. Crazy or not, I simply had to.

I took a deep, shaky breath and looked for Robert. Meeting my eye, he nodded, answering my unspoken question. He moved so he was sitting on the other side of Louisa. Robert understood this was something I needed to do, that maybe I needed to bury McNair just as much as Eric did. And if I was going to step away from Louisa, I wanted the strongest person in our group next to her.

I pried my hand from Louisa's and pulled myself to my feet using the tree for support, suppressing the groan that wanted to escape my lips. My side still smarted.

"Don't even think about it," my father commanded.

I slowly dragged my eyes from the scene of Eric furiously clawing at the ground beneath him to find my father staring me down. His eyes carried a depth, an anger, an authority that was never present during my childhood. I staggered back. The transformation of the man I called father, the quick change from the affectionate man he had shown me earlier, left me dizzy.

I swallowed. I had never stood up to him before. At least not in any important way. I had never had the chance. The council had seen to that.

I took a deep breath. This was the same man who'd checked my wound and touched my cheek. I didn't need to fear him. "It's the right thing to do. I owe him that," I said, my voice strong. Firm.

"Don't be ridiculous. There's no point in this. We need to go back to the community," he answered. Just like that, I was dismissed.

"The community?" Lockwood scoffed. Scoffing was second nature to the boy who had first befriended me in the community. Somewhere between teaching me how to milk a cow and teasing me nonstop, he'd become one of the people I trusted most in the world, and I was eternally grateful to have him at my side. "They won't let us back in," he continued. "We left. We defied Al. So we won't be welcomed back by anyone there. Not when our leaving could have led the council back to them. Not when our leaving got McNair killed." Lockwood had been unusually quiet since the encounter with George. He mostly just stood silently, watching over my sister, a girl he didn't even know.

"Lockwood's right," I said. "We all left knowing we wouldn't be able to return. So, unless you have some safe haven we can travel to, we need to come up with a new plan. And that means we have time to bury McNair," I explained, hoping to make my father see some sense. He had always been a reasonable man.

"I agree with Tess. There's no point wandering around aimlessly," my childhood friend Henry argued. "Not with Tess wounded and Louisa…" His voice trailed off.

I swallowed the bile that wanted to crawl up my throat at the thought of what my sister was facing. I had watched our older sister, Emma, die during childbirth. I wouldn't be able to do it again.

I still hadn't discovered the truth behind why so many of our women died while bringing life into the world; all I knew was that it kept happening, plaguing our species with little rhyme or reason. A sickness that appeared to have no hope for a cure. A sickness I was, somehow, immune to.

I turned my back on my father and made my way toward Eric, where I knelt down and began to help him dig. I kept my eyes focused on the earth, the many layers that would cover the body before me. It would hide another death I was responsible for. If McNair had just stayed in the community, refused to help me on my quest to save Louisa, he wouldn't have died. I closed my eyes and took a deep breath.

There would be time to mourn, but it wasn't today. I needed to help Eric. He had been there when I needed him, and he was my friend. I didn't have many of those. As I lifted my head to look at the people who surrounded me — Henry, Lockwood, Robert, and Eric — I knew I would do anything for them.

Months ago, I never would have imagined that Eric was capable of feeling anything close to devastation, but back then I had been so narrow-minded. I wanted to hate the world and everyone in it. I didn't see his thirst for vengeance against the deformed chosen one for what it really was — debilitating sadness.

The kind of sadness that made you or broke you.

I looked over at the man who had once shared a toast with me, a toast to our dead mothers. His face was beyond pale and his eyes watered. His jaw was set. He wasn't going anywhere till he buried his friend, and so I wasn't, either.

Strength meant doing what was right even when what was right felt foolish.

Henry, who was on his knees across from me, reached forward and lifted my chin. Our eyes echoed each other's sadness. We were all connected, everyone who shared the woods with me, by loss.

I opened my mouth to speak when I was suddenly yanked off the ground by my arms. I spun around, coming face-to-face with my father.

"Enough," he gritted out. "You will stop this second. We will go back to the community. I know Al. He's a weak man who stands behind a gun and calls it power. Trust me when I tell you this—they'll let us in. Now. Let's. Go."

My mouth fell open, and despite how hard I tried, I couldn't stop the tremble that ran through me.

"Take your hands off her," Henry snarled, next to me in only a matter of seconds.

"I suggest you mind your business. This is a family matter," replied my father, dragging me toward my sister. Louisa's hands moved to her ears and she began to cry.

"Family?" Henry yelled after him. "Last time I checked, you've been dead. Usually dead means, you know, not walking around and attempting to manipulate your daughters through fear and ridiculous displays of testosterone. Now, if she wants to stay here and bury her friend, that's what she'll do."

"Maybe we should all just calm down and talk about this," Lockwood suggested. "Take a deep breath. Everyone is an adult here." He shot a worried glance toward my sister, who had seemed to curl in on herself, an attempt to protect herself from the only people she had left.

I twisted out of my father's grasp. "He's right. We all need to settle down and talk about our next move. Sitting here and yelling—"

I didn't get to finish my sentence. Eric charged at my father, knocking me to the ground in the process. My side stung, sending pain up and down my body with the blood that flowed in my veins. There wasn't a part of me the pain didn't touch. I gasped, a layer of sweat covering my forehead. When Henry helped me to my knees, I watched as my father pulled Eric off him. He lay panting on his back as my father got up on his feet.

"I understand you lost someone, boy, and that comes with a pain that can make you crazy, hateful. But if you touch me again, I promise it will be the last thing you do," he warned, towering over a fuming Eric.

My father had always protected our family, and I knew he carried a strength in him that I had never wanted to see tested, but the man before me, once caring and loving, now seemed so cold and distant.

Seeing the look on my face, his shoulders slumped. "He attacked me," he said. He had never seemed so tired or so old as he did in that moment.

"I know. He's in pain. He's really a good—"

The slump of his shoulders vanished as he pulled his back straight, stalking over to me. He took my chin in his hand. "In case you haven't noticed, everyone's in pain," he replied, speaking to me just like he did in the days of our piano lessons—soft but authoritative. Strong but understanding. "That doesn't mean they stop. They won't ever stop. The council will keep coming and coming until they kill every last one of us," he continued, raising his voice so *every last one of us* could hear. "So, we move. We keep going. We don't stop and bury the dead because soon there'll be too many dead to bury. The war isn't coming, Tess, it's here. And there's no time to waste. No place to hide. We fight or we die."

Chapter 3

"You have to sleep sometime, Tess."

I looked over at Louisa. She slept so peacefully on the ground next to me that I could almost pretend her life wasn't ruined. If I covered her with enough blankets, I could even hide the fact that she was carrying a baby that would most likely kill her. She was too young to have gone in for inspection, so there was no way of knowing if she was like Emma or me. "I could but I won't," I whispered to Lockwood.

"I'll watch after her," he replied, plopping down on the ground next to me.

"You will, huh?" I asked, raising an eyebrow. We had been walking for two days, mostly silently. Our group was trudging back to the community I prayed would let us in. When Henry had dared to ask my father if we could return to whatever makeshift, backwoods camp he came from, he dismissed the idea with a grunt, continuing to stalk through the woods. Without the community, we had no home. No place to go. And looking at Louisa, it had become clear that we needed a home desperately.

"Not... I didn't mean like that. I just m-meant." Lockwood began to stammer, his skin flushing from his cheeks all the way down his neck. He had hovered over Louisa protectively during our trek, offering his arm to help her when the terrain got to be too rough. She never took it, but he never stopped offering, either.

I nudged Lockwood's shoulder with mine. "I know what you meant. Calm down. Though I have to admit, it's nice getting the advantage in our little war of wits. Especially now that I know you have a weakness for blondes," I teased, surprised that I could even joke at all. It wasn't that I didn't understand everything that happened only days before; it was just that I couldn't focus on it. Not yet. I had to get Louisa to safety first. That was all that mattered, all my little heart could handle.

Because if I thought of the other things...

I would become her again—the girl I fought so hard to bury inside me.

Lockwood opened his mouth to protest, but I cut him off. "I appreciate the offer. I just can't. I know I should sleep, but not yet."

"I understand," he said quietly. We sat like that, both lost in our own thoughts, staring up at the night stars through the canopy of trees. Insignificant in the grand scheme of things. The war would rage but the stars would always remain. At least until mankind brought the whole world down with them.

"What a fine mess we've gotten ourselves into," he finally said.

"You mean what a fine mess I've gotten everyone into," I amended, ripping at the grass that poked up between my fingers.

"Enough," Lockwood said. "You didn't make the world like this, and you didn't put a gun to anyone's head to bring them to these woods. I'm here because I wanted to be. Same with McNair. He came because he felt like it was the right thing to do. And your father was right. About fighting. It's time to fight," he finished, his voice carrying a passion I had never heard from him before. His eyes moved to my sleeping sister, and I understood.

Lockwood always had liked a lost cause.

• • •

"I have to go to the bathroom," Louisa whispered in my ear. The first words she had said to me since the exchange with George. She shifted and squirmed on her feet, darting her eyes among the men who walked on all sides of us.

"We need to take a break," I called out to my father, who was ahead of us, lifting my hand to block the sun that seemed to announce to the world where we were. Even in the woods with my father, I was starting to feel vulnerable. He had been right. This place wasn't safe. I felt it in my gut.

"No. Not now. We keep moving," he answered, refusing to even break his stride long enough to look back.

A small noise escaped Louisa's lips. I stopped and looked back to see her mouth pulled tight. "I wasn't asking for permission. I was telling you we need to stop. It'll only take a few minutes."

My father stopped dead in his tracks. I braced for his

anger as he slowly turned around to face me. But as his eyes moved from me to my sister, I saw the slight slump of his shoulders once more. "Make it quick," he muttered, turning his back on us. He couldn't keep his eyes on Louisa long.

"Come on," I told her, pulling her gently by the hand away from the group.

"Want me to come with you?" Henry asked, keeping pace with me as we moved deeper into the woods.

"We'll be fine. We only need a few minutes. Girl stuff," I said.

Henry put his hands in the air and slowly backed away. "That's all you needed to say."

Once we were safely away from the group, I turned around so my sister could have some privacy. My little sister. There were many things I needed to ask her. How far along was she? How did she feel? And then the darker questions, the questions that might cause me to kill a man—the questions that would turn me into Henry.

Was she forced?

"I'm done. We can go back now," Louisa said quietly. It wasn't the tone I was used to hearing from her mouth. We had spent the greater part of our lives fighting with each other, jockeying for the attention of our sister who was more a mother to us than the woman who gave birth to us. While I'd tried rescuing her from Templeton, the fact remained that I had abandoned her. There were many discussions we needed to have, but any tension that existed between us seemed temporarily gone. I turned around and reached again for her. She didn't hesitate in placing her small hand into mine.

I knew she didn't do it from affection; she was frightened out of her wits. She trembled when someone stepped on a branch or when the wind rustled through the trees.

Gone was her sauciness. Her fiery nature. She was a girl destroyed.

Almost.

I hoped I still had time to save her.

"Come on, they're waiting for us," I said, tugging on her hand.

Two steps…and all hell broke loose.

Two shots blasted into the air from a gun. Before I could reach my hand to cover her mouth, Louisa screamed. It ripped from her as if it carried her very soul with it. I jerked my sister around by the hand and ran, pulling her along with me. I pushed my legs as fast as they would go, but she flailed and stumbled behind me.

I yanked harder against her. I didn't know where we were running to; I just knew it was time to run. These woods had already taught me that. The leaves behind us crumpled and called out to us, alerting us that someone, or something, was close behind.

Louisa begged for me to stop, but I shut out her pleas. If we stopped, we would die. She hadn't lived inside the woods, hadn't been outside of council protection, so she didn't know what was possible.

An image blurred past me on the left as a man bolted ahead of us, placing himself directly in my path. I attempted to skid to a stop before running right into him. Falling forward with my sister in tow, I collided with him, and the man caught me in his arms before Louisa and I fell to the ground. Every muscle in my body tensed, ready to battle for my sister. When I managed to look up, I came face-to-face with Robert.

"What is it? I heard shots," I panted, my legs trembling so hard that my entire body shook.

Robert cupped my face with his hands. "It was your father. He shot into the air. Everything's okay. You're safe."

I sucked in air through my nose, gulping it down, forcing it in. "What do you mean it was my father? Why would he do that? Is he crazy?"

Before Robert could answer, Louisa slumped to the floor. She was no longer screaming or crying—she just sat on the ground staring forward, her eyes wide. Her chest heaved up and down rapidly as she rocked back and forth.

I crouched down so my eyes were level with hers. "Shhh, Robert said we're safe. Breathe. Just breathe." I tucked a hair behind her ear.

But she didn't reply. Didn't blink. Her shaking hands moved to her stomach, and she rocked with greater force. Her head began to rock slowly back and forth, and her lips moved, whispering something furiously over and over. I leaned closer so I could hear what she was saying. "I believe in the council. The council will protect me. Protect me from my enemies. Protect me from myself."

The words my mother had taught her years ago.

Louisa was still a believer.

"What the hell was he thinking?" I growled, looking up at Robert.

"I think it's better if you see it," he replied. He reached down and scooped his sister-in-law into his arms.

As I followed behind Robert, Louisa wrapped her arms around his neck and buried her head against his shoulder.

"You both okay?" Henry asked, jogging toward us.

"No, we are—"

"Everyone and everything is just fine," Robert cut me off. He looked back at me, warning that now was not the time. He then proceeded to move a little quicker, creating space between Henry and my sister and me.

As soon as Louisa was out of earshot, I turned to Henry. "No, we are not okay. What was he thinking? Did he feel like he needed to remind us who was in charge? He nearly scared Louisa to death."

Henry shook his head and clenched his jaw. "He did it to call them."

"Call who?" I asked, looking at his face, seeing it pulled tight with worry.

"Them. His people." Henry pointed ahead of me.

I followed his finger to find a ragtag group assembled behind my father. They were dressed in clothes not much better than those worn by the Isolationists in the community, but they sure were dirtier. It had been a long time since these people had been out of the woods. Men and women of various ages, guns held tightly, looking to my father as he spoke. Their bodies held straight with attention like they were an army listening to a commander.

It just so happened their commander was my father.

This was the resistance.

Lockwood walked over to us. "Your father is getting creepier by the day," he whispered.

"I'm assuming the package is still secure?" my father asked a man not much younger than himself. He was a beanpole of a guy, standing a good foot above my father. But the way he bowed his head and slumped his shoulders, not in some show of disrespect but more as a reaction to my father's show of dominance, it became clear who was in charge.

"Yes, sir. Safe and secure," he answered.

"Good. Take yourself and two others and make sure it stays that way. Without it, we have nothing."

Beanpole Guy nodded and walked back to the group. As he left my father's side, a female soldier moved forward. I walked closer to where my father stood, afraid that I would miss something, some clue or signal as to why he was back. Why he was acting so cold.

"Pardon me, sir, but I was wondering if you knew what happened to Harvey? Was she successful in her mission?" asked the young woman. She couldn't have been much older than me. Her muscles were tight, and her black hair was pulled back in a controlled ponytail. Her arms were crossed behind her back as her eyes stared straight ahead. Where the other man had seemed to cower before my father, this woman was holding her own.

"She was not successful. Unfortunately, she didn't stop the target from the rendezvous," my father replied with a sigh.

Unfortunately, she didn't stop the target from the rendez- vous. He was talking about the girl he had sent to stop me from meeting George.

"You mean the lunatic who took joy in sticking a knife in your daughter's abdomen? You don't mean you sent her, do you?" Henry charged.

"I never told her to hurt—" my father began.

"Don't you dare say a word against her! You didn't know her," my father's soldier yelled, her stance of control showing that it had cracks.

"She was a brave girl who died for the greater good. We're all proud of her," my father said as he placed a comforting hand on the girl's shoulder.

The girl nodded, her chin trembling with emotion. My father tapped her under the chin. "Head up, Stephanie. Harvey wouldn't have wanted you to waste your tears. She'd want you to fight on."

Stephanie swallowed and nodded again. "Yes, sir. What's next?"

"We will be escorting these people back to their camp. Once there, we'll gather supplies and men. Then, phase two."

"What's phase two?" I asked.

"Nothing you need to concern yourself with," my father replied, reaching forward and giving my shoulder a small squeeze.

"I can be useful," I argued, not liking the idea of being brushed off. I had survived a great many things. I was a fighter.

"Of course you are, Tessie. But right now I need you to look after your sister."

My father turned to face our group. Robert held tightly onto Louisa. Lockwood and Henry flanked my side. Eric, sullen and quiet the days after his fight with my father, stood in the back, glaring at the army assembled before us. Our army was smaller, less organized, but it felt like an army all the same. Despite sharing natural status with my father's people, I suddenly felt like we weren't fighting on the same side.

"Set up camp here. We move out in the morning. Our goal is to reach the community by nightfall tomorrow," my father clipped. Loud. Clear. No room for argument.

I blew air out from between my clenched teeth, spun on my heels, and headed deeper into the woods. I needed a moment.

"Tess, wait up. Please. Slow down," Robert called from

behind me.

"Not now. I just need to walk. I need a moment to myself," I snapped without hesitating. I sped up my movements, hoping to disappear in the sunset, melting into the crimson red.

"Come on, slow down," he begged, jogging to catch up with me. I knew he was doing so out of courtesy only; it would take nothing for him to stop me. He was a chosen one.

"Why is he acting like this?" I asked, my voice hitching. "He hasn't even attempted to explain where he's been all these years. He hasn't once asked Louisa if she was all right. How can he look at her and not care?"

"After your father rescued me from the center, I spent some time with a resistance sect much like the one that follows him now. These people, they become obsessed with their mission. It's their life. It's not born out of selfishness—or at least they don't see it that way. It comes from a place that longs to make the world better. They're desperate to fix it."

"Better? At what cost?" I asked. "Leaving your family? Abandoning them to make it through this messed-up world on their own?" I fought back the tears that threatened to spill from my eyes.

"But you left, too, remember?"

I gulped. "I had to. They were going to kill me. I planned to go back for Louisa."

"Maybe he had to make the same choice? And it's not the reunion you imagined, but he did come back for you."

I shook my head, crossing my arms against my chest. "The way he talks to them, worries about them…"

"Of course. He's their leader. They're his family."

"But…he already had a family," I said.

Chapter 4

I never could tell if the screams were real. In the seconds after my eyes popped open, my mind struggled to answer the question: nightmare or real life? It was getting harder and harder to distinguish between the two. But then one scream followed after another. And another. They got louder, more frantic. Shrill cries into the night sky that seemed to stretch before us like some black ocean with no end. And as my sister scrambled to her knees from where she slept beside me, I knew with dread coursing through my veins: this was real life.

"Robert!" I yelled with all of my might, pulling myself up onto my feet, blindly reaching into the darkness for my sister's hand. There was no point keeping quiet. The cries for help echoed throughout the woods that surrounded us, trapping our group with whatever was hunting us down. A cage of desperation and horror. A hand clamped down on my shoulder and I yelped.

"It's me," Robert said from my left, reaching across and helping my sister to her feet. I couldn't see him through the pitch black of the night. My eyes hadn't adjusted to being yanked from sleep. Besides, my reflexes weren't nearly as good as his.

Before I could open my mouth, a voice cut through the night. "Tess! Are you hurt?" Henry bellowed in my direction from the darkness of the abyss. I tried to answer back, but the yells and groans of the men and women who scrambled around us filled my brain, making it difficult to form a coherent thought, let alone words.

"What's going on? Can you see anything, Robert?" Lockwood called out from behind us. I hadn't realized he'd been resting so close to where my sister and I had slept, but I wasn't entirely surprised, either.

Robert and Lockwood continued to exchange words, but I couldn't make sense of them. All I could hear were the screams. The wound in my side stung, a sharp pain radiating down my spine. It was a painful reminder that this wasn't the first time I'd met danger in these woods. My heart pounded against my chest, and I found it difficult to breathe.

What now?

What dark thing would happen next?

The heavy beat of feet against the ground fell in sync with the rapid beating of my heart, and I thought I'd go crazy from it. Every voice around me sounded muffled and far away. Out of reach.

Get it together.

I couldn't be weak.

Not now.

Not ever.

The pounding of feet came closer and closer to where my sister and I stood huddled against our chosen one brother-in-law. I could feel him shift next to me, turning in every direction, searching for some escape route, but from the sounds of the screams that came sporadically from around us, it didn't sound like we had anywhere to go.

My father had demanded that Louisa and I rest inside the perimeter of soldiers he had created. I hadn't intended to fall asleep, but the weight of the past few days had caught up with me, and I had lost my battle with exhaustion. My father said we would be safe. We were surrounded by an army. An army of men and women who were now being attacked.

"Down!" Robert hissed. I didn't wait to be told twice. I grabbed my sister by her elbow, pulling her down hard onto the ground. "Try not to make any noise. Try not to move," Robert whispered, assessing the situation that I couldn't even see.

My stomach pressed against the uneven, rocky dirt, and the ground dug painfully into my wound. I grunted and lifted my head, resting on my elbows to squint, but I could only faintly see the shadows of men and women darting here and there across my line of vision.

The screaming had become less frequent, replaced with the rhythm-less beat of yelled commands and popping guns. Louisa pressed her forehead into the dirt, whimpering softly. The only music the world seemed to play anymore — a symphony of war and death. The song played on repeat; the world a broken record player no one knew how to fix. But there was something off about the song. Something different. A new instrument added to the mix, one I didn't recognize. Guttural. Slow. Drawn out. Raspy. And it was getting closer.

"What's out there?" I asked, my voice panicked. I cringed at how loud and desperate it sounded.

"Quiet!" Robert commanded.

The sound was getting closer. "Sir! I think I see them. They're safe," a voice I vaguely recognized yelled, and then the soldier was running toward us.

"Cover her eyes," Robert said to me, nodding toward my sister. I turned to find her looking up toward the man who claimed to be coming to our rescue. I furrowed my brow, trying to make sense of Robert's words. What was about to happen?

"Damn it, Tess! Do it! Now!"

Before I could reach my hand over, Lockwood covered my sister's eyes with one hand while placing a protective arm around her.

That's when I saw the first one.

The thing Robert knew my sister wouldn't be able to handle seeing.

It was worse than the deformed easterner I had seen months ago in these very woods. I didn't even know what to call the creature that sprang on top of the soldier, tackling him to the ground effortlessly, the soldier's bones cracking and snapping as he fell like a tower of blocks knocked over by a vengeful child.

It wasn't just that the creature was deformed. Appearance-wise he wasn't much different from the deformed chosen ones we had stumbled across from the Eastern sector. Enormous in stature, the creature lacked any of the beauty that made up the design of the chosen ones flashed across the television screens of my childhood—lavish and grand promises that an age of innocence was about to begin. It had been anything but that. Forced into compounds. Girls used and abused to suit the council's needs.

The beauty of the chosen ones was a lie. At least most of them. James's outer beauty was nothing compared to the soul that lived inside of him—a soul he insisted he didn't have.

But as the council became more and more sure they had properly subdued the naturals, they must have followed the lead of the eastern sector—mass producing killing machines to fight the war that continued to plague our borders, no longer caring about fooling naturals into believing these angelic, god-like humans were created to protect us.

The chosen one before me was an abomination. His skull was covered in ridges and bumps, sunken in places that made me feel like if I touched it, the entire head would cave in. His features were misshapen, haphazardly designed. Rushed. Grotesque. His head was covered in patches of long, stringy dark hair.

McNair's words from the day we found the eastern creature slithered into my ears: *They're losing the war, and they need infantry. So they commissioned these things. Strong. Brutal. Easier for us naturals to kill because of their lack of abilities, but good for mass-producing.*

No care was given to this creature's appearance. He wasn't designed to impress. He was designed to kill.

I began to pull myself up from the ground, knowing the only chance we had of surviving was to run, but Robert held me firmly in place. He gave a tight shake of his head.

The monster lifted his head back, howling into the night sky. That's when I saw the teeth. I gasped. Razor sharp and uneven, they gleamed with saliva, chomping into the night air. I reached a trembling hand toward my sister, placing it over Lockwood's, ensuring that she wouldn't see what was about to happen next.

With a raspy, wet howl, the creature brought his teeth down onto the man's neck. Nothing more than an effortless tug and the monster brought his head back up, ripping out the man's throat. The man who had run toward danger to help us.

Blood splattered across the creature's face, and as it landed on his lips, he licked at it hungrily. The taste of blood only increased his frenzy, and he brought his teeth back down onto the man's body. I couldn't watch anymore. I closed my eyes and pressed my head against the dirt.

"Their sight and hearing aren't that great. If we just lay here and don't move, he won't see us," Robert whispered to me.

"How many of them are there?" Lockwood asked.

"I reckon a dozen."

"Couldn't you take it out?" Lockwood asked, his voice hitching at the end. He had always been a farmer; he didn't want to be a solider. He only became one to help his friends.

"I don't want…" Robert's voice trailed off. He didn't want to leave us. He could have saved my father's solider, but that meant leaving us vulnerable, attracting the other creatures with the noise. No matter what he was created for, he didn't want to be a solider, either. He had wanted a wife and a child. He had wanted a family. Louisa and I were all he had left of that dream.

The pounding of my heart mixed with the noise of the fallen soldier's muscles being ripped apart and devoured by the creature created by the council. This was no way for anyone to die.

"Tess!"

My head popped up. I couldn't keep my eyes shut any longer. I knew that voice calling my name—it was Henry, and he was searching for me. Headed straight in the direction of the monster that wanted to feast on his insides.

"Robert!" I begged, pointing to Henry, who barreled toward us without a thought to his own safety. Unlike the others, Henry had always wanted this war.

Louisa shrieked. I whipped my head around to find a creature's hand clamped around her ankle. In the quickest of seconds, Robert flipped himself around, crashing right into my sister's attacker. Both chosen ones, devil and savior, fell to the ground, fists flying so fast and furious it was hard to make out whose limbs belonged to whom.

I turned away, trusting that Robert could handle taking out the second creature. I had to trust that he could do it.

I reached down and pulled the knife I knew Lockwood had hidden in his boot. I had watched as he distracted a female solider earlier at dinner with his lame attempts at humor, swiping her dagger when she wasn't looking. I didn't say anything to him at the time. I knew he took it in case something like this happened. Something like this always seemed to happen.

"What the hell are you doing?" Lockwood grunted, towering over my sister like a shield. Sweat covered his brow as he turned back and forth between Robert fighting the creature and Henry running toward us, failing to see through the darkness the creature before us.

As I clutched the knife in my hand, pulling myself up onto my knees, I knew what I was going to do. I knew what I was going to risk. I saw it all. Every bad thing that had happened in my life. Things that seemed out of my control. Things I had let happen to me. The chosen ones taking my father away, my mother committing suicide, losing Emma. Helping cover up the death of a young girl at Templeton, a girl I knew nothing about except that she was a servant like me, forced to pay for the sins of others. Burying the young chosen ones that Henry and his girlfriend had murdered, losing James over and over again. That's why the world was the way it was. My parents, their parents, all the generations before me—they had just sat back. A chain reaction.

I couldn't be the victim. Not anymore. It was stupid, but sometimes the stupid thing and the right thing seemed to be one and the same. These things were strong but not clever. Feral but not imperious.

"Tess!" Henry screamed toward us again. At the sound, the creature stopped feeding and slowly twisted his body around. He was hungry for seconds.

I looked back at Robert. While he had quickly and efficiently dispatched of the creature, three more had appeared. I would have to do this on my own. I had one chance. I looked down at my sister, forcing back the tears that pooled in my eyes. "Keep her safe until I come back," I spat out to Lockwood.

I had every intention of surviving.

I wasn't going out of the world like this.

The creature crouched, growling at Henry, who skidded to a stop, his eyes wide with fear. The monster began to stalk toward his prey, and I knew that this was it. I bolted, holding onto the knife until the handle dug into my skin. Melding with the weapon. With a wild scream, I flung myself onto the back of the creature. The abomination barely registered my weight, briefly staggering as he moved toward Henry. He thought I was weak. Insignificant. He had been programmed to take out the larger target first. He would deal with me later.

My enemy, the tool of the council, brought his fist down onto Henry's head before he could even lift a hand in defense. Henry toppled to the ground, knocked unconscious. I reached back and jutted the knife into the side of the creature's neck. With a roar, the monster threw me over his shoulder onto the ground. He fumbled for the knife that was still lodged in the side of his neck. Every bone in my body tingled and vibrated with the pain of being smashed onto the ground. I couldn't move. I could only watch as the thing before me yanked the knife from his neck, dark, angry blood spurting out.

The creature's nostrils flared as he reached down, grabbing my by the shirt. As he pulled me toward him, ready to tear me limb from limb, one thought crossed my mind: I was happy. I wouldn't die a victim. I would die fighting. Maybe Henry could still escape, and maybe he couldn't. But I would die fighting.

"Tessie!"

The monster turned his head in the direction of my father's voice, and I knew the distraction awarded me a second chance at taking the thing down. I balled my hand into a fist, pulled it back, and let it land right in the monster's throat. There was no way the hit would do any damage, but it was enough to startle him.

He dropped me onto the ground. As I frantically scrambled to my knees in an attempt to escape, I heard the shot. One shot. Loud. Clear. Perfect. The creature fell to the ground next to me.

As a pair of feet ran toward me, I knew one thing for certain:

My father had just saved my life.

"What the hell were you thinking?" my father barked, crouching down and examining me for any damage. With the exception of a few bruises from being pummeled to the ground, I was fine.

"Just go back to your soldiers. They need you more than I do," I muttered, crossing my arms over my chest and looking toward my father's army, who sat huddled against the fire where the bodies of six chosen ones sat burning, the smell of decaying flesh burning my nose and making my eyes water. It wasn't the first time I had come in contact with the smell, but that didn't mean it got any less horrifying. When Eric had asked why we were wasting time burning the bodies, when my father certainly had no time to bury McNair, he replied that it was what his men needed. It was what they had earned.

Our ideas of closure were certainly different.

"Tessie," my father said with a sigh.

I blinked furiously, refusing to let any tears fall. Hearing him call me that, hearing it again, tugged at some part of my heart. "I said I was fine," I repeated. "They need you." And they did. My father had lost five men to the attack. My sister, Lockwood, and even Henry and I had escaped with nothing more than shot nerves, a few bruises, and, in Henry's case, a concussion.

"Tessie," he said again, and despite my ironclad resolve not to give in, my eyes moved toward his face. "Take a walk with me," he said. His voice wasn't harsh, but it was a command all the same. When I hesitated, he added, "Unless you're hurt and can't manage it."

It was a challenge. I shouldn't have given in to it, but he was my father, after all, and he knew I would. I pulled myself to my feet, suppressing a groan. My father promptly turned and walked deeper into the woods, away from his army. We walked in silence for nearly ten minutes before he stopped, turned around, and leaned against a tree. Away from the men and women he commanded, my father seemed to relax a bit, shake off the tough exterior he wore around like armor.

"For centuries, scientists have argued over whether a child's personality is formed through nature or nurture. I always hoped my stubbornness wasn't passed along to you."

It took me a moment to respond. I had expected a scolding, at least a lecture, not a school lesson. My father continued to be full of surprises. "Nature or nurture? What do you mean?" I asked.

"It means whether we are who we are because we were born this way or because of the world we were born into," he explained. "But I left so long ago, and here you are, perhaps the most stubborn girl I've ever met. I guess nature wins out."

I offered a short laugh in return. "Maybe it's because you left me that I had to become so stubborn. Maybe it was the only weapon I had left."

Despite my wry tone, my father grinned. "And the debate continues."

I shook my head. "Is that why you brought me out here? To talk philosophy? If you ask me, I think we should be getting the hell out of these woods. Weren't you the one demanding that when we tried to bury McNair?"

My father's smile faded. His eyes narrowed as they searched something in mine. He took a deep breath and rubbed a hand across his jaw. "No. That's not why I brought you out here. When I saw you attack that thing, putting your life in danger to save your friend, I wanted to kill you myself for being so stupid."

Scolding and lecturing it was.

"Standing up for someone you care about is stupid, is it?" I challenged.

"That's exactly it, isn't it? The conundrum. The problem I caused and did everything in my power to avoid at the same time," he said quietly.

"Can we please stop talking in riddles? Why are we out here? If it's to tell me you think what I did was ridiculous, then let's get on with it," I retorted, tapping my foot furiously against the dirt ground. I refused to let him get a rise out of me. He couldn't play father one moment and commander the next and expect me to be all right with it.

"But it's the riddle that has come to define my life. I left my family to protect them, joining the resistance movement — "

"But I saw two chosen ones take you! Are you telling me they were part of it, too? That it was all an act?" I couldn't help myself. I was exhausted, every muscle in my body tight and wound up, and I was scared. Scared that we would never make it out of these woods. Scared that we *would*, and they wouldn't let us back into the community.

"I will tell you all that in time, I promise. What you need to know right now is why I did it."

I swallowed down the lump in my throat. "And why did you do it?" I managed.

"To save this world. To save it for you, and Emma, and Louisa. I am so close, Tess, to ending all of this. To bringing the council down." I opened my mouth to argue but my father held up his hand. "I know you will always see my leaving as a betrayal, but I had no other options. If I had stayed, I would have ended up in that compound. And there, I wouldn't have been able to do a damn thing. I would've had to live with the knowledge that they would destroy my family, take my eldest daughter from me and force her into servitude, make the women in my family hate everything about themselves that made them beautiful, and I couldn't do a thing about it. So I left. I left everything I loved. I became this man you look at with hatred. I became him to give you a better world."

"You could have been there. Did you ever think of that?" I said, unable to keep quiet any longer. "Maybe I didn't want a father who saved the whole world—maybe I wanted a father who saved mine."

"I wouldn't watch them destroy you. I couldn't," he said, his voice edged with some deeply buried emotion. Raw. Wild. "So, I left, and I am so close to ending it all." He took two giant steps toward me, grabbing onto my arms. "I need you to give me time. Listen to what I say. Follow my orders without question—"

"I'm your daughter, not one of your soldiers," I spat out.

"Did you see those things that attacked us? Did you really look at them? The council doesn't give a damn about us anymore. They want all of us naturals dead. Those things were created to search the woods for survivors. To eat us alive. If we sit back, we are asking for extinction, and I want you to survive, Tessie. That's all I've ever wanted."

My father took a deep breath and reached a trembling hand into his pocket. He pulled out a folded piece of paper. Tattered and worn, it looked close to falling apart. "I'm only asking for you to trust me for a little while. Just till the end," he continued as he unfolded the paper. "And when the world is once again as it should be, you can go back to hating me. I knew it was a possibility the moment I left, but it was a sacrifice I was willing to make."

I opened my mouth and closed it. I had heard these sentiments before. I had heard them from Henry, a boy hell-bent on doing whatever he had to do to bring down the council. And hadn't I given him a second chance? My father reached forward and took my hand, placing the piece of paper in it.

It was sheet music. It was our song. The very first song I ever learned to play. The song my father taught me. The song that led me to James. He had kept it this whole time. I couldn't stop the tear that rolled down my cheek, and for once, I didn't want to.

"There's one more thing, child."

I cleared my throat and handed the sheet music back to him, but he simply smiled, refusing to take it.

"About this boy you love…"

"James," I breathed, my hand clutching onto the song that defined the most important moments of my life. His curly, wild black hair. His endlessly deep mismatched eyes. The scar on his chin that was the most perfect imperfection I had ever seen.

The boy I loved.

"Would you like to talk to him?"

Chapter 5

I pulled on Louisa's hand so she stood right next to me. Lockwood moved to the other side of her. "Al will be pissed. He's not just going to let us return, not without making us pay. This is the same man who put a boy on trial for saving your life," he reminded me.

Put a chosen one on trial, I thought. When I had first entered the community, I expected life to be utterly different. But in a lot of ways, the most important ways, the people of the community and the members of the council weren't so different at all. Many in the community distrusted Henry and me for simply being outsiders, and we'd had to work hard to gain their trust.

When I had fallen ill and James had come to rescue me, they treated us both with such unbelievable hatred. I sometimes found it hard not to wonder if hatred was the only thing all humans shared. I wasn't entirely sure everyone was capable of love, but I had seen enough hate to last me a lifetime. The people of the community shunned and judged James and me. Not to mention they tried to kill him for simply being a chosen one. They hadn't even bothered to see what kind of soul lived inside.

The community hardened itself in order to survive; they weren't the most understanding species.

The community. The place I thought I would never see again was less than a mile from where we stood, shrouded in the protective cover of night and the camouflage of the trees. I could faintly see the wooden fence and lit torches that surrounded the safe haven.

"Somehow, I don't think my father's too worried about it," I replied, tearing my eyes from the place I wanted so desperately to return to, trying to make my voice sound blasé. I could feel Louisa shake beside me. As I looked down at her, I saw her eyes widen, darting toward where the lights of the community crept into the woods. We stood hidden in the darkness of the tree line. Robert and Henry huddled near the edges of my father's group. There, he stood, furiously whispering his orders to his standing army.

Appearing to sense my sister's nervousness, Lockwood cleared his throat. "You're right, Tess. I don't know what I was worrying about. Charlie seems to have everything under control," he said, nodding toward my father.

Henry and Robert joined our line. "So, what's his brilliant plan?" Eric asked.

"You're not going to like it," Henry said.

"Charlie wants you and Lockwood to walk ahead of us and call out to the men on watch," Robert said.

Eric laughed bitterly. "You mean he wants to put the most expendable people in front in case they shoot first and ask questions later?"

"He feels that if the guards first see people they know, people they trust, they will be more likely to listen to what they have to say."

"Will they hurt you?"

Her voice was so small my ears barely registered it. I turned my head to find Louisa staring up at Lockwood. If there was any fear on Lockwood's face at hearing my father's plan, it disappeared before her words were fully out. A slow grin spread across his face. "Shoot me? I'm too important. Your sister must not have told you. I was in charge of the livestock."

"He milked cows," Eric added drily.

"Yes, I did. And I was damn good at it. Now, how about we go broker peace, shall we?" he said as he began to walk toward the camp. He held his head up and walked without an ounce of fear.

"If your father gets me killed, I'm going to haunt you," Eric said before joining Lockwood on his trek.

I gave my sister's hand a squeeze. "Don't worry. Lockwood can talk anyone into anything."

"More like talk you to death so you just give him what he wants," Henry joked. "Your sister's right, though. He'll be fine."

I could feel the weight of my father's presence behind me without seeing him. It was like a sixth sense that I couldn't shake ever since we started heading toward the community. His eyes were burning holes in the back of my head; I wondered if it was like this for all fathers and daughters. I turned around, offering him a small smile. He merely nodded in response. He was back in commander mode. It had been years since he had to be a father, and it was clear it was difficult for him to negotiate between the two roles. He wanted his family safe, and he was going to get me in contact with James. If that wasn't reason enough to follow him, I didn't know what was.

James. I was going to talk to James somehow. My father had promised. He told me that he had men on the inside of the council's headquarters. Once his man decided if James was trustworthy, which I assured my father he was, he would help us pass letters across the lines.

I don't know how he knew about James. Maybe his spies. Maybe Robert. But he knew what James meant to me, and he had promised to do anything in his power to get my words to him. I had to trust my father. I simply had to.

I untangled myself from Louisa, trusting she would be safe with Henry for the time being. I walked to where my dad, our leader, stood, nestled amongst his people. "You sure about this?" I asked, glancing back toward the hazy lights of the community.

"I'm not worried if that's what you're wondering," he replied casually. Too casually for my taste.

"Al's not the most reasonable of men," I said.

"You think I don't know that? You think I'm not fully aware that he threw you in a jail cell and put you on trial?" I could have sworn that his hand tightened around his rifle as he spoke. I remembered the way he had killed the chosen one without flinching, and I hoped for Al's sake that he would hear my father out. "I know exactly how unreasonable Al is, but I also know that if I need to, I'll take this place by force."

I shook my head and bit the inside of my cheek. History was written, compiled from stories of men trying to take something that didn't belong to them in the first place.

"You don't approve of my methods?" my father asked.

"Does it matter?" I countered, raising an eyebrow.

"Trust me," he implored, his voice taking the gentler tone that I'd rarely heard since his mysterious return into my life—a tone that had filled my childhood with comfort and hope. Staring at him, a mixture of desperation and determination etched across his face, I reminded myself this was the man who promised to try and keep me in contact with James. The man who saved my life.

I reminded myself this man was my father.

I opened my mouth to reply when the sound of the safeties clicking off ten guns stopped me. The woods that separated us from the community rustled and warned us of the men who approached. I scrambled over to where Henry and Louisa stood. Working together, we pulled Louisa behind the line of my father's army. Her limbs froze and locked, protesting both fight and flight. She was simply ready to give up.

This was exactly the natural the council wanted her to be.

Eric and Lockwood were the first to appear, their hands held up in the air. Both of their faces were tight with worry. A group of ten men, rifles in hand, followed them. Several men lagged behind the community's row of guns with makeshift lit torches in tow.

And behind them came Al.

I tightened my grip on my sister's hand.

"It's been a long time, Charlie," Al said, lazily leaning against his rifle. His smugness had always driven me crazy.

"That it has," my father replied, shifting his gun so it

was pointed directly at the man who stood between us and
safety—even if that safety was temporary. For the briefest of
seconds, I was glad my father was pointing his gun at Al; I'd
do just about anything to get Louisa inside the community.

"I think we can lower the gun. There's no need for it.
Not when we both know you won't use it," Al sneered. His
slimy, slippery grin refused to leave his face.

"What makes you so sure?" my father asked. Despite his
age, his aim was steady, firm. It never wavered.

"'Cause I know you. Don't think I don't remember those
early days. Back then…I heard you. When we traveled from
community to community, passing intel, gathering men for
the great rebellion that never came, you cried in the night
when you thought no one could hear you. You cried for your
children. Sometimes even your wife."

"I suggest you shut your mouth. You have no idea what
you're talking about," my father warned. He was attempting
stoicism, but it was crumbling quickly. He squinted and
leaned forward slightly, his gun still aimed directly at the
man who McNair once told me would never be happy. Not
because it wasn't possible, but because he never wanted it.

"Nothing is going to get solved while you all have those
damn guns pointed at each other," Lockwood said. "Why
don't we just go back to the community, get Sharon to check
in on Louisa, and talk this over."

The man holding his gun trained on Lockwood jutted
the butt of it into Lockwood's stomach. He lurched forward
onto his knees and coughed so violently I worried he was
going to burst a blood vessel in his forehead. Louisa hid her
head against my shoulder and began to whimper.

Henry grabbed my wrist to hold me in place. If it wasn't

for Louisa, nothing would have stopped me from running to Lockwood. I breathed in and out through my nose and could hear Henry doing the same next to me.

"I remember telling you to keep your mouth shut! You lost the right to speak the minute you left," Al snapped at Lockwood. All the while he kept his eyes on my father.

"Is it any wonder you've never been able to inspire loyalty? And I'm not talking about using fear to get a bunch of weak-minded folks to stand behind you with guns," my father replied.

Al laughed slowly, moving his head back and forth. As the sound of his chuckle weaved throughout the woods, mocking the brightness of the stars that covered our heads, it became louder. Sarcastic. Taunting. "Says the man who travels with a pack of wild things, half-crazed morons propelled by dreams of a war that will never come."

"Let me shoot this son of a—"

"Hold your ground, Stephanie," my father commanded. I glanced back and see her grit her teeth, her eyes holding nothing but contempt for the man who insulted my father, his army, and everything they stood for.

"Just leave, Charlie. There ain't nothing for you here. Go back to wherever you came. No rebellion to chase after in these parts. The most we got is a bunch of boys who call themselves resistance fighters, but all they do is go out and collect supplies. Chase your pipe dream somewhere else. We're just trying to survive."

"That's always been your problem, Al—you're too concerned with just surviving," my father countered. "Don't you want something better than hiding in the woods like a convict?"

"Better to rule in hell than to serve in heaven. You really think you can take me down? How? With a few malnourished lunatics and a pregnant slut?" Al spat, pointing his gun toward my little sister.

That was all it took. My father's resolve was gone before the smoke from his rifle drifted toward the sky. Al screamed in agony, grabbing onto his leg as he crumpled to the ground. As Al's men moved to shoot my father, Stephanie took two of them down, matching my father's shot to Al's leg.

Louisa yelped. My mouth dropped open and my eyes went wide as a wave of nausea washed over me. The three men from the community cursed and moaned, rolling around. I would never get used to this violence. I didn't *want* to.

"Anyone else?" Stephanie screamed.

The rest of Al's men dropped their guns and held their shaking hands into the air. My father lifted his gun and rested it on his shoulder, sauntering over with half his mouth turned up into a grin.

"I let you say your words, but I'm done now. The next time you open your mouth and say anything against me, I'll jam this rifle down your throat."

"Go to hell," Al spat.

"Look around." Without another word, my father stepped over Al and headed toward the community. "We're already there."

Chapter 6

"I need more bandages, sheets, anything to help soak up this blood," Sharon yelled, nearly knocking me over as she ran toward the community's makeshift infirmary. Despite being ready to give birth at any moment, she moved with a quickness that defied logic. But, then again, she had always put others before herself.

My father's soldiers ungraciously dragged Al and his wounded men into the gates of the community by their arms. When the other members saw us enter, their guards following behind us with bowed heads, our men holding their guns, they scurried back into their rooms, rushing what children they had left far away from us.

The community had always feared invasion by the council's chosen ones; they never thought they would have to fear their fellow naturals.

My father had told me that this was the way it needed to be done—the way he could protect us all. I knew the community would have a hard time accepting that. Especially considering he had shot one of their leaders…but they really didn't have a choice.

While my father went to work setting up a perimeter, replacing the community's watchmen with his own trusted guards, I ran as quickly as I could behind Sharon, dragging my little sister with me.

"Please, Tess, I'm tired. I can't run so fast," Louisa said.

I shut out her pleas. There would be time for her to complain and moan later, but now we needed to search for the truth. That was all that mattered in the end. Inside the walls of the community, I could almost understand my father's frenzy, his willingness to do whatever it took to protect his own. I would do just about anything to find the answers I needed for my sister. Was she going to die? The only person who could even possibly tell me was off tending to the wounds of three men my father was responsible for shooting.

When I busted into the small infirmary, my hair sticking to my forehead with sweat, the sight of blood nearly made me throw up. Towel after towel lay abandoned on the floor as Al and his men cried out, cursing my father. Sharon and two others, a man and woman I vaguely recognized from my time in the community, were exchanging a lightning-quick series of medical terms I didn't understand.

"You won't take my leg, Sharon. I'd rather die. You hear me?" Al screamed, his face beet red from exertion.

"The wounds aren't too deep with these two, but I'm afraid…" The woman's voice trailed off, her face grim as she stared down at Al.

Sharon gave the woman a curt nod, hustling to a drawer and yanking it open. I recognized the needle and thread from my own experience getting stitched up. Sharon threw it to the woman.

"Lazarus? I need you to go find Eric and Lockwood. We're going to need help holding Al down." Sharon panted, running a trembling hand through her hair.

I swallowed, forcing down whatever food was left in my stomach. I had seen a lot of blood and death in my life, but something about watching Al pray and beg not to have his leg cut off caused my very being to shake. Under the monster was a man, and for some reason, that made this all the more frightening.

My sister urgently tugged on my hand, but I wouldn't leave. If I had learned one thing in the past couple months it was that life was unpredictable, wild — the bitch of fate itself. This was where my sister needed to be, and I wouldn't move from this space until I attempted to make sense of a world that seemed increasingly senseless.

I just couldn't.

Sharon turned back to the drawer and pulled out a saw. At the sight of it, my sister gasped and grabbed my hand. "I...I can't. I can't — " A frantic, high-pitched squeak issued from her lips and she fell to the floor.

It was only then that Sharon saw me. Her eyes traveled to where my sister lay on the floor, stirring slightly. Her eyes fluttered as I gently shook her back to consciousness. Sharon placed her hand over her abdomen. "Oh, Tess," she whispered.

Her voice didn't sound helpful. It only sounded sad.

I gasped for breath, suddenly finding it near impossible to breathe. "You...you have to help her. Check her," I begged. I didn't care about the men behind her that were also calling for Sharon's attention.

Sharon nodded and pressed her lips together, pulling in air through her nose. I don't know where in her mind she went during that brief moment of silence, but it certainly wasn't with those in the room. When she returned, her eyes met mine. "One crisis at a time."

"Lazarus said you needed us?" Eric called out from behind me.

"Louisa! What happened? Is she all right?" Lockwood called, clearly panicked.

"Lock, take this girl into the other room. There's an extra cot out by the dining tables. I'll be there as soon as I can." Sharon turned to me. "I promise."

I blinked away tears and nodded as Lockwood bent down and scooped Louisa into his arms. My resolve, my control over the hurt and fear, was slipping.

. . .

Later that night when everyone was fast asleep, I scrounged up some paper and a pen and crept away from the group, calling back the skills I'd learned while sneaking around to see James. Back then, life had seemed so difficult. I was falling in love with a boy who was created to hate me. It was complicated.

Now, I longed for the problems of those days. Because back then, those problems only affected me. Now there didn't seem to be anyone left untouched by the darkness. Not even Al escaped from it; he had embraced it, claimed it as his own, and it had taken his leg.

Sharon had yet to check in on Louisa. Hours after leaving her, she was still deep in the blood of Al and the other men shot during what felt like a part of some nightmare that never ended.

Blood.

Always so much blood.

It continuously hunted me, and I didn't know how to outrun it anymore. I needed the hope my father offered. His words continued to move about in my mind. There was a possibility that I could speak to James through letters. Words. It was words that had brought us together in the first place. Sitting on his bed reading the outlawed passages of *Jane Eyre*, our fingers aching to reach for each other in between the space of the words we read aloud. What would I write to him? What could I say? How does one put their very soul onto the page?

I could only hope that the cool, brisk night air and the stars above would help me write my letter.

When my father and his men set up camp in the dining hall, and I was sure Louisa was safe, watched over by a trio of personal guards—Henry, Robert, and Lockwood—I pretended to fall asleep. It wasn't long before the others around me went to sleep, too. We had traveled far, further than any distance measured by miles. It felt like we were constantly traveling from one world to another. None of us sure which we were meant to live in.

I welcomed the cool air that greeted me as I stepped outside of the dining hall. The makeshift command center had grown hot and stuffy. While living in the compound, I had gotten used to sharing cramped sleeping quarters with others, but there was something about sharing a space with a bunch of soldiers sprawled out on tables, their hands protectively around their guns even while they slumbered, that left me feeling antsy.

I grimaced as I took a seat on the wooden steps of the building that had served as everything from mess hall to courtroom to infirmary. My side was still sore from the stabbing. I leaned my head against a post. It was only then, alone with nothing but the crickets and other mysterious noises that made up the night's symphony, that it all truly hit me.

Louisa. James. My father. McNair. Al.

My eyes pricked with unshed tears. I tucked the paper under my leg, so I wouldn't lose it, then squeezed the bridge of my nose with my fingers, hoping I could force the tears back down. It was hard to swallow. Even harder to breathe. I pulled my knees to my chest and rested my head against them, my heart pounding painfully against my chest. Like a beacon calling for some ship distressed at sea to return home, wondering if it ever would. I clutched onto the fabric of my shirt, hoping, willing myself to reclaim control.

Even if my father could get my letters to James, they wouldn't change our situation. We would still be apart. It would be easy to lose it, crumble. But I couldn't believe that my destiny had already been written. Our last moments in the woods didn't feel like an ending. The memory of him was almost enough to save me, but I wanted more than some idea of him.

I wanted him back.

I closed my eyes and searched my mind for something, anything that would quiet the fear that was screaming inside me. And then I saw him, the boy I now knew I would never stop loving. Even if I never saw him again, I would love James till my dying breath. If there was anything after death,

I was pretty sure I would love him then, too.

I remembered our time together in the woods. I let the memory sweep over me like the waves that McNair had once told me he dreamed of seeing, waves that moved and crashed, echoing the feelings that made life, no matter how difficult it got, worth living—passion and freedom.

It had happened in the woods, the vast land of greens and browns that separated council-controlled territory and the settlement the community was so desperate to keep safe. We had made that bit of woods our own. We had always been able to do that—take a place and define it to suit our needs. The piano room. The closet after the party. The jail cell.

Knowing full well that death was a possibility, I had given myself to James in those woods. I hadn't wanted to risk missing out on anything. Not when I knew that our meeting with George could mean the end of it all.

But it wasn't the only reason I had had sex with James. I'd done it because it was what I wanted to do. Want. Desire. All the things the council programmed us to think were dirty and wrong.

But it hadn't felt wrong.

I didn't have sex just because I could, either. I knew what it meant for me, and I knew what it meant for him. Whatever the council wanted to make of it was up to them. Even Sharon had changed it to suit the needs of the community. For me, it had been about intimacy.

It had been everything.

It was the first time I had ever completely and utterly trusted anyone in my whole life.

"You don't have to be careful with me," I had whispered.

"Won't it hurt?" he'd asked, moving closer to my lips, his hand running up and down my back.

"Yes." I'd nodded. "But don't worry, I won't break."

James had hesitated, and, to be honest, it drove me a little mad. I bit on my bottom lip and tugged on the waist of his pants. His breath caught and he looked down at me. His face flashed red as the heat traveled down his neck. I unbuttoned his pants.

And then he had been helping me shed my clothes. It was as if we were both taken over by a frenzy, a fiery fit of emotions. I hadn't been able to help but giggle. Both naked, we just sat there and stared. My eyes traveled across the body science had perfected, and when his eyes moved across mine in turn, I didn't feel embarrassed by the randomly flawed construction. The way James looked at me left no room for mortification. His eyes only carried awe.

James had licked his lips as he reached for me, placing a gentle hand on my hip bone. His fingertips grazed my skin, and my whole body erupted into goose bumps. His hand traced its way up my torso. Ever so slow, ever so adoring.

James cleared his throat. I couldn't take one more second of waiting. I closed the very small distance between us and pressed my hungry lips against his. James, who had always been so careful with me, wrapped his arms around me and pulled me to him with a force that left me breathless.

His tongue pressed against mine, moving not like a teenager afraid of the voyage he was about to take, but, instead, like a man who didn't worry if he made a mistake. Because no matter what happened in these moments, we had chosen to share them together. Once I realized that, I didn't feel nervous anymore. We would always be each other's first. No one, not the council or the community, would ever be able to change that. As we fell to the ground, moving and shifting together, becoming one with each other and the woods that protected us, I knew there was nothing more natural, more human in the world than this.

Maybe sex could mean all the things the council said. Betrayal. Lust. Weakness. But it didn't mean that's what it had to be to us.

For us, it felt like hope and love and promise.

• • •

"Tess, you should come inside. Your neck's going to hurt like hell if you sleep like that."

I reluctantly opened my eyes, letting free the weighty breath I held trapped in my throat. I left the comfort of that moment—the moment that would forever only belong to James and me.

Henry reached down to help me up.

"Do you mind sitting here for a bit?" I asked, nervous for the conversation I was about to have, knowing I owed it to the boy in front of me to attempt it.

When I'd thought that I would never see James again, I had allowed myself to feel something for Henry, something I had never been able to completely define. He was my first friend, and when we lived together back in the compound, he had distanced himself from me because we had been taught that love was wrong, But together in the wild lands of the Isolationists, we had grown close. Closer. Henry had always been sure of the way he felt, but I never had such clarity. All I knew was that the shared kisses between us never stirred my soul like the ones I shared with James.

"Of course not," Henry replied, taking a seat next to me. "But why do I get the feeling I'm not going to like it?"

"Because you won't. I need to talk to you about James," I said softly.

Henry sighed. "We don't need to have this conversation tonight."

I reached over and took my best friend's hand in mine. "Yes, we do. We should have had this conversation a long time ago, but I messed things up."

"Let's not go feeling sorry for yourself." Henry rolled his eyes. "We both messed things up."

I couldn't help but laugh. "I guess you're right."

"I usually am," he said. He paused, looking at the night sky above us. "Actually, I never am. I don't know what I'm talking about," he said, and then he started to laugh, too.

"It's time I make things right, and that means talking about James. And me. James and me. I know that George took him back to the council—"

"Would it be a waste of my time to explain to you that the likelihood of ever seeing him again is slim?" he asked.

I offered a small smile. "Yes, it would. That's where I went wrong before. I convinced myself that I was never going to see him again, and I didn't let myself feel the weight of that. At least not completely. So, I tried things with you. I wasn't ready. I tried to be, but I wasn't."

Henry pulled his hand from mine, turning his face from me. "Don't sit here and tell me you didn't feel anything for me. I remember the way you kissed me."

I swallowed, knowing the next thing I said would destroy him. But it would be a temporary destruction, like burning down a forest so it could grow again. "I did feel something for you. I'll probably always feel something for you. But even in those moments when I convinced myself I would never see James again, I was still more in love with the memory of him than I was with you."

I braced myself for Henry's reaction. Instead of arguing, he sighed and ran a hand over his face. I realized he was probably just as tired as I was. "I know," he said.

I pulled myself to my feet and placed a hand on his arm. "I wish it could be different."

"You know what's crazy? There's a part of me that doesn't care that you'll never love me as much as you would him."

"You say that right now, but you would mind one day. And then you would hate me. I can take you being mad at me now, but I could never handle you hating me," I said.

Henry nodded and walked off into the darkness without another word. I stared after my best friend as he moved further and further away from me, and despite his slumped shoulders and bowed head, I knew I had done the right thing.

For once.

Chapter 7

Tess,

There are no words to express the utter astonishment I felt at receiving your letter. I never even let myself hope to see you again; it didn't feel fair. You were alive. You had your sister. What else could I ask for? And then your letter arrived, handed to me by one of the creators under my plate at dinner. Effortlessly. The smallest of gestures with the greatest of impact.

Despite half of your letter being crossed out, no doubt by someone to keep hidden any fact or detail that might lead them to you, I lost myself in every word that crawled across the page.

I have always moved through life blindly. I have always stumbled, reaching my hand out, searching for the wall, needing something to help me along. This is the way it has always been with me, and I sometimes think it's the one part of my being that will never change.

You have been my guide since that first day in the piano room. When I think back on you, our times together, I don't want to change. The council is wrong. Kendall was wrong.

Needing someone isn't weakness.

The council is trying to change me. When George returned me to them, taking me right to the center, the headquarters, he was welcomed back a hero. It was almost as if the man who processed us was expecting George to show up with me. The things he knows, Tess, are enough to make any man tremble with fear. Every dark thing that has ever whispered seductively in my mind, he has recited back to me.

I believe George used his ability to gain acquittal for his crimes. It probably didn't hurt that he had me as well. Once I went through debriefing (don't worry, I said nothing of you or the community, I swear it. I would never tell them. I would die before giving them a way to hurt you more than they already have) I told them I had left the compound because I sought to find out what lay in the woods. I was curious. Once they were done questioning me, George and I were both assigned to different creators, and I have only seen him once since.

That's what they do with chosen ones here. Each one of us is assigned a job based on our ability. You were right when you guessed that I would be selected as a bodyguard for someone important. Once they ascertained the extent of my ability from George, they assigned me to a man named Scott Harper. He is the son of Abrams, one of the original creators of the first batch of chosen ones presented to the public. No one dares to call him by his first name, though. Just Harper. I suspect they are afraid of showing disrespect. Even his two sons call him sir.

I believe the council has been making genetically engineered humans for quite some time, much longer than they have let on. I have only been given a little bit of information because I am still rather new, but things are worse than either of us ever knew. There are whispers of things I shudder to write down, not out of fear that someone will read them, but more from a deep-rooted nervousness that by writing them, they will be true. No denying the rumors anymore.

Needless to say, when they assigned me to Harper, they forgot one important detail. When Kendall created me, he wired me so that I could only sense when someone was in trouble when I cared for them deeply. So, while I followed Harper for days, I was unable to prevent him from receiving an injury while awakening a new batch of chosen ones. One of them bolted straight up and attempted to strangle him. It was the oddest thing I have ever witnessed. Once everyone had regained their composure, they looked to me, wondering why I hadn't foreseen the event and stopped it.

I am not certain, but I believe they spoke with George, who decided to share what he left out about my gift. No doubt he gives and holds information in ways that suit his personal agenda.

He told them about you.

Not about the community or even meeting in the woods. I still don't understand why he kept those things secret, but he did. He told them I had fallen for a Templeton girl, and since meeting her, meeting you, my loyalties have been shifting.

That is when they decided to get to work on re-programming me. As you must remember from your time at Templeton, while we are incubating, the creators flash images into our brains that depict naturals in the worst possible way. Images of war, betrayal, wanton lasciviousness. So, when we wake up and begin our training, our minds are more apt to listen to the propaganda—the countless history lessons on how time and time again the naturals, due to their emotional weakness, turned on each other and their governments.

Chosen ones are not created to rebel, let alone think for themselves, so the creators have decided that I must be re-programmed. Every morning they tie me down and make me watch those films, the images that made up what I can only call my childhood. At first, I struggled against the ropes and tried to keep my eyes shut. But without scaring you, they have ways to make me watch, Tess. They have ways.

In the afternoons, I sit with a creator, a man so

old I sometimes foolishly wonder if he was there at the start of time itself. He talks to me for hours and hours about the council, their beliefs, and even you. I don't mind talking to him of the council. I have millions of questions that I want answered, but when he brings you up, I cannot speak. I cannot say your name in this place.

You are the brightness.

This place is the darkness.

And I don't want to risk it destroying you. So, I say your name a thousand times in my head and write it here, knowing they cannot take it from me if I don't give it to them.

When I refuse to talk to them about you, it makes them angry. And so a man appears, and he has ways. So, I talk. I am so ashamed by it. But I never say your name.

And when I'm done talking about you, they take their turn. They try and convince me that you have tricked me, manipulated me with your natural ways. They want to corrupt my feelings for you, but I never let them.

When I return to my room, my head hurts so much that I wonder if it would be better to just bash it against the wall. Then I think of you. If there is even the slightest chance I will ever see you again, I must keep going. I won't give up. Every day, I thank the God that created you, asking him to bless you for that letter. I am so happy to hear you are trying to reconnect with your sister. I will continue to hope to receive another missive. Just the thought of it makes all the pain worth it.

George came to see me this morning. He told me to pretend. He told me if I didn't, they would wash my memory completely. Re-start me. Re-make me.

I have to pretend to hate you.

Because if I don't, they'll make sure I don't remember you at all.

And for some reason, George wants me to remember.

~James

Chapter 8

"It's all right to be nervous," Eric told me, scratching the back of his head, clearly more apprehensive about the day's lesson than I was.

I gritted my teeth and held my gun level with the target. "I don't have time to be nervous." I didn't have time *or* patience. Every time I re-read James's letter, I was filled with rage. If I ever came into contact with the men who tortured him, I would murder them. I would.

I took a deep breath and squinted my eyes, trying to bring the can into focus. The hardest part about shooting a gun was shutting out the rest of the world. A good shot had to maintain complete composure, focus, control. At least that's what Stephanie had told me during breakfast.

While she refused to break my father's orders and teach me herself, she always sat with me during morning mealtime and offered me tips. I could tell there was a part of Stephanie that didn't think it was right that my father forbade me from learning how to use a gun, a part of her that knew in this world it was wise a girl learned how to defend herself. But she would never go against her commander. Luckily for me, Eric had no problem disobeying my father's orders.

He was pretty much the only one brave enough to do so. Hours after arriving at the community, my father called a meeting with all of the leaders. By the time the meeting concluded, the community was under his control. He and his army walked the streets enforcing their own brand of law and order. For the most part, things remained how they were, but it still bothered me how quickly the Isolationists, ancestors of those naturals who ran from government control, gave up their rights.

No one dared to question me or any of the men who traveled with us into the woods to meet George. We may have forced our way back into the community, but no one treated us as outcasts. Whatever my father had told them must have been pretty damn convincing. Another reminder that words carried just as much power as the gun I held in my hands.

Needless to say, I hadn't seen much of my father since the early days after our return to the community. I couldn't shake the feeling that he was avoiding me. Despite his attempt at reconciliation back in the woods, I hadn't had much contact with him. He begged me to trust him, told me it would all be over soon. Maybe I needed to let him do what needed to be done.

"I'll take your cow milking for the rest of the week if you make that shot," Lockwood called out from behind me.

I spun around to remind him that I had been covering both of our cow duties the past two weeks, since he spent all of his time doting on my sister. But both he and Eric fell to the ground. "Whoa! Whoa! What the hell? You never point a gun at someone unless you plan on shooting them," Eric yelled at me.

I lowered the gun. "Who said I wasn't planning on shooting Lockwood?" I joked, but my cheeks were red from embarrassment. I cleared my throat. "How is she?"

Lockwood pulled himself off the ground and shrugged. "The same," he answered, instinctively knowing who I was speaking about. Of course he knew; Louisa consumed both of our minds. Sharon couldn't offer the answers I sought. Not without access to medical instruments and machines that were near impossible to find in the wilds of the Isolationist territory. "She'll barely eat. She won't talk. She just sleeps and stares at that wall," he continued, kicking at the dirt beneath his feet.

I nodded and turned my attention back to my target. "I'm ready to try it," I growled, figuring the best way to stem my anger was to shoot the hell out of a tin can. Of course, if Eric knew how angry I was, he'd probably take the gun right out of my hands and tell me to walk it off.

"All right, then," Eric said. "Breathe in and out. Steady your aim, find your center, and shoot. Your stance is important, and, please, for the love of God, remember the recoil."

"Um, should I back up? Like go back inside back up?" Lockwood teased from behind me.

"Shut up, Lock. Tess has this. She's a strong son of a bitch. She can do it," said Eric, his voice firm.

I replayed all of Eric's rules and reminders in my head, doing everything he told me. I closed off my mind, shutting out all my anxiousness and fears about Louisa. I focused and did what Eric, my great teacher, had taught me.

And then I shot.

I promptly and ungraciously fell straight on my ass. My chest burned with adrenaline, and my breath escaped from me like the birds that flew from the trees upon hearing the shot.

"Hot damn!" Eric yelled, running toward the fence post where the can had been placed.

I stood up, furiously wiping the dirt off my pants. "I'm sorry. I thought I was prepared for the recoil. I'll do better next time."

"Better? You shot it dead on. Right in the middle." Eric beamed, running over with the can so I could inspect it.

I couldn't help but grin too. "Well, hot damn indeed. Of course, I did fall on my butt—probably not the most useful thing if it ever comes to fighting," I admitted a little sheepishly.

"You just need some practice. You did fantastic. We'll continue tomorrow," Eric replied. When I opened my mouth to beg for another go, he cut me off. "I have border duty, and I don't feel like hearing your father's mouth if I show up late. Don't worry. Tomorrow," he promised, punching me playfully in the arm before heading toward the dining hall. One day, I would have to remind him how hard those punches were.

"Wait!" I called out after him. Eric stopped and turned around to face me, raising an eyebrow. "Would you mind if I kept that?" I asked, pointing to the can. He laughed and tossed it to me.

"So, what are we going to do about your sister?" Lockwood asked as soon as Eric was out of earshot.

I rolled my eyes and tucked the can into my coat pocket.

Then I slung the rifle over my shoulder and walked to the shed where the community stored the weapons. "There's nothing to do but wait. Unless you know how to time travel, I suspect you're going to have to learn a bit of patience."

"She's freaking out, Tess," Lockwood countered, closing the shed and locking it once I had returned the gun.

"Louisa's main occupation in life has always been drama. Don't get swept up in it," I warned, pushing past him and striding back toward the dining hall. Between working all day with the livestock and training, I was near famished.

Lockwood grabbed onto my arm and halted me. "So, we're back to being this girl? The *I don't feel anything* girl? Let me tell you something about that girl. She's a real bitch, and nobody likes her."

"Nobody likes a potty mouth either," I countered, trying desperately to lighten the mood.

Lockwood continued to stare me down. I looked up at my friend, paling at his words. He was right. *I* didn't even like that girl. But it wasn't as simple as all that, either. I was frightened. Not for myself, but because I was certain that, once again, I was going to fail my little sister. Emma had always taken care of us, during the worst of my mother's drinking episodes and after my father left; my sister hadn't been dead for a year before I abandoned Louisa, leaving her to be manipulated and used by the likes of George.

"What am I supposed to do?" I asked, my voice cracking. "Look at my little sister and tell her I don't know if she's going to die? Tell her that I was wrong when I thought Sharon could help her? Remind her that I'm the reason she's stuck in this backwoods place, away from all the comforts the council could offer her? I mean, if she's going to die, at least she could do it without starving."

"Backwoods place? Even you have to admit the community is better than the compound."

I sighed. "Of course. But she won't see it like that. She grew up believing everything the council told us. Now, she just sees us as the people who took her from that safety. Brought her to a place where she's scared all the time. You saw her in the woods."

"Maybe you could help her be less scared."

I pulled my arm from his grasp. "She knows what happened to Emma. She remembers. Now she's stuck out here waiting for that thing inside her to crawl its way out and kill her."

"It's not some thing, Tess. It's her child. When I sit with her, she, well, she tries to protect the baby. I can see it in the way she curls in on herself."

I crossed my arms and tucked my chin down. I couldn't look at Lockwood, not when I was sure my face radiated all the characteristics that defined the old me. It was the one part of myself that hadn't been changed since leaving the compound. Even after seeing how great Sharon was with her kids and despite knowing I wouldn't share my sister's fate, I couldn't see the point of bringing any child into such a messed-up world.

I had learned the hard way that us humans, naturals and chosen ones alike, were fragile. And not just in a physical way. We hurt each other with wounds and scars that no one would ever see, but that didn't mean they didn't exist. Often, they were the injuries we could never come back from. My mother certainly hadn't been able to.

I couldn't even begin to fathom why women like Emma

even thought of risking childbirth. So, how was I supposed to offer hope when it all felt so hopeless? Either Louisa was like me and would bring a fatherless child into a world where there were no certainties, only millions and millions of questions that no one bothered to answer. Or, she would be like Emma.

She would die.

I still could remember every moment of watching Emma's death. Despite the fact that I was currently standing in the middle of a makeshift town miles and miles from the place where she had died, I saw and felt everything from that day. It replayed in my mind like a warning—a more convincing propaganda film than any produced by the council itself.

She had screamed. I'd been able to hear it stick in her throat, caught in a mixture of saliva and blood. I didn't know what I was supposed to do.

She'd reached out her hand to me. I'd hesitated.

I had glared at the midwife who was vainly trying to keep my sister breathing. I wondered what it would feel like knowing no matter how hard you tried, you would always fail. The midwife looked to me and I could read the emotion in her eyes: she was asking my forgiveness. I gritted my teeth and moved my gaze away.

I'd knelt down beside my sister, hoping the action would quiet her unnerving, unceasing cries for me. Her bright, feverish eyes bore into mine. "Did she live?"

"She?" I asked skeptically.

Emma repeated her question. Her longing for an answer was evident in her voice.

"No," I'd said. "It didn't live."

Now, I swallowed, forcing down the shame that washed

over me every time I thought about how I'd acted during Emma's final moments. That was the reason I couldn't be any comfort to Louisa. That was why I had to wait. Let whatever ending fate had decided for her play itself out.

I wasn't strong enough to be there for her. I could stand up to a room full of people I barely knew and threaten to sacrifice myself for the boy I loved. I could learn to shoot guns, willing and able to fight if the need arrived.

But I couldn't be a good sister.

I cleared my throat. "I...I just can't."

Lockwood clenched his jaw and looked away from me. For the first time in our friendship, I felt his disappointment in me. He threw his hands in the air and walked away without saying another word.

As I watched him disappear back toward the infirmary where they had permanently placed Louisa, I felt my chest tighten. It heaved up and down, vainly trying to gather air. But I couldn't breathe. I clutched at the collar of my shirt and pulled it from my neck, but still I couldn't manage to force air into my lungs. I stumbled back. My eyes went wide, searching for someone, anyone to help me.

It had been so long since I'd had a panic attack.

I couldn't watch her die. I couldn't do that again.

Not again.

Not ever. Not ever again.

A gentle hand landed on my shoulder, and I spun around to find Robert. As soon as I saw him, I fell apart, crumpling into his arms.

"Let it out, Tess. Just let it out," he urged.

And so I did. I sobbed and sobbed into the chest of my brother-in-law. The more I cried, let go, the better I felt, until

my wild, incessant sobs turned into a quiet whimper. "I'm
so sorry," I managed, pulling back so I could look up at him.

Robert's brow furrowed. "Sorry for what?"

"How I treated Emma during that last day. I should
have been there for her. I was so selfish and scared. She took
care of me my whole life, and I abandoned her when she
needed me the most," I admitted, my voice hitching as the
tears started to fall once more.

"Abandoned her? What are you talking about? You
think she didn't know you were frightened out of your
mind? The most important thing was that you were there.
That's always the most important thing," he assured me.

As I stared up at the man who traveled with me into the
unknown because he had once loved my sister, I knew he
believed it with all of his heart.

He had always been there.

"I'm scared," I whispered.

"So is she," he answered back.

Later that afternoon, when I was sure any trace of my
breakdown had left my face, I went to my sister's room. As I
moved to open the door, I heard Lockwood's voice coming
from inside.

"I brought a new book today. I think it's right up your
alley. It's by a woman named Jane Austen. Quite a witty one,
that Ms. Austen. The book is called *Pride and Prejudice*."

I smiled to myself, remembering how a boy once tried to
help me with books. Happy to know that even in the wilds of
the community, people believed in the power of the stories

of our past, the stories the council wanted to silence.

I knocked gently on the door before pushing it open. "Mind if I sit and listen? I've never read this one," I said quietly, bracing myself for whatever Lockwood, or Louisa for that matter, had in store for me.

Instead of accusations or judgment, Lockwood smiled. "Not at all."

I smiled back. It was shaky, but a smile all the same.

My sister lay on her cot, curled, like Lockwood had told me, in on herself. Her eyes stared vacantly into the distance. I took a seat on the edge of her cot.

Lockwood gave me a small nod and began to read the witty Ms. Austen's work.

And somewhere between the arrival of Mr. Bingley and the Netherfield ball, Louisa took my hand in hers and squeezed it.

Chapter 9

The door to the infirmary flew open, banging loudly against the wall. I bolted up from the chair where I had fallen asleep watching over Louisa when Lockwood left to take a break, instinctively grabbing for the rifle I always kept at my side since Eric told me I was ready to carry one.

"Sharon needs you," Lockwood panted, his face red from exertion. He had clearly run from wherever he was—and fast.

"What is it?" I asked, putting the rifle down and grabbing for my jacket, pulling it on quickly. Despite the nearness of summer, the air remained cool and crisp.

"She's… Sharon's having the baby."

My stomach dropped. "What…what does she need me for?"

"I don't know. She just keeps asking for you. She's going crazy about it. Melinda begs her to breathe and push, but she won't. She says she needs you."

I looked back at my sister who, somehow, managed to remain asleep despite Lockwood's dramatic entrance. She had been sleeping more and more lately. In fact, her health seemed to be getting worse as the days went on. Her skin had turned an alarming shade of gray. Her hair was always matted to her forehead and cheeks with sweat. She was too weak to even sit up. Sharon had tried to tell me that for some women, especially frail ones like Louisa, pregnancy was harder than usual. My little sister had always been sickly, an affliction that seemed to affect most of the last natural-born children, but this was different. Every time I looked at her, all I could see was Emma writhing and crying out.

But I wouldn't abandon her. Not again.

"Don't worry. I'll watch after her," Lockwood promised.

I hesitated. I hated leaving her. Once my livestock shift was done, I always came straight to the infirmary and sat with her. Louisa still didn't speak much, but I could tell by the way her eyes lit up when I entered the room that she was just as happy as I was to spend time together.

"Okay. I'll go," I said hesitantly, trying to ignore the butterflies in my stomach. "But you have to promise me. The second she shows any sign of...well, anything that doesn't seem right—"

"I'll come get you. I swear it," he interrupted, knowing the dark places my mind wandered to. Most likely because when it came to Louisa, his mind wandered there, too.

Lockwood was the only person who spent as much time with Louisa as I did. Even her own father failed to show up much. He came by now and then, popping his head in and asking how she was. All we could ever tell him was that she was the same. My father usually appeared satisfied with this brief assessment. I knew he was busy, but that didn't mean being with us wasn't important as well. I thought of how hard it was for him to look at her. I understood his fear, but wasn't he supposed to be a fearless leader? How brave could he really be?

Lockwood, on the other hand, was forever by Louisa's side. The more time he spent with her, the more she seemed comforted by his presence. I even heard her ask him to bring another book last week. He had chosen *Vanity Fair*. I liked that maybe she could find a friend in this place. Perhaps, if she survived, she could think of the community as home. Lockwood wanted that as much as I did, and I was eternally grateful to have found such a great ally. Besides, if she lived through the childbirth then it meant she was like me, immune to the illness that killed so many mothers, and the community would beg her to stay.

I ran to Sharon's room as quickly as I could. Unlike back in the compound where women were brought to a special room to give birth, surrounded by medical instruments that couldn't save them, the women of the community did not find it strange to attempt giving birth right in the comfort of their own home. I thought the whole process rather primitive considering the dirt and dust that covered each room no matter how hard one cleaned, but Sharon had given birth to five children successfully, so who was I to judge?

I heard her screams before I could even open the door. It seemed like I couldn't go a day without being reminded of what I'd lost when Emma went away. It was painful enough having to look at Louisa, but hearing Sharon's screams caused a sensory overload.

My hand shook as it reached for the doorknob. I took

a few deep breaths to try and steady my nerves. Sharon went out of her way to check in on my sister every day, so I owed her this. I owed her for other reasons as well. She had given me so much, despite the way I had judged her during my early days in the community. Back then, I thought her simpleminded, nothing but a mule with no other purpose than to bring babies into the world. But she was so much more. She was the mother I never had and always wanted.

As I pushed the door open, Sharon's screams stopped. She lifted her head from the cot where she lay sweating. "I've been waiting for you," she managed between uneven, labored breaths.

Melinda, the other woman who had assisted her the day Al and his men were shot, stood at the foot of her bed. Two of Sharon's eldest daughters huddled in the corner, one holding a basin of water.

"I came as fast as I could," I explained, slightly embarrassed by how shaky my voice sounded.

Sharon, whose hands gripped onto the sweaty and bloody sheet beneath her, unclenched her fist and reached out a hand toward me. "I was waiting and waiting. I needed you to see this."

I stepped gingerly into the room. "See what?" Sharon threw her head back and groaned.

"You have to push," begged Melinda. "Tess, tell her she has to push."

"You heard her. Push, Sharon," I implored, still unsure what power I had in this room of life itself.

Sharon blew air in and out of her nose, gritting her teeth. "Come hold my hand," she managed.

I saw her again. Emma. The way she held out her hand

to me. The way I didn't take it. I swallowed as I rushed to Sharon and clutched her hand to my chest, falling to my knees by her bedside. "Tell me what you want me to do."

She reached up a hand and tucked a strand of hair behind my ear. "Look at how scared you are. That's why I needed you here. I need you to watch. To see."

"We can't wait any longer," Melinda insisted, looking under the sheet that covered Sharon's legs.

"You ready?" Sharon asked, turning her head up to look at me.

I couldn't help but laugh at the insanity of her question. "Are you?"

"I was born to do this," she replied, narrowing her eyes, readying her body for what was about to happen.

Born to do this. That was the idea that separated us. Sharon felt it was her duty to help the naturals continue. She gave herself willingly to the men of the community because she thought God had chosen her, selected her to save mankind. It was her responsibility.

It felt more like a burden to me.

As Sharon pushed and pushed, her body contorting and shifting in ways I didn't think possible, I thought of the millions of women who came before her and all the reasons they had for taking on the task. I wasn't naive; I knew some women had no choice at all. But others, like Emma, wanted it so desperately.

Sharon lifted her back off the cot and reached forward with her free hand, reaching into the unknown. She stared straight ahead. Her brow was furrowed, sweat dripping down the side of her face.

I had always seen her choice to mother the children

of the community as weak; giving up so much of herself to some larger idea that, in the long run, probably wouldn't matter. The council wasn't just going to disappear, and the community wouldn't remain hidden forever. No matter how many children she brought into the world, the end was near for mankind.

But as I watched Sharon, her determination never wavering for even a second, I saw it for what it was—strength. She was a warrior just like Eric or my father. Maybe I didn't agree with her reasons for fighting, but I was glad she was fighting on my side.

I clutched onto Sharon's hand, which still rested over my heart, until the cry of the newborn baby filled the room. The shrill noise caused my arms to erupt in goose bumps. I pulled myself to my feet in an attempt to get a look at it.

This was the part I never got to see with Emma.

Melinda took the baby to a table in the corner of the room and went to work, checking and rechecking to make sure it was healthy.

"Look how anxious you are," Sharon said tiredly, squeezing my hand.

I felt my cheeks burn. "I just want to…"

"Just wait. This is my favorite part." Sharon squeezed my hand again.

Melinda wrapped the baby in a white blanket and brought the child to her mother. Sharon untangled her hand from mine, and I had to uncramp my fingers from the pressure she had exerted on them during the labor. As Melinda sat the baby in her arms, Sharon burst into tears. Not the sad kind. Not tears of loss. But, rather, tears of the purest joy I had ever seen.

When I looked down at the baby, I found myself crying, too. A warmness, an unconditional lightness, one that had no beginning and no end, a lightness that I had never felt before, filled me to the brim. This was the beginning, not the ending, Emma should have gotten. The one she always wanted. "She's beautiful," I choked out, wiping a tear from my cheek.

"Life always is. That's why I needed you to see. I needed you to know what this could be," she whispered, her eyes becoming heavy with exhaustion.

I heard the words she didn't say—Sharon needed me to see what it could be in case it wasn't like this with Louisa. Because even if I watched her die, Sharon still held out hope that one day I would be a mother.

"Tess," Sharon called to me.

"Yes?"

"I want you to name her," she said.

I stared down at the baby who looked up at me, her eyes furiously blinking, unused to the sun that streamed in through the windows. I didn't know if I would ever choose to be a mother, but it was a choice I was glad I got to make. I had seen this battle lost too many times.

It was good to know that sometimes we could win it.

"Emma. I want to name her Emma," I said.

Chapter 10

Tess,

Have you written since your first letter? Are you safe? I haven't heard from you. Things are getting worse. Much, much worse. If I knew you were okay, I could handle it. I need to know you still exist because they are trying to erase you.

I don't know how to pretend like I hate you. I've tried. But somehow, the council can tell. I repeat all the lines they have given me about your people, the naturals. I've told them how you used your body, your smiles, your words to make me think that you loved me, used that love as a weapon to destroy me. Bent me to your will, so I would follow you till the end of time. Forever leaving and forgetting about the council.

I tell them all of these things day in and day out, and they still don't believe me. The funny thing is almost everything I have told them is true. Love is a weapon. It has consumed me like a fire that burns and rages, spreads and consumes. And I love all of you. Your smiles. Your words. Your body. You never had to bend me to your will because wherever you went, I wanted to follow. Not out of some weak obsession, but, rather, because when I am with you, I am my best self. My only self.

The council wants me to be something different. Darker. Violent.

I even tried to bring forth that side of me. I was created as a weapon. It is in my very being. You would think it would be easy to pretend, but I am constantly failing at it. I thought about every bad thing my kind has done to yours, every heartbreak they ever caused you. But still they could tell. Knowing you has changed me in ways science cannot undo; science couldn't even predict it.

So, they torture me.

At least I know why. They're scared. Petrified. I can overhear them talking when they think my mind is too dulled by the pain. Someone took something from them, and they want it back.

They are in a panic. All of my fellow chosen ones talk about their assigned creators. The long meetings they are called into. The sleepless nights. The uneaten meals. I don't see my creator very often. I only know that the accident I didn't stop nearly took his life. He's having a hard time healing due to his old age. I overhear the rumors about his father—Abrams. Horrible, twisted stories. Have you heard of this man? It's all anyone seems to talk about around here. Especially when they think I have passed out from the pain.

I wish they would just leave me alone, but they need me. I'm not sure why, but I'm the key.

They want me to save the council.

So, I continue to try. Maybe if I can pretend long enough, well enough, I can find out what they are so desperate to get back.

If I can, I'll make sure they never get it again.

~James

Chapter 11

My father had been holding onto my letters. James needed my words, and my father had never sent them. At least not after the first one. I practically ran to the dining hall where my father was holding a meeting with his advisors. With every step I took, James's desperate pleas went round and round inside my head. He was living in hell and he had no one. Not even my letters.

I was going to kill my father.

Abrams. James had mentioned that the men around him kept whispering about his creator's father. It was a name I'd heard growing up, a memory I had to work hard at pulling out from all the other thoughts that muddled my mind. Abrams was a story told at night to scare little children, no more real than a bogeyman or the monster that lived under the bed. Hardly anyone talked of the original creators, nameless men who had faded away in time. The chosen ones were the face of the council now; no one bothered to spend time learning the history of the creators. They were merely the workmen; the council and its army of genetically engineered superhumans were the real stars.

But Abrams had been different. Stories floated around about this particular scientist. It was rumored that he had killed the original five creators, those responsible for the first batch of chosen ones, in the midst of some psychotic break. Included in that mix, his own father. The council had even used the story as part of its propaganda—see how even the best of us naturals can fall? He had been a scary story to me. Nothing more. I had too much to hate right there in front of my face growing up; I didn't have time to hate a legend.

"Your mother would have hated those pants."

I skidded to a stop, nearly colliding with my father. He was standing on the steps of the building that served as the dining room. Somehow, he knew I was coming for him. He let out a low whistle. "I mean it. She would have never let you out of the house wearing those."

"My mother hated a lot of things," I fumed, attempting to wipe some of the dirt off the trousers I had taken to wearing.

For some reason, my father smiled. "You and I have always been alike in a lot of ways. Misunderstanding your mother being one of them."

"Where are my letters?" I yelled, refusing to waste another second on some pointless battle of wits with my father.

He swallowed, kicking at the dirt beneath his feet. "I guess you read about that in the last letter from your boyfriend?"

Of course. He knew James had told me. "You've been

reading my letters from James, haven't you?" I asked, appalled.

My father lifted his head and looked me dead in the eyes. "Did you really believe I wouldn't? Don't go thinking I'm playing father and trying to make sure you two are keeping it above board. I'm no idiot. I've got no right telling my girl who she can date. But I can't pass up the opportunity to search those letters for anything that can help the cause."

I bit the inside of my cheek, shaking my head. "Is that why you said I could write him? So you could have a chosen one on the inside?"

"I'd be lying if I said it wasn't part of the reason. He can see and hear things my men can't. But it wasn't the entire reason I let you write to him and him to you. I could see what he meant to you. I'm not completely heartless." He took a step closer to me.

"Then why hasn't he gotten any of my letters? I know you've been going through them, crossing out anything you think can lead them back here."

My father reached forward and placed a hand on my shoulder. When I tried to shake it off, he gripped onto it. "I never kept anything he said from you. But I can't let you write to him anymore. It's too dangerous. It's clear from his letters that they already know too much about you. I'm sorry, Tessie."

I clenched my jaw and looked away. It made sense, and James would want to keep me safe. But it wasn't fair, and I didn't know how to deal with all the unfairness anymore. Hating the world didn't end it. Loving didn't end it, either.

"Why even let me have his letters? Just for your damn intel?" I charged.

"We all need something to hold onto," he explained quietly. "Despite what you think, I'm not a total monster." When I didn't reply, he sighed. "What I told you a few weeks ago was true. Everything I have done and everything I am planning, I do for you and your sisters. Sister," he amended. "I'm going to fix this world."

"You? You're going to fix it?" I asked. "How do you plan on doing that?"

"It's better if you don't know all the details. In fact, you're safer if you don't. But when this is done and—"

I held up my hand to stop him. "I don't want to hear it. It's better for me if I don't hear all the details? I've been told that line before, and let me just say, I'm *never* better off. Besides, you don't get to make those decisions for me anymore. I can fight, you know. If that's your big plan. I know how to shoot a gun."

I wanted to fight. If loving and hating didn't make the pain go away, maybe fighting would.

"Fighting is more than knowing how to shoot a gun. If you had a halfway decent teacher, you'd know that."

"I had a great teacher," I said. "You'd agree if you got to know Eric."

With a growl, my father grabbed onto my elbow, yanking me along with him. He moved so fast through the community that I could barely keep up. He didn't stop till we reached one of the barns that lay outside of the borders. Five of his men stood guard around the fenced-in area where we kept a few horses. Only there weren't horses in the pen any longer.

Inside stood a deformed chosen one. Well, not so much stood as crawled. His legs had been chopped off at the knees. Despite a steady flow of blood that streamed down onto the ground, the beast thrashed against the dirt floor, hissing and foaming at the mouth. Before I could speak, my father lifted me up and threw me into the pen.

"What the hell are you doing?" I screamed, scrambling to my feet. At the sound of my voice, the monster stopped moving, lifting his torso high off the ground with his arms. He dropped his head back as his nostrils flared, taking in my scent. I stumbled to the fence post and turned to climb out when my father pulled a gun from his holster and held it at my head. On cue, every gun in the vicinity was trained on me.

"So, you're ready to fight?" my father yelled, his face turning red. "What happens when they take that gun away from you? They'll definitely try. In fact, once they do, you're pretty much done for. A gun is a weapon; it's not any sort of safety guarantee. That weapon up there is just as important as any gun." He pointed at my forehead.

A guttural, wet groan came from behind me. I flipped around to see the creature pulling his body toward where I stood, and the fear came rushing over me. The pounding heart. The sweaty palms. The millions of cells inside of me that flared alive. But I didn't have time for any of it. I had to fight.

I looked around at my father's men, but none made a move to help me. "I don't get you. Any of you," I yelled, scurrying away from the creature. I had the advantage of speed, but that was about it. "You walk around like you have all the answers, but if you did, then why are our women still dying? Why do we have to hide away in the woods, praying that they won't find us? You don't know how to fix this world because there's no fixing it. This is all just about power.

That's why you hate the council. Not because of what they took from us, but because you weren't smart enough to take it first!"

"Don't think that thing won't tear you limb from limb. He gets ahold of a leg and you're done for. How long can you run around that pen till you get tired?" my father asked, ignoring my tirade. "He'll *never* get tired. That's the way he's been made. He's an exterminator. And there are two ways to take him down — the heart and the head. But you got no gun. So, what do you do?"

I had no gun. I wouldn't be able to take him out with my fists alone. I continued to move around the perimeter of the fenced-in cage, searching the ground for something, anything to use. A large rock lay just outside of the post. If I lay down, I might be able to reach it.

"It's a risk," my father called out, seeing me eyeing the rock. "It means turning your back to it. It means you have to be fast."

"It's the only option I've got," I spat back. The monster roared, snapping his teeth furiously. He was tiring of this game as much as I was. I took a deep breath. I didn't count to three. I didn't have time.

With a grunt, I threw myself down to the ground, stretching my arm as far as it would go under the fence. My side was still tender from the stab wound, and it burned as I pushed my body to grab for the rock. I felt pressure before I could react. The creature bit down on my foot, the hard sole of my shoe saving me from getting it torn clear off, but it wouldn't save me for long.

I didn't scream. I didn't panic. The minute I did, I would be dead. I pushed my arm even further, and I nearly wept when my hand clutched onto the rock. I knew I had only one shot, and I hoped one shot was all I needed. I lifted my free foot high into the air and brought it down right onto the back of the creature's skull. It was enough to leave him disoriented. Enough to get me to my feet.

Now came the moment of truth.

Would I be strong enough to bring it down?

I lifted the rock high above my head and it came down with the force of a hundred scared girls. Girls who were told they were nothing. Girls who were abandoned. Girls who weren't as lucky as me. And then I brought it back up and down again. And again. And again. Until I couldn't lift my arms anymore.

The creature wasn't ever going to move again.

I turned around, my face covered in blood, and looked up at my father. He was smiling. "We start training tomorrow," he said proudly. He reached forward a hand, helping me over the fence.

Once I was safe, I planted my hands on my father's chest and shoved as hard as I could, considering my strength was spent. "Who the hell do you think you are? Are you crazy?" I screamed. Before my father could open his mouth to speak, I shoved him again. "I could have died!"

The fear that I had buried washed over me. I could barely contain the tears that threatened to spill. My hands hummed and buzzed with an energy I had never known in my entire life. I clenched them into fists. My father stared down at me, seemingly calm except for the way his eyes narrowed. "But you didn't die," he said slowly.

The hair on the back of my neck stood up. I looked around to see my father's soldiers enclosing us. Sensing their alarm, my father held up his hand. "Everything is fine. Leave us," he commanded.

"But, sir…" One of his men hesitated.

"I said leave us," my father clipped in response.

Without another word of objection, my father's men disappeared, leaving me with the man who had set up my demise and the chosen one I had killed.

The chosen one I had killed.

I had killed something. I slowly dragged my eyes to the bloodied mess of a creature that lay on the dirt ground. I brought a shaky hand up to cover my mouth; I wasn't entirely sure I could keep at bay the nausea that was coursing through me.

"It deserved to die," my father said softly. I wasn't like most of the naturals, who would consider the death of any chosen one a good thing. Because I loved a chosen one. I couldn't just write off his death because he was different. Just as James could not write off the death of my people because we were naturals. And while in the end I knew it was the deformed chosen one's death or mine, and I would always choose life, it didn't mean I would be happy about it.

"You learned a good lesson today, Tessie," my father said, pulling my attention away from the body.

"A good lesson?" I scoffed. "This isn't the piano! This isn't the kind of lesson a parent should teach his child," I spat.

"Isn't it, though? Look at the world we are in. Isn't this the best lesson I could ever teach you?"

I shook my head. "And what am I supposed to learn from this violence? This death?"

My dad placed both of his hands on my face. "You're

supposed to learn how much you want to live. You're supposed to learn what you'll have to accomplish in order to do so," he replied, his voice cracking. "I wish it were different. This world. Us. But it is what it is, and it won't ever change unless we change it. And that means doing things, ugly things."

I reached up and pulled my father's hands from my face. I swallowed back the emotions that crept up from within me as I saw the tears pool in his eyes. "What's changed?" I asked, averting my eyes from his face. "You didn't want me involved. You wanted me to sit back and follow your lead. Trust you."

"I wanted to keep you safe. But I was foolish to think you'd sit back and let me. You're a fighter — I can see that. Too much like me. So, if you're going to fight, I'd rather be the one to teach you."

I pressed my lips together and nodded. Despite everything, a part of me soared at hearing my father tell me that I was like him. That I was a fighter. Even though his bloody lesson was nowhere near that piano from my childhood, for a second, just a second, I felt like that little girl again.

"I wouldn't have let the thing kill you. If you needed me, I would have saved you. But I knew you wouldn't need me, and I needed you to know that, too."

I should have been angry with him, but I wasn't. I felt different as I walked with my father back to the community in silence. Like some fire had been lit inside of me. It didn't burn me through like Henry's fire, but, instead, it guided me. A light in the darkness.

A purpose. Was this the feeling my father searched for when he left?

"I'm sorry for not telling you about the letters," he said when we reached the dining hall. "I know what it is to love like that," he added quietly.

I raised an eyebrow. I hadn't ever remembered seeing affection shared between my parents.

"Your mother wasn't always the woman you knew. She was different before the world completely went to hell. She was a lot like—"

"Louisa," I finished. "I know. They were always so close. You should go see her." My father opened his mouth to reply, but I cut him off. "She needs you. I know things with us haven't been easy since you've been back, but I'm still glad you're here. She needs you, too," I repeated.

My father took a deep breath, running a hand over his face. "I'll go see her now. All right?"

I nodded. Everything, momentarily, was all right.

• • •

"If you're not going to eat that, I'll sure as hell take it," Stephanie said to Henry, reaching over and grabbing a piece of meat off his plate with her fork.

"Who said I wasn't going to eat it? You know what they say about people who assume things?" he asked. I looked up at Henry, expecting to find a scowl or at least a sense of stoniness, but he was grinning at Stephanie.

When I had spotted Henry and Stephanie sitting together at dinner, I didn't think I would be interrupting something if I sat with them. My body was still tingling and jumpy from my encounter with the chosen one, and I had hoped listening to them prattle on would be enough to calm my nerves.

Stephanie laughed. It was much brighter, lighter than I had expected from someone like her. "You were batting it around like you had invented a new sport," she said, reaching over again for a second piece.

Henry chuckled and pushed his plate in front of Stephanie. She grinned even wider. "And what exactly do they say about people who assume things?"

"That you make an ass out of you and me," I spoke up, finishing their lame joke. For some reason their happiness was rubbing me the wrong way, and it wasn't because of jealousy. As I shoveled the food into my mouth, the high I experienced after proving I could handle myself was fading. Something else was replacing it.

Something darker.

"I thought you had duty tonight?" Henry asked Stephanie.

"I did. Charlie let me off early. We all hate when he does that. He's so important to the cause, you know? But there's no telling him otherwise. When he gets an idea in his head, well, he — "

"I have no problem telling him otherwise," I cut in, attempting a smile. Penance for my earlier grouchy behavior.

"You're his daughter. I think all daughters are wired for that," she replied good-naturedly.

"You told him, right? About my involvement with the resistance movement back at Templeton?" Henry asked, choosing to ignore my remarks.

I wondered what he had told Stephanie about his involvement in the murder of young incubating chosen ones. His girlfriend at the time, Julia, had pulled the cords on the machines that kept them alive. He had never bothered to explain to me exactly what his role was in the event. The council never found out he was a part of it, but Julia was executed.

Stephanie nodded, stuffing a forkful of food into her mouth.

"Well, what did he say?"

Stephanie held up a finger as she finished chewing. As she took her time, I suspected she was trying to come up with an answer that, while truthful, would still please him. Henry must have picked up on the stalling tactic as well because he reached over and placed a hand on her arm. "Don't worry about it. I figured he wouldn't let me in."

My eyes widened as I watched Henry's hand lingering on her arm. Even more surprising, she didn't seem to have a problem with it. I cleared my throat, and he pulled his hand back.

"That's not it at all. He appreciates your dedication to the cause, but he just has a lot on his shoulders right now. I mean something big. Maybe when this is over, you two can talk," she replied.

"No, I get it," Henry said casually. Too casually. He was putting on a show to make her feel better. I knew how much Henry's need for revenge against the council propelled him—it was what drove him. And I didn't entirely blame him. He had watched the council brutally attack and murder his mother and sisters. I thought of Louisa, pregnant and scared, and I wanted a bit of revenge myself.

"Seriously. Once this is all done, we'll both go and talk to him. We could use a good man like you," Stephanie said.

The side of Henry's mouth pulled up in an attempt at a smile. "A good man, huh? You obviously didn't hear that from anyone I know."

Stephanie blushed again, and I was sure this time it had nothing to do with me. "Sometimes you can just tell."

As I left the dining hall, I nearly knocked into Eric. "Whoa, there. What's got your ass on fire?" he asked, grabbing me by the elbows in an attempt to steady me.

"Nothing," I lied. I still couldn't shake the dark feeling that had grabbed hold of me.

"Doesn't seem like nothing," he teased, looking over my head into the dining hall. "Aren't those two cozy? What do you think that's all about?"

I shrugged. "Nothing. Henry wants in on whatever my father is cooking up."

"Nah, it's more than that. They're looking pretty intimate if you ask me. There's all kinds of wants and needs bouncing between those two," he noted, leaning back against a post. A lazy smile graced his face, and I could tell there was a part of him that enjoyed making me uncomfortable. I imagined this was what it would have been like if I had ever had an older brother.

I decided to give in to his bait. "Wants and needs?" I asked.

"Yeah. That's how people work. How they size each other up. Whenever you meet someone new you gotta ask yourself two things: What do I need from him? What do I want from him? And for most people you'll meet it's usually a pretty good mixture of wanting and needing, but when you find that person you want more than you need…well, that's got trouble all over it."

Eric's smile disappeared. "McNair told me that once." He pushed himself on the post and began to walk back and forth. "Something's not right about this, Tess."

"What do you mean?" I asked, not liking the way a chill had danced its way up my spine at his words.

"So, your father rescues you and just sits around the community. For what?"

"He says he's planning something." But at Eric's words the feeling I had been trying to push down almost consumed me. Something wasn't right. Why *would* my father tell me he wanted me out of this only to train me to fight? Why the sudden change? Was it just to teach his stubborn daughter a lesson? He told me it was because I was going to fight anyway, but it still seemed so sudden. Now that the adrenaline had worn off, my lesson seemed demented, brutal.

"Yeah, but what? If it's some sort of attack, then why base yourself here? We're quite a ways from the council headquarters."

I shrugged, forcing my face to hide my doubts. "We have our own rebel sect here."

"Yeah, but all they ever do is gather intel. They're not really the fighting kind."

"Well, if they're into gathering intel then maybe that's what my father is doing. Gathering information so he can set his plan into motion," I suggested.

"It doesn't feel like he's planning anything. It feels like he's hiding from someone, and he drags that group of yes-sir men and women around with him for protection," Eric said.

"Hiding? I don't think my father's the run from a fight type. He left my family to fight in the resistance."

"Maybe he's not hiding," Eric said. "Maybe he's hiding something."

"What would he be hiding?" I asked. But something

whispered in the back of my mind. Mention of a package. Could that be it? But what object could be so important?

Eric stared off into the slowly fading sunlight. A sign that the one thing we could always count on was that light would give in to darkness. "I don't know, but I intend to find out. If you hear anything, you'll let me know?"

Eric could read my hesitation. "You're one of us now. You're part of this community. Whatever your father is hiding, by keeping it here, he's putting everyone in danger. People who took you in, Tess. Despite everything, you should remember that."

I thought of Lockwood and Sharon, and I knew I would do anything to protect them. They had become my family out in the wildness.

"The people who live here didn't come to this place because they wanted to fight. They came here because they wanted to live," Eric said softly.

I nodded. "You're right. And I'll do whatever I can to make sure they're safe."

Eric exhaled with relief. "Now, we just need to find out what he's planning."

I looked up at my new co-conspirator. "I think I may have an idea. How long does it take to make that shine stuff? You know, that drink that makes you drunk?"

Eric simply grinned.

Chapter 12

Later that evening, I trudged toward the infirmary where Louisa was staying. I lifted my hand to knock on the door when I heard her laugh drift out from underneath it. I stilled. It was one of the most beautiful noises I had ever heard. I cringed thinking about how shrill her laughter had always sounded to my ears. Now that I could lose her, it brought me joy.

I leaned my ear against the door. Lockwood's muffled voice called out to me, and I couldn't help but smile, shaking my head slightly. Of course Lockwood would be able to get Louisa to laugh. He was a pro at making people feel better.

"You really think I'm like her? Emma is my favorite of Ms. Austen's characters," Louisa said.

"Of course I do," Lockwood replied, an airy, amused lightness to his voice.

"I guess she really isn't that likeable though. She can come across as pretty selfish. I guess I *am* like her."

"People only say that because they don't know her. Her intentions are commendable. She wants the best for everyone she cares about. Sure, maybe she goes about it the wrong way, but she never tries to hurt anyone."

"I don't think anyone has ever misread me," Louisa said. "I've always done and said exactly what I wanted. It's funny. I could always fool the others—my oldest sister and the rest of the compound people—but never Tess. She always saw me for what I was."

"Maybe she saw you for who you were, but now she gets to see who you become. Besides, I don't think you're selfish. And any girl who says exactly what she wants is appreciated by this man," Lockwood teased.

Louisa laughed again. Louder. Stronger. "You're a rare find! When I worked at Templeton, that's the way they wanted us. Shy. Eyes down. Simpering like we didn't know that we could want anything for ourselves at all. Even George…"

I gritted my teeth at the mention of his name, pressing my ear harder against the door. Louisa sniffled. I placed my hand against the door, wanting to comfort her but knowing I had to pull myself together. I had to be strong when I entered that room.

When I reached for the doorknob, Lockwood's voice stopped me. "Shhh, it's all right. I promise it's going to be all right."

"But it isn't," Louisa insisted. "Nothing will ever be all right again. Either I die or I become a mother. I'm not ready to be a mom. God, I was so dumb. Silly to believe all the pretty things he said to me. I didn't care who said it; I was just so desperate to hear them."

"What he did to you is one of the most vile, sickening

things I can imagine one person doing to another. What right do any of us have to wreck people's lives for our own personal gain?"

"He didn't force me. I gave myself to him willingly. It's my fault as much as his," she said. "Even if I make it through this, I'm ruined. Who would want me? I gave myself to a chosen one."

"You listen to me, Louisa," Lockwood demanded. His voice carried a tone I had never heard before. "Maybe you were naive. Maybe you share the blame, but in no way should that bastard not be damned a thousand times for how he used you."

"But—"

"No," Lockwood interrupted. "I'm not done. I want you to understand one thing. You are not ruined. You are not beyond repair. When you make it through this, and you will, you deserve to find happiness just as much as anyone else who walks this world."

I dropped my hand and took a step away from the door. I wouldn't interrupt their moment. I knew what it meant to have a person like Lockwood in your life. A person who was there for you and guided you, not out of some assumed family obligation, but because he wanted to be there.

I walked into the night air. I walked and walked until I reached the border. I nodded to the guards, my father's men, who patrolled. Unlike before, when we could go if we wanted, my father forbade anyone from leaving the community unless it was to report to one of the farms for work. I leaned against the gate and looked up at the stars.

Somewhere, James was just as trapped as I was.

I thought of the morning after we'd had sex. When it was

over, we'd lain with each other, curled against one another, never beginning and never ending. We'd stayed like that till the sun began to rise.

James had reached down and pulled me off the ground. He'd worn a satisfied grin on his face. "Someone is mighty proud of himself," I teased.

He'd laughed. It bounced through the forest, calling it awake. Readying it for the day. "I'm just insanely happy."

I stood on the tips of my toes and kissed him gently on his scar. "I'm insanely happy too," I whispered.

James looked down at me, and I was lost all over again. I would never tire of looking into those mismatched eyes. They didn't make him different. They made him *him*. He chuckled as he reached over and pulled a leaf from my tangled hair. "They'll know just by looking at you that we've been up to no good."

"No good?" I said. "I thought it was very, very good."

James growled and lifted me up into the air. I wrapped my legs around his waist and he pressed his lips hungrily against mine. I moved my hands to his hair, curling my fingers into it, attaching myself to him. I never wanted to let go. Every part of me ached to be touched by him, and every part of me ached to touch him right back.

"Do you know how much I love you?" he breathed into the base of my neck. His lips fluttered against my skin.

I nodded, kissing the top of his head. "As much as I love you."

James slowly put my feet back on the ground. On the way down, I pressed my body against his. He cradled my face in his hands. "That will never change. No matter what."

I looked deep into his eyes. "I know." Because I did. It

was one of life's few assurances. I would always love James.

I pressed my lips once again to his scar. "I adore this," I whispered, unable to hide the smile that seemed etched on my face all morning.

"Only you would love a man's fault." He chuckled.

"I love every part of you," I replied, running my fingers down his chest.

"You're enough to drive a man crazy," he said. The tremble in his voice caused my toes to curl. I wanted him again. And again. And again.

My fingers traced the waist of his pants. "Tonight?" I said, knowing full well it was a promise I wouldn't be able to keep.

James grabbed my hand and brought it to his lips. "Tonight," he echoed.

As the sun climb higher into the sky, I knew our moment was coming to an end. James reached down and placed his hand over my heart. "Thank you," he said.

"For what?" I asked, my voice choked with emotion.

"For everything."

As the memory slipped away, I looked back up at the night sky. Praying and hoping that James knew how much I wanted to thank him, too.

For everything.

Chapter 13

Tess,

The memories are slipping. They have always been what I clung to in those moments when the thought of never seeing you again seems like the only possible ending to our story.

I flip through them like the pages of the books we used to share. I see you that day in the piano room. I remember how you played with such reckless abandon. I think I loved you even then. I loved the idea of you. So much passion within those delicate fingers as they pressed against the keys. You were already so different than what the council told me you would be. I saw it in the way you looked at me. An intelligence, a need that echoed mine in so many ways. The wish to be defiant.

When I got past the idea of you, the projection

of everything I was told would undo me but only made me, I was a goner. Because when I learned about the girl who sat on my bed with me, traveling to the worlds kept from us, I knew I would never love anyone else.

I always imagined that when you went off to the community, you would love again. I would never blame you for seeking happiness. I want you to have it so badly. But just as I knew you would find it, I knew there was no other for me but you. I'm sure I sound like one of the characters from some long-ago-outlawed novel, but why not love like them? Why not love forever? I have always been told that love is a weakness, but I think it is my salvation.

But they mean to take these memories from me.

I have tried not to write about these moments. I have been worried what they will do to you if you ever read these letters. Only, I fear what these moments are doing to me. I try so hard to fight back, but the council, as you know, is strong. Their strength does not come in the way their armies move across the lands, though that in itself is a force to reckon with. Rather, it comes in the way they control our minds. I believe that is the true danger.

So, I will write these dark moments here. In case I cannot fight them off. In case they take you from me. I want you to know I fought, and what they are capable of.

They have abandoned the notion of trying to talk you out of my brain. They had even stopped showing me the propaganda videos. They have moved onto newer, more specialized tactics.

These are the people who created me, Tess. They cooked me up in a lab like I was a three-course dinner. Kendall picked my hair color, my weight, and size. He played around with my brain to try and foster my ability. They molded me into a fighting machine. So, they will do what needs to be done to keep me.

The creators are my God, and I am supposed to bow to them.

Their methods are torturous. A few mornings ago, they tied me down to a gurney and wheeled me into one of the headquarters' labs. Without any kind of sedation, they inserted a wire up through my nose. They shoved and shoved until the cord, which seemed to come alive on its own, attached to my brain.

I know they wanted me to scream out, but I held it together. I thought back on you. I was saving you. At least the you that exists in my brain. So, I gritted my teeth and bore it. But that was only the beginning of the procedure.

Two of the creators watched a tiny screen, which beeped and blipped at them. Somehow through the machine, they could read when I was thinking of you. Perhaps it was my accelerated heartbeat or some chemical being released, but every time I reached for you within my mind, the pain came.

All kinds of pain. The first time it was an intense wave of nausea. It almost felt as if my stomach was turning in on itself. It was so strong I was sure I was going to vomit all over myself. Still, I did not cry out.

I searched my mind for another memory of you. I thought of the first time we kissed. How you so hesitantly asked me if I wanted to kiss you. How long I had dreamed of the words. I never thought it would actually come true.

As I thought of that bliss, that moment I will treasure as long as I am still me, they started the second round. This time it was as if my nose had been broken. I swear I even heard the crack. I couldn't help it; I gasped out. One of the doctors smiled at me. The sight of his pleasure at my pain called forth what strength I had left inside.

I took a deep breath and closed my eyes. I let every memory I had ever shared with you rush upon my mind. I lavished in them. Despite the pain in my nose, I couldn't help but smile. The machine blared wildly, signaling that this would not be an easy battle for them.

Then came the third round of pain. Slowly, they broke every bone in my body, snapping and splintering like trees caught in an angry storm. I managed to lift my head up to scope out my injuries. To my utter astonishment, every bone was perfectly fine.

They had used the wire they attached to my

brain to make me think I was feeling these things. The second I started to feel better, they began the process again. Nausea and broken bones.

This went on for hours. Until it happened.

I don't even want to write it. I am so ashamed. I have betrayed you, Tess.

The last time I went to think of you, I stopped myself. Your image came into my mind, and I shut you out. I forced you away. My body tensed and cringed, trying to shield itself from the pain they would fool it into feeling.

But after I shut away thoughts of you, they stopped. They pulled the wire from my nose, and they were done with me.

The next day I held out a little longer. I had spent the previous night preparing myself. But the day after that, I lasted a little less. And the next day, I gave in even quicker.

This has gone on for one week. Today, I didn't get past the nausea.

Please forgive me.

~James

Chapter 14

"I see she's dragged you into this as well," Henry deadpanned.

"Well, she needed a supplier, didn't she?" Eric replied, pulling a jar of tannish liquid from his coat pocket.

"Will you guys just come in already?" I asked. "You're causing a scene."

Time was not on my side, and I needed answers. I had to know what my father's plans were. Despite training for an hour with him every morning for weeks, I was no closer to the truth. And James was fading. Every morning I re-read all of his letters. His words, his pleas, were what kept me going. Any time I began to doubt what I was about to do, I clutched the letters to my chest, closed my eyes, and reminded myself exactly what I was fighting for.

Cramped into the tiny hallway outside my room stood Eric, Lockwood, and Henry. I opened the door wider and ushered them in. "Where's Stephanie?" I asked when Henry walked past me.

"Oh, Stephanie's coming? I didn't know that," he said, feigning ignorance. He had looked toward the stairs about a million times in the brief moments he stood outside my door. He had been the first to arrive, so we both made pathetic attempts at conversation to avoid entering the room we once had shared alone. Henry bunked with Lockwood now.

I needed Stephanie for my plan. I had made sure she didn't have duty, practically begging her to join us. Once I let it slip that Henry would be attending our small party as well, she couldn't agree faster.

Not that I had created some genius master plan. I'd simply thought back to the last time I had drank the community's mystery liquor, and how easily words and truths slipped from my mouth. Like rain that had no choice but to fall from the sky and touch everything. I assumed that since Stephanie committed her life to the great cause, she was just as unused to the potent drink as Henry and I had been. If I could get her drunk enough, maybe she would spill information about my father's plan.

"You brought me here to drink?" Lockwood asked. His brow furrowed; he was clearly not impressed. It had taken forever to convince him to leave Louisa's side, until Sharon volunteered to sit with her for a few hours. Despite giving birth only weeks before, she was back up on her feet, attending to the needs of everyone.

"I think we could all use a little fun. One night, Lockwood. Think about the last month of our lives. It's been pretty stressful, no?" I said.

Lockwood sighed, a deep, soul-shaking sigh. His shoulders slumped as he released all the tension that he held inside. "Yeah. I guess I could use a night off. Not that staying with Louisa is a job. Because it isn't. I didn't mean it that—"

I placed a hand on his shoulder. "You don't need to explain. I understand."

"Are we going to sit here all night and rationalize every decision we make, or can we just damn drink already?" Eric said. "I, for one, prefer drinking. The best part about it is you won't ever think of making decisions at all. This beautiful stuff makes them for you." He brought the jar to his lips, then handed it to me. "Ladies first," he said.

"I'm not sure I would call you a lady, Eric. There are a few other words that might fit," Lockwood said.

"Let me rephrase. Ladies after stunningly macho men who could kick your ass," Eric countered.

I laughed and shook my head. I tipped back the jar and pretended to drink; I even made a face as I pulled the jar from my lips. Eric had made me practice my expression what felt like a hundred times earlier in the day. He didn't think I was good at keeping my emotions in check. I tended to think he was right.

There was a soft knock on the door. Henry, who had been sitting on the windowsill, shot up at the sound. "I'll get it," he chirped.

"Wants and needs," Eric muttered beside me.

"Sorry I'm late," Stephanie said as she walked into the room. My mouth fell open.

Stephanie was stunning. Gone was the tight ponytail and dirty uniform. Her black hair was free, cascading past her elbows. She wore a long pale blue skirt with a white blouse pulled tight enough to prove to anyone who wondered that she was all woman, not a girl. The sleeves of her blouse were shorter than what most women wore in the community, showcasing her tight and toned arms. She was the perfect mixture of toughness and beauty.

I crossed my arms on my chest. Between worrying about Louisa and trying to spy on my father, it had been weeks since I had bathed. I was dirt and dust, tiredness and lost hope.

I looked over at the other boys, who were also caught in the brightness that Stephanie brought with her into the room, entrapped as if all sense had been stolen from them. I cleared my throat. "You're not late at all. We just got started," I said, trying to keep a smile on my face.

I walked over to where Stephanie stood and looped my arm around hers. I pulled her into the room and motioned for Henry to shut the door. "You're up next," I said to her, handing off the jar of shine.

Stephanie hesitantly took it and brought it to her nose. She sniffed and made a face. "What is this?"

"It's the community's finest water." Eric beamed. "It would be rude not to at least try it."

"Yeah, I've heard that line from guys before," Stephanie said. She rolled her eyes and took a sip. Once the liquid made its way down her throat, her cheeks flushed red. She coughed into her fist. "You might want to get your water source checked out," she said.

"Look, if you can't handle it…" Eric began.

"You'd be surprised what I can handle," she retorted before taking a longer drink from the jar. If the second sip bothered her, she didn't let it show. She turned to Henry and handed him the jar. "Your turn."

Henry glanced at me, and for a second I thought he knew I was up to something. I braced myself for his accusation.

Instead, he brought the jar to his lips and drank.

"Why do I feel like we're all going to regret this in the morning?" Lockwood asked, shaking his head as Henry handed him the shine.

• • •

Two hours later, the shine had claimed its first victims. Lockwood lay on my bed. His head hung over the edge while his feet rested straight up against the wall. Between the blood rushing to his head and the effects of the alcohol, his face was the deepest red I had ever seen it.

Henry and Stephanie sat on the windowsill. I watched as their arms and legs casually touched. Her shoulder would brush against his. His fingers would graze hers. Their limbs swayed like the breeze—all movement and no order.

Eric and I sat on two wooden chairs in the center of the room. Neither one of us was drunk, and neither one of us was pretending any longer. The other three were so far gone that we were sure none of them would notice that we were completely and utterly sober.

I nodded toward Eric. He leaned forward in his chair, placing his elbows on his knees. "So, Stephanie, how do you like the community? It has to be a lot different than what you grew up in. I mean, you did live in a compound, right?"

Stephanie leaned her head lazily against the window. "No. I didn't come from a compound." While Eric had been the one to ask her the question, she stared deeply into Henry's eyes as she spoke.

"What do you mean you didn't grow up in a compound?" Henry asked her. He stared right back.

"I was born in the woods," she mused, a slight smile on her face.

"You mean like another community?" I asked. "Another Isolationist outpost?"

Stephanie shook her head. "No. In the woods."

Henry laughed. "Like one of the creatures from that play Lockwood tried to get me to read."

"*Midsummer Night's Dream*. That's what he's talking about," Lockwood called from underneath his arm, which he had thrown over his face.

Henry leaned forward and pressed his forehead against Stephanie's. "Are you a fairy?" he teased.

Stephanie threw her head back and giggled, hitting Henry in the chest. "Hardly. My parents were resistance fighters just like me. They met on a mission. I was born on the move. Hell, I've always been on the move."

Her mother, like mine, was from the last generation to successfully carry children, but even they suffered more miscarriages than births. It was my generation, and every generation after me, that would suffer Emma's fate. Unless they were like me. Was Louisa? I pushed her image out of my mind; I had work to do.

"That couldn't have been a very fun childhood," I said sympathetically. I felt sorry for her. I couldn't imagine constantly living my life on the run.

"Don't feel bad for her," Henry scoffed. "She was free. No compound or community to tell her what to do. Growing up knowing that she would be part of the group that would take the council down…"

I bit the inside of my cheek and looked away. Of course that would be the life Henry would have preferred.

"Free?" Eric asked, narrowing his eyes at Henry. "You said it yourself. She was born into it. What choice did she have? My people came here so they could be free."

"Your people aren't any freer than those suckers back in the compound," Henry spat.

"We don't rape mothers and sisters in the woods while a little boy watches. Don't you dare compare us to them!" Eric sneered.

Henry's face went white. "How do you know about that?" He turned and glared at me. While darkness seemed to attach itself to everyone I knew, it seemed particularly attracted to Henry. Sensing the hypocrisy of the council, his mother had tried to run with him and his sisters when he was a child. When the chosen ones caught them, they brutally attacked the girls, leaving Henry alone, returning him to the world he would spend the rest of his life hating.

"I…I didn't tell him," I stammered.

"Lockwood told me, and only because he thought it would garner some sympathy for you. You come across as a real asshole, you know that?"

Henry turned his icy-cold stare to Lockwood, ready to lay into him. But the poor boy was already passed out. I was sure it had more to do with the long nights watching over Louisa and less to do with the effects of the drink.

"I'm sorry to hear about what happened to your family. My parents were killed, too. They both died on a mission," Stephanie said, reaching over and taking Henry's hand in hers. "My sister, Harvey, as well. I guess you all know how she died." She turned and stared out the window.

I gulped. I hadn't known that the girl who stabbed me, the girl my father sent to stop me from meeting George, was

Stephanie's sister. I stole a glance at Eric. He had been the one to kill her sister. He'd shot her in the head.

After a prolonged silence, Stephanie dragged her eyes from the blackness of the night and looked at Eric. "So, what were you saying about how different you were from those who ran the compounds?"

Eric clenched his fist. "That's different. Your sister was a lunatic who stabbed Tess."

Stephanie yanked her hand from Henry's and wobbled to her feet. "She was following orders!"

Eric bolted up from his chair, knocking it to the ground. "That says a lot about your leader—the one you follow around without question. The man was willing to sacrifice your sister and wound his own daughter to suit his needs. What kind of man does that?"

"A man who believes that sometimes we have to make sacrifices!" Stephanie exclaimed. Something shifted in her eyes, and suddenly the solider was back. Albeit a drunk, enraged one. The situation was getting wildly out of hand.

"The same man who asked you to live and work among the very people responsible for killing your sister. The man who asked you to do it without question," Eric continued.

"Don't put this on Charlie. You were the one who killed Harvey," Stephanie retorted. She turned and looked back at Henry. "Can you walk me home before I do something we all would regret?"

Eric laughed bitterly. "You think Henry didn't want her dead? I just got to the gun faster. He was too worried that the girl he loved was going to bleed out. Tell her, Henry. Tell her how crazy Harvey was. Tell her how you wanted her just as dead as I did."

"She wasn't crazy! Shut your mouth before I shut it for you," Stephanie warned.

"We both know you won't. Charlie wouldn't like it." Eric grinned, sitting back down in his chair. Smug. Satisfied. "When you're ready to realize how much you've been used, you come and talk to me, sweetheart. You can tell me what your precious leader needs to hide so badly that he'll stab his daughter to keep her in the community. Not because he wants her safe, but because he needs a reason to come back. That's why he sent you all those messages, Tess."

My stomach dropped. He was right. It all made perfect sense.

My father had insisted I stayed within the walls of the community, so he would have a reason to come here. He could have shown up with his army under the ruse that he was here to reunite with his long lost daughter. Only Al and the other leaders would have to know why he was really there. The rest of the community wouldn't have to live under this new form of martial law.

But I had messed it up, and he needed me alive, so he sent Harvey to stab me. Knowing that those who traveled with me wouldn't let her truly harm me. He sent Harvey because she was crazy. Her wits muddled by whatever had claimed her mind. My people, protectors, would be quicker.

He banked on the fact that the people of the community would let me back in because of what I could do. And when Al said he didn't care, he forced his way in anyway. My father didn't think of me as his daughter; he thought of me as his bargaining chip.

I was going to be sick. I pressed the back of my hand against my mouth, turning away from the rest of the group.

I slammed my eyes closed, refusing to see the pity that lived in their eyes. Even after I took a few deep breaths, my body felt heavy with the weight of it all.

Henry cursed under his breath, and I knew he saw the truth just as I did. He scratched the back of his head and looked over at Stephanie, who stood fuming at Eric. "Come on, let's get out of here," he told her.

Stephanie shook her head. "I don't want anything to do with you people. And I sure as hell don't need you to walk me back. You're just like them," she charged, her voice broken with emotion.

As she turned to storm out of the room, Stephanie's hair flew to the side of her shoulder. Two faded branding marks glared at me from the back of her neck. Instinctively, I reached up and felt my own slash marks. These marks were the way the council kept track of the transgressions of girls. I had received my first mark as a result of my sister, Emma, getting pregnant. My second mark came when I spoke out for Henry's girlfriend, Julia, during her trial for treason. George gave me my third, claiming I would need it to help him bring down the council.

"How do you have those marks? You said you never lived in a compound," I asked, pointing a finger toward her.

Stephanie furrowed her brow. "Your father made me get them years ago. In case..." Her voice trailed off.

"In case what?" Eric asked.

We were almost there.

Glaring at Eric, Stephanie pushed past Henry and stumbled out of the room. Henry turned to me and clenched his jaw. "Great party, Tess," he said dryly.

"Things didn't exactly go as I planned," I admitted.

Henry raised an eyebrow. "Really? What exactly did you plan to happen here tonight?"

I didn't like his tone. I couldn't stand how he stood judging me after everything he heard. "I planned on getting Stephanie to tell me exactly what my father is doing here in the community and what he's hiding."

"You planned on attacking her! She's not your enemy."

"Maybe she's not my enemy, but she's certainly not on our side," I countered.

"Our side? What makes you think I agree with you? Just because it's the side you picked? I think we both know those days are gone," he said, his voice carrying a tiredness that I wondered would ever leave.

I lifted my head to meet his eyes. "Not my side. The side that puts people before the cause. That's the side you belong on."

Henry shook his head and took a step away from me. "You don't get to tell me what side I belong on anymore."

And then he left.

Chapter 15

The streets of the community were eerily quiet the following morning, but I could still hear the angry words thrown about the previous night banging inside of my head. I hadn't meant to hurt Stephanie. I had intended to convince her we could be friends, so she would feel comfortable enough to let the effects of the alcohol take control. Then she was supposed to tell us everything. In the pale light of morning, it was hard to see my actions as noble.

My stomach tightened when I thought of the way Eric had bragged about killing Stephanie's sister. He wasn't a bad man; not that she would ever know that by the way he had acted last night. He was just fiercely protective of those he cared about. It was our common ground.

The whole night was one colossal mess. Despite his terrible tactics, Eric was right. We needed to protect the people of the community. Maybe they hadn't always welcomed me with open arms, but they had offered me safety. Twice. I couldn't forget that.

I sighed and pushed my feet faster toward the infirmary. Louisa had been moved there due to her failing health. The closer she got to her due date, the worse she became. Cramping. Shortness of breath. Loss of color. Despite being only a few months along, she didn't look like she was a survivor; she looked like she was losing the battle. When I had returned there last night to relieve Sharon, she took one look at me and told me to turn around, go back to my room, and get some rest. She left no room for arguments.

The night before, I'd slept curled up on a chair, checking every so often to make sure Lockwood was still breathing. When I finally pulled myself from my restless slumber, I was excited to spend the morning with Louisa. She had started to talk more and more with both Lockwood and myself, and I was really loving our moments together. We still weren't close by any means, but our relationship was going. It was a start.

I was lost in the memories of the night before and dreams of my sister's future, when the sounds of footsteps running behind me broke my trance. They pounded heavily against the morning silence, fighting for control with the breaking dawn. I turned around to see a man sprinting down the dirt road toward me.

He was covered in blood.

A thousand different scenarios ran through my mind. Maybe he was one of Al's men finally exacting his revenge on me because of my father's actions. Maybe he was some spy from the council. Maybe he was another one of my father's crazed men, putting into action some plan I wasn't made privy to.

Hadn't we all argued about that last night? Desperation was man's greatest ally and darkest villain.

I looked wildly around me for a sign of anyone or anything to aid me. No one but the bloodied man and me were to be found. Considering the speed at which the man ran toward me, there was no hope of outrunning him. I would have to face him straight on.

I gritted my teeth and braced myself for his attack. His eyes were large, scared, frenzied. He was getting closer and closer. The blood he wore covered almost every inch of his tan cotton shirt. It splattered and marked his face like war paint from the books my father used to read about the Native Americans who once ruled these lands; men desperate enough to do just about anything to protect their own.

The man running right at me was definitely a man of war.

I inhaled and clenched my fists. The bloodied man looked right past me. He narrowed his eyes and stared straight toward the infirmary. The place that was protecting my sister. I couldn't let him get there.

Logically, he could have been one of my father's men. I hadn't met all of them, so it wasn't out of the realm of possibility. But being one of my father's men didn't hold the same sense of security as it once did. I didn't entirely trust my father anymore and that distrust extended to his crew. I'd rather be wrong than dead. I'd rather be wrong than something happen to those I loved.

I planted my feet firmly on the ground. I bent slightly at the knees, knowing from my training that if I tensed my body too much I could do some damage to myself on impact.

I took a deep breath and then I was off. I sprinted toward the man, throwing my body onto his, bringing us both to the ground.

Slightly disoriented, the man cursed and yelled, throwing me off him as if I weighed nothing. He must have used his last bit of strength to push me because he struggled to pull himself to his feet. My father always told me victory would only come if I could pinpoint my opponent's weakness. This particular enemy was near exhaustion.

I mustered everything I had left inside of me and scrambled to my feet. With a grunt, I threw myself onto the assailant's back, wrapping my arms around his neck. Once I had a good grip, I let my body go limp, using my weight to put pressure on his windpipe. I would hold onto him as long as it took.

I had to.

"Let him go!" a voice pleaded with me, but I didn't budge. "Tess, I said let him ago!" It was only the second time that I recognized Sharon's voice. Hearing her urgency, I loosened my grip and stumbled backward away from the man. Once he was free, the man bolted toward the infirmary.

All the air I kept trapped inside rushed from me. I slumped forward and placed my hands on my knees, trying to regain control.

Louisa.

He had run into the infirmary where Louisa was. Even if Sharon told me it was safe to let him go, I had to see for myself that my sister was safe. I spun around, running as fast as I could.

Sharon met me at the doorway and held up her hands. "Tess, I'm gonna need you to stay here with Louisa," she said calmly. She was standing next to the wild man. He sat in a chair near my sister's bed trying to catch his breath.

My eyes darted from the man to Louisa to Sharon. Louisa's eyes were wide with shock, but otherwise, she seemed unharmed. Sharon walked over to me and patted me on the back. "She's not in danger. I need to go help Sam," she said, nodding to the man.

I returned her nod, trying to stop my body from trembling. A mixture of unused adrenaline and overwhelming relief. As I stared at the man, I noticed something. With the exception of being a bit winded, he didn't appear to be hurt. "That blood isn't his, is it?" I asked Sharon.

She smiled tightly.

"Whose blood is it?" I asked, my voice turning cold.

"I can't answer that," she replied, bending down and pulling a variety of medical supplies from a trunk kept at the foot of my sister's bed. "I'll be back to check on Louisa later. I promise."

Sharon handed the man the supplies and gave him a curt nod. With a sigh, he pulled himself to his feet and left. Sharon turned to me, opened her mouth, and then closed it. I took a step toward her and grabbed her hand, pulling her out into the hallway. "What is it? I know you want to tell me."

Sharon looked behind her to make sure the man was gone. "It's not my secret to tell. You should really talk to your father."

I rolled my eyes. "I've tried talking to him. He says I already know everything I need to know." I paused, taking a moment to note the worry in Sharon's eyes. "But I do need to know. Don't I?"

"Ask him again," Sharon said. "He's your family."

"You and I both know that doesn't always mean something." I swallowed. The doubt had been growing inside of me like a parasite, slowly taking over, destroying me from the inside. What was my father's end game? What was he willing to do to achieve it? As much as I wanted to know, there was a part of me that couldn't trust him. At least not entirely. "I'm closer to you and Lockwood than that man who calls himself my father, so if he's putting us in danger, I need to know about it. Now why was that man covered in blood? Does it have something to do with what my father's hiding?"

Sharon pressed her lips together. I clutched harder onto her hand. "Please," I said. "Help me protect our family. Blood doesn't always make family."

"You don't think I know that?" she replied, placing a hand against my cheek.

I opened my mouth to entreat her help once again when a loud ringing cut me off. It was the loudest bell I had ever heard. I unhooked my hand from Sharon's and placed both of my hands over my ears.

"What is that?" I screamed.

Sharon paled, and she looked over my head toward the infirmary. I turned around to see my sister shaking, clutching the blankets to her chin. Sharon grabbed my elbow and pulled me close.

"We're being attacked," she yelled into my ear.

Chapter 16

Tess,

It has been so long since I've written you. I am ashamed that I have tried not to think about you. In my defense, it has not been entirely for selfish reasons. The torture the council put me under worked. Every time I reach for your image or a memory, my body is taken over by pain. They mean to burn you straight out of my mind.

My greatest fear is that they are quite close to succeeding at their mission. Even as I write you this letter, I am overcome with sweats and shakes. Even though I'm on the verge of another episode, I must write to you.

I will write to you. I need to explain.

I realized that the men who tortured me had almost forced you out of my mind entirely, so I hid you. I shoved your presence deep inside my head where neither they nor I can find it. If I don't think of you, if I choose not to think of you, then they can't burn you out of me. That's what the pain is like, Tess — fire. It burns and burns, and then I heal only to burn again.

So, I have forced you away. Not forever but long enough to make them forget. Make them think I have fully given myself to their whims. It has already started to work. They have assigned me back to the family. I now live in the estate on which the council headquarters sits. This place... If you thought Templeton was all pomp and circumstance, it is shambles compared to this place.

I spend my days getting to know my assigned creator, Harper. The hope is I will bond with him and be able to protect him. He is important. Though I am yet to be informed as to why.

That is why I am writing to you. Thinking of you. Aching for you.

Our bond.

Tonight, I woke up with only you running through my mind, and I knew you were in danger. Only twice before in my life have I been filled with such dread. I must admit that there is a small part of me that is comforted that I had a premonition concerning you. It means that our connection, despite the work of the council, is still as strong as ever.

But then what I saw keeps playing over and over in my mind, and I have no way of stopping it. There are guards always outside my door. So,

I write you like some useless man who can't do anything else. I write, because if I am correct, I will see you soon. Because leaving here won't stop what I saw happening to you. I will make sure you get these letters. You'll need them. You'll need to know what you're in for.

You're in danger, Tess. Even though I will not be able to stop the first of what appears to be a long line of chain reactions that lead you to the moment that torments me worse than any torture ever exacted on me, I write to you.

I see you here. You work in the headquarters in the service of the council you hate. I don't know much about the women here, but I will make it my duty to find out. They are rarely seen in the main labs. They, like us chosen ones, are assigned to families. While I don't hear much about them, what I saw concerning you — I can barely write it.

I keep thinking of the third mark on the back of your neck — the third branding that George gave you back in the woods. I can't help but wonder if this is what he planned all along. I will search him out in the morning. I don't know if I can trust him. I don't know that I can trust anyone.

Three marks. That is the first image that came to me in my vision. The back of your neck. Your hair was tied up into a bun. I couldn't see your face, but I knew it was you. You were trembling. You stood in a room fancier than anything I have seen yet.

There was a noise behind you and you

crouched down. You crawled across the floor and hid behind a curtain. But the darkness did nothing to protect you. He found you. I couldn't see his face, but he grabbed you and pulled you from your hiding space.

The last thing, the final moment of my vision, was you screaming.

So, I write to you now. I'll have to find someone to trust. My only hope is that these letters can get to you. Because without a doubt, I know one thing is for sure. You're coming here.

~James

Chapter 17

"You have to lock the door behind me!" Sharon commanded.

"What do you mean?" I asked. My heart was pounding like war drums. My mind once again thought of the people who first settled this land; the land we had done everything to destroy since then.

One long history of war and bloodshed.

Sharon took hold of my face. "Tess, I need you to breathe."

I hadn't realized I'd been hyperventilating. I nodded and closed my eyes. I counted to ten. I sucked the air in through my nose and pushed it out of my mouth. Inside my head, I hummed the song James and I had played together on the piano back at Templeton. I tried every trick I knew to calm the panic attack, and while it was easier to breathe, I still felt the fear claim me. It was like the feeling had attached to me like some parasite, waiting to show itself whenever I felt safe.

"Look at me," Sharon urged. I forced my eyes to hers.

They were steady. Calm. Ready for whatever was next. This was the life she had chosen, and she knew that this day would come.

We all knew.

"We don't have much time. As soon as I leave, you lock this door, and you don't open it for anyone. Not till morning. Not till there's nothing but silence," she said.

I shook my head. "No. You have to stay here with us," I pleaded, reaching my hand forward and clutching onto her.

"I have others to protect," Sharon said quietly. Her eyes welled with unshed tears. She kissed my cheek and walked past me deeper into the room.

The bell continued to ring like a banshee in the night. If I made it through this, I promised to destroy any bell I saw for as long as I lived.

I turned and watched as Sharon pulled a chair up to a wardrobe. It was half broken by years of misuse and carelessness. She stood on the chair and reached up, fumbling around the top of it till she found what she was looking for.

Dust fell to the ground like snow. I couldn't help but wonder if any of us would see another winter. I remembered playing in the snow with James; it would be easy to lose myself in memories of him in this moment.

Sharon sighed with relief when she located what she was searching for. I looked up to find her holding the precious item in her hands—a rifle.

She got down from the chair and placed the gun in my hands. "I understand that you know how to use one of these things?" Gone were the tears. She was back to being the mother who would do anything to protect her children. Back to being the mother any child would be blessed to have.

I wrapped my fingers around the rifle. "I can handle it," I said. I sniffled, attempting to force it all back in, trying to put on the brave front that Sharon had shown me.

"I know you can," she answered. She took two steps toward the door before I halted her. I pulled her into my arms and hugged her as tightly as I possibly could. "What's this for?" she asked, laughing slightly.

"Everything," I mumbled into her shoulder.

Sharon gave me one final squeeze, and then she was gone.

As soon as she left us, I bolted the door. Louisa cried quietly, and I didn't really blame her. Everything in my soul told me I should be running. But Sharon knew as well as I did that I couldn't leave Louisa, and I certainly wasn't strong enough to carry her.

I could fight. So many around me had taught me strength. Sharon. Eric. Robert. Henry. Even my father taught me how to use my wits when weapons weren't enough. And they were all out there fighting. I could join them in battle, but I was needed here.

Sometimes staying safe was the bravest thing you could do.

I sat on the bed next to my sister and wrapped an arm around her shoulders. She whimpered into my chest. After a while, the bell stopped ringing, and an eerie silence moved through the community like a slithering snake—all *shhhh* and foreboding. I knew it was only the calm before the storm.

Louisa lifted her tear-stained face. "What do we do now?"

I leaned down and kissed my little sister on the top of her head. In so many ways, she wasn't a child anymore, but nothing could stop me from protecting her. I should have made it my mission to protect her years ago.

"We wait," I said simply.

"For what?"

"For dawn. For the end. For whatever comes next."

Chapter 18

The screams were the worst.

They filled the air. There was nowhere Louisa or I could go to hide from them. They started slowly at first. Random. Intermittently punching the air. It was as if the horror itself was a creature playing the most twisted game of hide 'n' seek in all of history.

A piercing shriek would blast through the air and then the silence would follow. Cat and mouse. Louisa would stop trembling and crying long enough to look up at me with questioning eyes, begging me to tell her that it was over, but moments later, the screams would return.

Every muscle within me trembled with need—the need to go and defend the ones I loved. I reached for my sister's hand, clutching onto it to help tether me.

This went on for nearly an hour, and then there was no space for silence at all. The world exploded into chaos. We listened as the sounds of men and women running, desperately trying to save themselves from whatever was out there, filled our ears. Gunshots echoed and vibrated painfully against our eardrums.

I couldn't take standing still any longer. I began to pace around the room, searching out objects that I could possibly use as weapons. Within five minutes, I had a pile ready in the center of the room. Broken shards from a mirror. A splintered broom handle. A heavy porcelain water basin.

Louisa's cries became short, rapid shrieks each time we heard someone yell for their loved ones below. A crazy, distorted Morse code between the terror outside and the anguish within our room. And somewhere between the duet of her cries and the sounds of war, I thought of all the people outside. There were people I loved in the community. Henry. Robert. Lockwood. Sharon. Eric. My father.

My father.

Where was he? Didn't he command an army of vigilantes? No doubt, he, Stephanie, and the rest of them would fight, but who or what were they fighting against? My father's words whispered to me as I clutched my little sister tighter: *So, you're ready to fight? What happens when they take that gun away from you?*

A gun is a weapon; it's not any sort of safety guarantee.

That weapon up there is just as important as any gun.

If the community was up against an army of chosen ones, there didn't seem to be any hope of winning. I had seen one or two chosen ones taken down with quick wit and guns, but a whole army of them? Even my father, a man who had dedicated his life to fighting, knew that was a battle he couldn't win.

I let the tears fall freely then. I let them fall because I

didn't know how much longer my friends had, and I didn't know how much longer we had, either. I let them fall because my friends deserved my tears. Their loss would be felt even if I wasn't alive to feel it.

The world would be a lesser place without them.

I closed my eyes and leaned my head against my sister's. I cleared my throat. "Louisa? I know I haven't been the best sister, and I am so sorry for that. I wasn't particularly a joy to be around," I admitted with a short, pained laugh.

"Neither was I," she said, echoing my laugh. It was funny that now, so near the end, we were finally speaking the same language.

"I guess we were both pains in the asses," I replied, laughing harder as the tears streamed quicker and quicker down my face. It didn't feel odd laughing. It felt natural. It felt like the most natural thing in the whole damn world.

"But we loved the same people," she whispered. Her words were interrupted with small, breathy sobs.

"Yes, we did. So we should have loved each other better," I replied. It was a mistake that time had allowed me to at least start to remedy. I was thankful for that. As the end came closer, I realized I had spent way too much of my time hating and not enough time loving.

Louisa looked up at me. "I love you, Tess."

"I love you, too," I said. I suddenly didn't feel like laughing anymore.

So, we sat like that in silence. Both of us jumped at the noises that continued to bounce against the walls of the building; the noises attempted to shatter our bond, but they wouldn't succeed. I rocked my sister back and forth, humming my mother's favorite song. Eventually, Louisa started to hum with me, and we filled the tiny infirmary with our own brand of warfare.

Minutes turned into hours.

The waiting became worse than the screaming. Somehow, Louisa and I had managed to make peace with the end. Louisa had even stopped crying. She took my hand and placed it over her swollen abdomen. Neither one of us spoke.

Then the banging started.

The war had come to our very door.

I jumped from the bed and snatched the rifle. I held it straight and steady toward whoever was attempting to break in. I knew it was likely they would overtake us, but I wasn't going to go without a fight. There was a muffled gargle of words yelled at us from the other side of the wooden barrier, but neither of us could make out their meaning.

"We're ready for you!" I screamed, using everything I had inside of me. I would not be drowned out. I would make sure they heard me.

The door buckled and whined as it was nearly torn from its hinges. I clicked the safety off my gun. I found my center. I remembered my stance. I aimed my gun. "Come on, you bastard," I whispered as I narrowed my eyes.

With a deafening crack, the door split in half. Much to my astonishment, Lockwood stumbled into the room. His face was swollen nearly twice its size. Covered in a broken map of cuts and bruises, he spat blood onto the floor and fell to his knees.

Louisa yelped behind me and scrambled off the bed. With a grunt, she knelt onto the floor next to him. "Oh, God! Are you all right?"

I held my gun at the now opened door, only glancing down at Lockwood. "What's going on out there?"

"It's a bloodbath. There are chosen ones everywhere," Lockwood coughed, more blood spilling from his mouth.

"Can you get up?" I asked.

"Get up? He's barely breathing!" Louisa exclaimed.

"I can get up," Lockwood said, slowing pulling himself to his feet.

"I need you two to try and move that wardrobe in front of the door. It might give us some time. I'd help, but I've got to keep this gun right where it is." While I was happy to see Lockwood alive, I wasn't thankful that he broke down the door that provided what little resistance we had.

"No, Tess! We need to leave," Lockwood said. "He's gonna blow it all up. The whole town. He wanted to lure enough of them in first, so at least some of us could make it out. Turns out he's planted damn bombs all over."

"Who?" I asked.

"Your father."

A gun is a weapon; it's not any sort of safety guarantee.

That weapon up there is just as important as any gun.

My father had a plan, all right.

I tore my eyes from the door and looked at Louisa, who managed to get up. "But we can't leave," I said quietly. She wrapped her arms around her torso and looked to the ground. Louisa couldn't run. She knew she would slow us down.

Lockwood, nearly broken, stalked over to Louisa and lifted her in his arms. "Yes. We. Can," he gritted.

My eyes welled with tears once again. I would never stop owing Lockwood. "So, what's the plan?" I asked, pulling myself together and focusing on what was ahead.

"Can't quite say we got one. Just run like hell for the woods."

I started to speak when an explosion cut me off. My hands flew to my ears instantly. Louisa buried her face in Lockwood's chest.

"We have to go now!" he screamed.

"Wait! There's one thing I need to do first," I pleaded.

"There's no time!"

I ignored him, snatching the sheets from the bed. I threw open the trunk that lay at the foot of Louisa's bed and laid the blanket on the floor. I grabbed anything that looked useful from the trunk, a variety of medical instruments and aids that I had no idea the purpose of. I wrapped the sheet around them, creating a makeshift satchel.

I forced the bag into Louisa's arms. "I need you to help us. You need to hold onto this bag with all your might. Don't let it go. Can you do that?" Louisa nodded furiously. "Good. Let's go."

I took a deep breath and spun toward the exit.

"Robert!" Louisa yelled. Her voice was the brightest I had heard in hours.

A wave of relief rushed through my body. Despite being covered in dirt and sweat, he appeared to be unharmed. "Let me carry her. I'm quicker," he said, looking toward Louisa.

I watched as Lockwood hesitated for the slightest of moments. He didn't want to let her go. "He's her best chance," I said.

Lockwood lifted Louisa into my brother-in-law's waiting arms. He then walked over to me and grabbed onto my hand, clutching it in his. "On the count of three," he ordered.

"One. Two. Three."

We ran. We ran faster and harder than I have ever run before. We sped through the crumbling community. Buildings built long before my arrival sizzled and burned as the sun faded into darkness. I tried to ignore the bodies that lay sprawled all around us. Grotesque shapes of human suffering and death that littered the ground. I didn't want to see someone I knew. There was a time to mourn, and I had to live long enough to do so.

There was no rhyme or reason to the bombs that went off. Of course, that was probably my father's plan all along. He knew he couldn't beat the chosen ones in combat, so he created chaos in hopes that the strongest and fastest of the Isolationists would have a chance of surviving.

Always survival of the fittest.

As the bombs detonated, we zigged and zagged, praying that our random patterns would give us an edge. But we all knew deep down that nothing but luck would get us to the woods.

The entire time, Lockwood never let go of my hand. Almost seconds after reaching the outside, Robert sprinted past us. I knew that Lockwood shared my thankfulness. Neither one of us minded being left alone, not when it meant Louisa would be safe.

Besides, we weren't alone. We had each other.

As each bomb went off, there was a distorted, horrific symphony of screams and groans. I couldn't tell the cries of the chosen ones from the naturals. The explosions caused a dust storm that made anything further than three feet ahead of us nearly impossible to see.

At one point, I thought I heard Lockwood yell that we

were almost there, but my ears rang so loudly that all I could hear was my heartbeat thudding and thudding and thudding against my eardrums—begging desperately to be allowed to live to see another day.

As I continued to push my legs forward, I vaguely made out the tree line. A sense of hope surged through me. I wasn't sure what awaited us in those woods, but it felt like escape.

How strange that the random collection of earth, trees, and rocks could be both heaven and hell. Of course, I knew it was just a place; it held no meaning except what man assigned to it.

Lockwood tugged against my arm. As the dust began to lessen the further we moved from the community, I could see the forest more clearly.

We were going to make it.

We were going to survive.

And then the world went black.

Chapter 19

My eyelids fluttered open.

As the light of a new day broke through the darkness that pursued me constantly, my eyelids shut again.

It was the light that pained me now.

I was afraid of what I would see. The minute they opened, the world would once again be changed. It was always evolving and becoming something new, altered in ways that if I was going to survive, I would have to learn to live with.

"I think she's waking up."

"Robert?" I whispered. I still refused to open my eyes. I had to make sure it was him first. I needed to know I still had someone. That was the trouble of letting yourself need people—it made you strong and weak all at once.

"Yes, Tess. It's me."

I slowly let my eyes open. Robert's face looked down at me from above. "Welcome back." He smiled.

"What happened?" My voice was scratchy and sore from a mixture of screams and dust.

"One of your father's bombs went off next to the entrance. The force of it blew both you and Lockwood back. You hit your head pretty hard on the ground," he explained.

My stomach dropped. "Lockwood?" I tried to sit up. My head felt like it had been stuffed with bricks.

Robert gently held my shoulder down. "Easy there. You've been out almost twelve hours. Slowly," he urged, helping me to sit.

I reached up to find my head covered in a bandage still damp with blood. "Lockwood?" I asked again.

"He's fine. A bit bruised but living."

I exhaled. "Who?" Robert raised an eyebrow at my question, but I swallowed back my fear. "Who?" I repeated. I wasn't going to back down. He knew what question I was asking: *who did we lose?*

Robert searched my eyes. Whatever he found in them, he could no longer look at me. "What matters right now is that you take it easy. Your father is re-grouping, and then we'll decide what to do from there. Till then, you need to rest."

I blinked back tears, surprised they even came to me at all. The smallest mention of my father and I was ready to fall to pieces. Fall to pieces over a man who chose war over family. Had it all been a lie? Every last moment he played the role of father since he had been back? "So, my father is all right then?"

Robert gave a small smile. "Yes, he's just fine."

I took a shaky breath and tried to still my nerves. Fear and relief danced inside me wildly, bumping and jostling against each other. "Will you help me up?" I asked, a slight tremble to my voice. Robert opened his mouth to protest, but I cut him off. "I'm awake now. There's no point pretending I can just sit here and not know," I challenged, forcing strength into my voice.

Strength I didn't quite feel.

Robert reluctantly helped me to my feet and linked his arm around my shoulders. I leaned against him as we walked through a makeshift medical station that seemed to go on for a good hundred feet. A road of blankets and moaning victims. Men and women. Children. As we moved down the line, I saw all sorts of ailments—injuries that ranged from minor cuts and bruises to amputations much like the one Al had to get.

Al.

The first body I came across. Littered among the suffering naturals were the bodies of those who had died during the hours of my unconsciousness. I didn't feel much as I stared down at the body of the man who had tried to have James killed. If anything, I felt sorry for him. But I didn't feel loss.

I thought back to one of the last conversations I had with McNair. He had called the community a new country. He said he hoped it would be a place where they could all start over and avoid the mistakes of the past. But as I looked at one of its former leaders, broken and dead, I wondered if there was any place to start over again.

It seemed like the naturals would always be running from their past.

As we moved down the line, Robert squeezed my shoulder. "What is it?" I asked, looking up at him. I felt the blood drain from my face. He had been trying to warn me. Whatever I was about to see would be terrible.

Except that it wasn't. It was Henry. He sat on the ground huddled with an injured Stephanie. Her arm was in a sling and several shallow cuts marked her forehead. Seeing me, Henry jumped up and pulled me into his arms. "You're awake. I tried to get to the infirmary, but everything was so damn crazy."

"You should have seen him. He was so brave." Stephanie beamed. "Practically took out one of the chosen ones on his own."

Henry actually blushed, and for a moment, I felt the need to look away. He reached down and helped Stephanie off the ground. "She's exaggerating. When I woke up yesterday morning, I went to apologize to Stephanie for…you know."

I nodded. I did know, but that seemed like another lifetime ago.

"I got to her room and Eric was there. That's when the attack happened. We didn't make it down the stairs before we were ambushed," he said.

"Eric?" I asked, wondering what he had been doing in Stephanie's room.

"He came to apologize," she said quietly. I raised an eyebrow. Eric was a lot of things but apologetic was never one of them. "He saved my life."

"When he saw what was happening, he pulled that damn bottle of shine from his pocket and lit the blasted thing on fire. Threw it right at the bastards. Then everything just went nuts. Fighting and running," Henry said.

"Somehow, I lost the two of them," Stephanie continued. "I fell behind. One of the chosen ones cornered me. I had no gun, no way out. Then there was Eric. He threw himself in front of me. Took on one of those things by himself. It didn't take… He…gave me enough time to get away," she added.

Stephanie took a shaky breath and reached for my hand. "I'm sorry. I know he was your friend."

I pulled my hand from hers and took a step back. My throat felt painfully dry. I shook my head. "I…" My voice trailed off. I wanted to discredit everything they had told me. To demand that what they were saying was impossible, but the truth was, in this world, it was entirely possible. Even probable.

"Is his body here?" I asked, my voice cracking. He would have wanted to be buried. I remembered how important it was to him to bury McNair.

"I buried him this morning," Henry said. "I tried to wait for you, Tess. I swear it. But I didn't know how long it would be before we would have to move out, and I knew—"

I threw my arms around Henry's neck. "No, you did well. It's what he would have wanted. Thank you," I whispered into his ear. I detangled myself from Henry and looked at Stephanie. "I'm glad you're all right."

She nodded. "Glad you're safe too. I really am sorry about your friend."

"He died doing what he wanted to do—protecting naturals. You two probably had more in common than either of you thought," I offered with a pained smile. I took a deep breath. "Who else?"

I watched as Henry and Robert exchanged a look. "Who else?" I demanded.

"Sharon," said a voice from behind me.

I turned around to see Lockwood. His face was caked in dirt. Long dried tear streaks marked his face. I slowly shook my head. "Impossible." Because losing Sharon just couldn't happen. People like Eric, soldiers, could die in wars.

But not people like Sharon.

Lockwood's face crumpled. "We lost her."

I continued to shake my head as an odd sort of lightness overtook my body. It was like I was outside of myself watching some horrific story unfold. I didn't want to see the ending to this narrative. Robert reached out and placed a hand on my shoulder, and I flinched. I didn't want anyone to touch me. I didn't want anyone to bring me back to my body. I didn't want to feel the things it was feeling.

"You're lying," I said.

Lockwood began to sob into his hands, falling to his knees on the ground. I tore myself from Robert's grasp. I crouched down next to Lockwood and grabbed him by the shoulders, shaking him as hard as I could. "Show me her body!"

"There is no body," Henry said softly from behind me.

I froze. I couldn't breathe. I closed my eyes and counted to ten. "Tell me how," I commanded.

"She was taking her children to shelter. One of the bombs got her. Killed one of the boys and her. There was nothing left," he answered.

A wild sob broke free from my lips. I pressed my fist over my mouth to keep another one from getting free. Robert offered his hand to help me up, but I smacked it away. I closed my eyes again, willing my body to return to its unconscious state.

I had lost another mother.

Through the darkness, I heard Lockwood's pained, desperate cries. I realized he had lost a mother, too. I forced my eyes opened and stared at my nearly destroyed friend, then reached forward and pulled him into my arms. Lockwood hugged me back, crying into my shoulder. I held him tighter. I forced back my tears because my friend needed me.

Once Lockwood settled down, I asked the question I was most afraid of. "And Louisa?" His face fell. He covered his eyes with his hand and began to cry again.

"She's not dead," Henry quickly clarified. "It's just that—"

"She lost the baby," Robert explained. "She's in a bit of pain, and we have to watch for infection, but she should be fine."

"But...I don't understand. How could she still live?"

"She lost so much blood. They had to make a decision. Your father chose to save Louisa," Lockwood said quietly.

"How? I don't understand," I said again.

Lockwood swallowed, turning his eyes from mine. "He had it cut out."

The baby. She lost the baby. The thing we had been so worried about. I shuddered at the mixture of relief and horror that rushed through me. Was that what war really was? An endless battle between these two contradictory emotions?

My sister would live. I would get to keep her. There was no way of knowing if she would have been able to deliver the baby, but it was devastating all the same.

"At least there's that," I said dully.

• • •

After one of my father's men denied me access to my sister,

claiming she was sleeping, I found a bit of secluded woods. I needed to be away from the road of anguish. I sat and leaned against a tree, attempting to find some sort of sense in the events that had taken place.

I remembered a story my father had told me when I was younger. It was a story connected to the Native Americans. A government that once ruled this land had made these people leave their homes and travel thousands and thousands of miles to some new place. They were called inferior. The government tried to take everything from them. My father had explained that thousands had died on these death marches. They had called it the Trail of Tears.

I wondered if that was what awaited the survivors of the attack on the camp. Where would we go now?

I reached up and touched my forehead. Somehow, I had reopened a cut. I brought my hand down to see my fingers covered in blood, and a fiery anger flared up in me. I was sick of us naturals being bossed around, hunted, and murdered for being who we were.

It didn't need to be this way. There had to be some place where this didn't exist. McNair's words came back to me then: *I figure there has to be a place all this is a bad memory. Eastern and Western. Chosen Ones and naturals. We've got to put a name to everything. I want a place with no name.*

And it was in that moment I made a promise to myself and McNair — I would find that place. It had to exist. I would do whatever it took to locate it. I would take the people I loved there, and we would be free from this madness.

But not before I did something else. I took my bloodied finger and began to make slash marks against the backside of my hand. The council had burned their slash marks into the back of my neck, marked me their property. I would mark them, too.

Sharon.

Eric.

Louisa's child.

Emma.

James.

James still existed, but they had tortured him. Altered him. And I would make them pay for it.

I would get revenge for what had been done to them.

"You need to add another one." Henry sat down next to me, and I furrowed my brow. "Sharon, Eric, Louisa, Emma, and James. But you forgot a name on that list."

"List?" I asked. I hadn't realized I had been saying the names aloud.

"Don't think I don't know what those mean. You forget who you're talking to," he replied. He took my hand gently in his, then wiped a bit of blood off my finger and added another slash mark.

"Who's that for?" I asked.

"You."

As Henry and I sat together against the tree, watching another day give in to darkness, I swallowed. "Is this because of me? Did they come here because of what I can do?" I asked. "Did I bring this on my people?"

If I had, I would never be able to forgive myself. Eric. Sharon. My sister. All touched by tragedy because of me. It didn't seem right that so many should have to suffer so I could live.

"No. This isn't about you," Henry said. He leaned his head against mine. "It's about your father."

I turned slightly in order to look at Henry. My forehead pressed against his. As I watched the sun dance in his eyes, I knew, in that moment, what I had given up. He hadn't been the destiny I had chosen, but that didn't mean the path with him would have been a terrible one. It just wasn't the path for me. I took his hand into mine.

"You said this was about my father. Is it about what he's hiding?" I asked. I held my breath while I waited for Henry's answer. If he told me yes, then everything Eric had feared would have came true. The people of the community had suffered because of my father's actions. He had never cared about them. The fact that he had planted the bombs proved he knew an attack was likely.

"Yes, Tess. According to Stephanie, they didn't even know you were here. They've been tracking your father."

I sat straight up and stared right into Henry's eyes. "Stephanie told you, didn't she? What my father is hiding?" I reached up and grabbed his chin, forcing him to look at me. "What the hell was worth the death of all these people?"

Henry gently removed my hand from his chin. "One of the original creators. Your father kidnapped him."

My mouth fell open.

Chapter 20

I stalked past the many victims of my father's actions. I ignored the countless protests that Henry hurled at me from behind. He had to have known they wouldn't have stopped me. Once I had recovered from the shock of finding out that my father had kidnapped a creator, the creator who had been talked about for years, more bogeyman than man, more legend than human, I wasted no time in hunting him down. We needed to talk.

One of the last things Sharon had told me was to talk to my father, and it wasn't too late to listen to her. He had to answer for her death.

He had to answer for a lot of things.

And then there was the other reason I sought him out — I wanted to see the man responsible for hurting and nearly destroying everyone I ever cared about — natural and chosen one alike. My father had held one of the creators in the community for weeks. A man who possessed the answers to so many questions, including questions about Louisa, had been so close. When I thought about it, and the fact that my father kept it from me, knowing how I worried for her, I could rip his head off.

I had been so stupid for placing even the smallest bit of trust in him.

I had pried from Henry where my father had set up camp. Not that it took much to figure it out. I just needed to follow the line of mindless soldiers who held their guns like compasses.

My father stood amidst his army, and I pushed through them without any attempt at civility. Upon seeing me, my father nodded. "Would you all mind giving me and my daughter a few moments?" he asked the men and women who helped him wipe out the community. It may have been the council's chosen ones who initiated the event, but it was my father's bombs that killed Sharon.

Bombs had been a staple of the resistance during its early stages. My father's letters had mentioned how desperate men and women strapped makeshift, dodgy explosives to their children in some horrific symbol of their anger at the many failures of their government. It made me sick even now to think of it.

Were there any limits to the things people would do?

Neither side seemed to care much about collateral damage.

The men and women mumbled to each other as they went off and busied themselves with the next steps of my father's master plan. "How's the head?" he asked casually, like he was talking about the weather.

"Compared to most, I'm just dandy," I replied bitterly.

With a groan, the first sign of his age I had seen or heard since he placed himself back into my life, my father sat down on the ground. "Yeah, I heard you lost some people. I'm sorry about that." He pulled his rifle into his lap and began to clean it.

I balled up my fists. "That's all you have to say? You're sorry?"

My father wrinkled his forehead. "What else would you like me to say? Because I feel like we keep having this same conversation."

Father and commander. He seemed to slip into each role effortlessly whenever it suited his needs.

He was right. There was nothing he could say that would stop me from wanting to yank that gun from his hands and aim it straight at him.

"Need me to show you how to clean one?" he asked. I frowned, unsure which part of my short speech had given the impression that I wanted to learn anything from him except the location of the council leader. "You're staring at my gun," he explained.

I crossed my arms and stared him down, trying, in vain, to regain my composure. My father knew exactly what buttons to push. Instead of yelling, he retained an air of stoniness during our conversations, and it always drove me mad.

He squinted, then sighed. "You're thinking of using this on me. Aren't you?" There was a slight air of amusement to his words. It seemed like everything I did or said reminded him of some inside joke he had forgotten to tell me.

"I wouldn't be wrong if I did."

"Some anger is good, Tess. It can fuel you. Give you purpose and determination when things seem impossible.

But too much anger and you'll implode. It muddles your brain." He went back to cleaning his gun.

"I'm not here for a damn lesson," I snapped.

"Then what are you here for?"

I lifted my shoulders back and stood straight. "I want you to take me to him."

"To who?"

"Abrams."

"Who the hell told you?"

"Does it really matter? I want to speak to him."

"Like hell it doesn't matter! If I have a leak, I need to stop it," he countered. He stood and hoisted his gun over his shoulder. "It shouldn't be too hard to trace. I'll start with your friend Henry." With a grunt, he pushed past me.

I spun around. "You owe me this!" I yelled.

My father froze. I watched as every muscle in his arms and back tensed. Temper. Despite trying to hide it from me, it was something we shared. He took a deep breath before turning around to face me. "Owe you?"

"Yes, owe. I don't even care why you left anymore, but the fact remains that you did. I had to sit there and watch my mother drink herself to death. To watch Emma die in childbirth. To trek through the woods to find that my little sister was manipulated. That she could die. And I did it without you!"

I clenched and unclenched my fists before continuing, trying to ignore how heavy my head felt. "I got your letters. I know that you always wondered if having children was the best idea. But that doesn't matter because you *did* have children. Children you abandoned."

"I left because it was the only way to stop—"

"Who? The council? The government that you feel abandoned *you*, right?" I walked toward my father, forcing my anger down, pulling up an emotion that I liked to keep hidden. "You came back here and made me believe you were that person—that man I cried for at night, but you're not him. Are you?" I asked, my voice cracking.

"No one is who they were back then. That's how we've survived," he replied, averting his eyes. Maybe he did it because saying it meant acknowledging everything we lost, or maybe he looked away because it was a lie. I wasn't sure, and I probably would never be sure about his intentions again.

"But at what cost?" I countered, blinking back the tears. When my father couldn't answer, I nodded. "Right. You brought that man into my home; you risked the lives of everyone I loved to keep him hidden. I deserve to know why."

I swallowed the lump in my throat. "Five minutes. I just want five minutes," I said "Show me that all of this has a reason. Prove to me that I wasn't just a pawn."

"I…" My father's voice trailed off, and I could sense that his determination was wavering.

"If you did this for Louisa and me, then give me what I need. And I need to talk to him."

My father gave a curt nod. "Fine. Follow me."

. . .

As I trudged through the woods, I went through my list of questions for Abrams. Questions I feared the most because they would lead me to the answers that changed my world.

Would the answers make me feel better? Or was I better off not knowing?

James's letters had told me the council knew Abrams was missing, and that they were doing everything in their power to find him. Despite his notoriety, he was still important to them. I couldn't help but wonder why. There was no way he was an active creator; it was some miracle of science that he even still lived. But what would the council want with a man who could only bring them shame?

"How did you get Abrams?" I called out to my father, who walked ahead of me.

"The council kept the monster moving. Always on the go from one compound to another. They kept him gagged, chained, hiding in cellars and basements. Naturals never knew the reason for their damnation lay right under their feet."

"But why?"

"Why does anyone keep something? Because it has purpose," he said, looking back at me over his shoulder. "They needed information. Information Abrams refused to give, no matter what they did."

I furrowed my brow. "What kind of information?"

"The kind that could change the world." He paused. "We ambushed one of the transports. Killed the captors and took him."

"Just like that?" I refused to believe that anything to do with my father was so simple.

"Just like that," he deadpanned.

"I can see where I get my great communication skills from," I said.

My father came to a stop, pointing his finger toward a

scrunched up, haggard creature tied to a tree. Its head was covered in a burlap sack.

Abrams.

"But how? Isn't he supposed to be dead? He's like a billion years old," I said. Even seeing it, it was still hard to believe.

"Come on, Tess, we both know there are no bounds to what science can do," my father replied.

"That's what those creatures were looking for? That's why they were in the woods. And why they attacked the community?"

My father nodded grimly.

"How did they know where we were?" I demanded. My father had put the whole community in danger by bringing this man there, but it still didn't explain how they found us.

"I'm not entirely sure. I can't figure that one out," he admitted, wrapping his hand tightly around his gun, an edge to his voice. "Right now, all you need to know is that we have him. And we will get what we need from Abrams: the knowledge we need to take the council down. For good. I never thought they would find us in the community. I brought Abrams there because I needed a place to try and get the information. Somewhere safe. Somewhere off the grid."

I remembered the bloodied man who had run toward Sharon only days before. The blood hadn't been his. Had my father attempted to torture Abrams as well?

I stepped gingerly closer to his prisoner. I lifted my hands toward the bag. I wanted to see him. I wanted to put a face to the pain I had felt all my life. It would be so much easier to hate one person than an entire government.

As my hand met with the rough texture of the bag, my

father's voice halted me. "You sure about this?"

No. But there was no turning back now. There wasn't time for that anymore.

I grabbed onto the bag and pulled it off.

All the air rushed from my lungs.

Abrams was right before me. Tied to a tree like a prisoner of war, bruised and bloodied, was one of the men responsible for almost every dark and twisted thing I had ever seen.

Except it wasn't a man.

It was a woman.

• • •

I couldn't speak. I couldn't move. How was this even possible? The council despised women, blamed them for everything that was wrong with the world. Claimed our emotions and natural-born wantonness weakened the men, leading the country to ruin. Was I to believe that this creator, one of the original masterminds behind the creation of the chosen ones and the downfall of the naturals, was a woman? The very thing that the council warned against had given birth to the council itself?

"Are you going to stare at me all day?" Her voice was quiet and wispy, like the leaves that crackled and crunched under your feet as you walked through the woods.

Her age showed in every crease and wrinkle that covered her face. And there were a ton of them. She was the oldest woman I had ever seen. Decrepit. Sandpapery. The blues of her veins broke through her skin like some sort of beacon, calling to whoever was looking for her. Bright curves of color against her alabaster skin. A bit of drool mixed with blood slipped out of her mouth. Her eyes, which once might have showcased color, were covered with a milk white slip of film.

Something so weak had destroyed so many.

I had a thousand questions for her. But at the mere sight of her, I lost all my power again. She was like the villains of stories living only on the pages. Except this villain was far more dubious than I could have even begun to imagine. It was hard to believe that she could actually be real.

"You have five minutes," my father reminded me. I nodded numbly as he moved to stand behind me. He didn't bother to explain away my shock. He simply held his rifle pointed at the woman he had hidden within the community. Apparently, despite the ropes and men who stood guard in the tree lines, my father didn't trust her. Of course, she had fooled an entire country, so I could understand his fear.

"She looks like you," Abrams said to my father. "Your daughter, I'm assuming?"

I opened my mouth to speak, but his voice cut me off. "Don't you tell her anything about yourself. If you have questions, you'd better ask her. You're running out of time."

I closed my mouth and stared at the enigma in front of me. Even broken and weakened, the woman spoke with such an air of authority that I was half ready to follow her every command. It wasn't the way a woman was taught to speak.

There was a part of me that liked the way it sounded.

"Ask away, child." Abrams grinned. The whispery static of her voice caused me to shudder. Under the power lay the threat, and while I would never give up fighting for my own rights, I would never take my power at someone else's expense. Yet she seemed to enjoy it.

"I don't know where to begin," I whispered.

"Of course you do," she whispered back.

I closed my eyes briefly, then pulled forward the image of Emma. I let the moment of her death play inside my mind. When I opened my eyes, it wasn't so scary to look at her anymore. "I want to know about the women," I replied, my voice steel.

Abrams raised an eyebrow. "The women?"

"I want to know what you did to them. Why they can't give birth. Why they had to d-die," I stammered. I could feel my hands shaking. Not out of fear, but out of something else — something darker, feral. Something more lethal.

If this was the fire that Henry walked around with inside of him, I didn't blame him entirely for giving himself over to it. It buzzed and burned inside of me, killing the fear. But I couldn't let it consume me. If I did, I risked becoming like my father, and I wasn't entirely sure he was so different from the villain tied up before me.

Abrams sighed and leaned her head back against the tree. "And I thought you had a good question for me. I do get so incessantly tired by these mundane ones."

Something inside of me broke. I flew at Abrams and snatched her by the collar of her shirt, pulling her tight against the ropes that kept her entrapped. My father had taught me how to kill, and I had never felt the desire to do so burn so brightly inside of me. "You listen to me, you maniacal monster! I know it was you and your kind! You did something to them. Put some damn chemicals in the water supply or poisoned them with those damn vaccinations. But I know you did it. I want to know what you did."

"Look at those tears," Abrams purred. "Such weakness."

I hadn't even realized I was crying. "Shut up," I yelled, slamming her head against the tree. Part of me expected my father or his men to intervene, but they all stood by and watched.

Abrams chuckled. "Do you want me to shut up or do you want me to answer your question?"

I slammed her head again. Her eyes rolled up to the back of her head. I unclenched my hands from her shirt and staggered away, then paced back and forth. My hands clutched onto my hair to keep from wringing her neck. Never before I had felt anything like this. The fire was getting strong, burning out of control.

"You're asking the wrong question," she managed to squeak out between coughs.

"What are you talking about?" I kept my feet moving. As long as I was pacing, I wouldn't resort to violence.

"It's not how but why."

It's not how but why. I had always thought the council could be responsible for the death of so many women, but to hear it confirmed, to know my sister's death could have been avoided, was staggering in its simplicity.

I fell to my knees. "Why?" My head dropped into my hands. I couldn't look at Abrams; it was one thing to dream of confronting your enemy, but it was entirely different to do so in person. This weak, deathly ill thing had taken my sister from me. My enemy was human.

"They were already sick."

I lifted my head, narrowing my eyes. "You mean you didn't make the women like this?"

Abrams gave the slightest shake of her head. "No, we

didn't do this, but we didn't do anything to stop it, either. Actually, I had very little to do with the illness that plagues the women. My father, and men like him that made up the council's team of scientists in the early days of the war, noticed that more and more women were dying during childbirth. Dying at alarming rates. They searched out the reasons everywhere. Maybe it was the effects of the nuclear war. Maybe it was a biological attack from the eastern sector. Maybe it was something in the water."

"So, what was it?" I asked. My heart picked up speed. It was as if I were at the edge of the mountain, and whatever Abrams said next would send me to the bottom of the ravine or save me. Was it possible that I could absolve the council of this?

"Rubella."

"What the hell is that?" I looked over my shoulder to find my father towering over me, glaring at Abrams.

"You see, child, I find it much nicer to talk to you than him. He beat me for hours trying to get me to talk, but he should understand that a woman never does anything she doesn't want to do," Abrams said with a sly smile and a wink.

With a growl, my father aimed his gun at her. "My daughter Louisa almost died! Now, answer Tess's question!"

Abrams's eyes lit with delight and she gave a lazy shrug of her shoulders. I got back onto my feet and placed a hand on my father's shoulder. His gun trembled in his shaking hands, and I knew, without a doubt, despite his questionable ways, my father had feared for Louisa's life. He dropped his gun, taking several steps away from Abrams.

"What is rubella?" I asked.

"I'm not surprised you haven't heard of it. For hundreds

and hundreds of years, most naturals received shots to protect them from it. Nothing more than a case of measles that science learned to control. But here's the thing that man always forgets about nature: it's a real smart bitch. She'll wait. Hide until you think you're safe. Morph into a new beast while your back is turned, and just when you've almost forgotten her power, she'll come back for you with a vengeance."

"So a virus killed my sister?" I asked. "Not the council?"

"Yes and no. The virus mutated, becoming almost an entirely new beast. It held many of the same properties of its original parent. With the primary strand, sometimes people didn't even know they were carriers. Our rubella shared this trait, showing no outwardly signs. Seemingly harmless. But its real threat, even back then, had been to unborn children. It caused birth defects, premature births, and even miscarriages. Some children survived back then but not with this new strand. It kills the baby, taking the mother with it," Abrams explained. Gone was the glee that oozed from her as she talked about the power of science. Her eyes took on a far-off look.

I knew that look.

"Who did you lose?" I asked, my throat suddenly dry.

Abrams blinked as if her eyes were pooling with tears, but there was nothing there. An old habit, perhaps. "My mother. I watched as my father wept over her body for days. He and I had never been close before then. He had always belonged to the council; he had never been a father. Always off in a lab doing God knows what. In those moments after my mother's death, I saw his human side. I thought we had connected. It was years later that I discovered what a monster he had become, and that was when I discovered I would have to become an even bigger monster to survive."

I swallowed. My throat still burned because I knew Abrams wasn't done with her story, and I knew it would only get worse. "You said the council didn't stop it. But could they?"

"I don't know. All I know is they didn't try. The whole world was falling apart. Nuclear war happened because the government couldn't control its people. People—that's always been the variable the scientists couldn't predict. And here was a virus that promised to wipe them clear off the earth. They had already begun attempting to create life— chosen ones as you have called them. The originals were disasters. Deformed. Monsters, really. They had no idea what they were doing."

With a shudder, I thought about the creatures that attacked us in the woods.

"You've seen one?" Abrams asked, reading something in my facial expression. "I heard my son had used my father's plans to create an army of exterminators. I haven't seen them myself. Not since those early days. I always liked my creatures a bit prettier. What can I say."

"You liked them prettier?" I asked, unable to stop myself from walking closer to Abrams. I knew I was way past my five minutes, but my father, seemingly entranced as I was, failed to stop us.

"I was four when my mother died. After that, I spent every waking moment in the labs with my father. Watching and learning as they created life. When I wasn't with him, I studied everything I could get my hands on. It's a hard thing for a man to see his daughter become smarter than he is.

Especially when he and the rest of his simpleminded chums went around blaming the whole lot of the world's problems on female existence. But he didn't understand—that was the way genetics, science, had made me. It wasn't my fault. I was fourteen when I found the fault in their formulas. I was fifteen when the first chosen ones were created based off my work. Back then, we could create and awaken a fully grown chosen one in three years. Three years. That was a mistake; I rushed it. They weren't ready. That was my mistake. We all made mistakes back then. My father was underestimating me. He never saw it coming."

"Why would you let the council use them against us? Why would you make the world like this?" I desperately grabbed onto her shirt. Abrams pressed her lips together and avoided meeting my eyes. "Please! I have to know."

"I fell in love with one of them," she said quietly.

I froze, my hands falling from her shirt. "A chosen one?"

She nodded. "But he betrayed me in the worst possible way. He said he loved me, and yet he knew about the women. He was my father's right-hand man. He watched them die and came to me in the night. Both he and my father used me to get what they needed, all the while teaching the world to hate who I was. Watching as we all died. My father had always told me they had tried to find a cure, and I had believed him. But fathers lie," she sneered, darting her eyes toward my father.

"So, you killed them? The creators?" I gulped, re-membering the legend that had surrounded Abrams.

She nodded. "They killed my mother. They told the whole world I was weak and dangerous when I was the one who created the world they wanted to live in."

"So, knowing how the women were dying, why didn't you try and find a cure?"

Abrams's eyes met mine. She leaned forward, pulling on her ropes. "Because I finally saw the world my father and his men feared—a world filled with betrayal and hate and darkness. A world not worth saving. I killed those men, and the minute I did was the minute I realized how weak mankind was. The council was appalled by my actions, but they couldn't kill me. They needed me."

I felt sick. She could have stopped it. She could have found a cure. My sister could have been saved. "To create more chosen ones?"

She nodded.

"But now they know how. Why still keep you alive?"

"Because I ensured they would need me. I invented a fail-safe. Protection against the council built into the chosen ones themselves." Abrams grinned.

With the mention of a fail-safe, my father appeared at my side. This was the information he had been seeking out. My chest heaved with my unspent energy. "What are you talking about?"

"When I helped my father build the chosen ones, I believed we could make a newer, better world. And when I found out the world wasn't worth saving, I made sure I could keep that power to myself."

"That's God's choice. Not yours," my father barked.

Abrams pulled against her ropes, leaning her frail body even closer to me. "God has abandoned you. If he is master of the universe, then he's responsible for what has happened to our species. And when you realize that," she continued, "then you realize that the thing you hated for so long—us—

is gone. Then you'll be like the rest of us...empty."

"Five minutes is up," my father interjected.

I felt dizzy. Like I still wasn't quite awake—that odd in-between place between sleep and consciousness where everything seemed possible and impossible all at once. It reminded me of the morning I woke up after escaping the compound. I had reached for the numbers lasered onto my arm by the council, taking comfort that something of my old life still existed.

I cleared my throat, forcing the words out. "The virus... When I went into my inspection, they found out I was immune. I wouldn't die in childbirth. How?"

"We're done here. Step away, Tess," my father demanded.

"Won't you let me answer her question?" Abrams said like she was asking him to pass the milk. "It's the least you could do, considering everything I told you."

"I want to hear what she has to say," I begged without looking up at my father.

"One more minute," he said.

"You'll have to come closer. It's a secret only you can know." Abrams smirked.

"The last time I did that, a girl stabbed me," I replied.

"I have about five guns pointed at me. I don't think I'll be stabbing you," she countered.

I leaned closer to Abrams as she pressed her paper-thin lips against my ear. Her words slithered in and traveled down to my very soul. "Nature, my love. Science never could control it. It chose you like it chose me. There is no rhyme or reason to it, but you're special. Unique. It is a blessing and a curse."

So I was a freak. I began to pull away from Abrams when

the short cluck of her tongue stopped me. "I'm going to tell you something. Something your father wants to know, and I'm going to let you decide whether you want to share it." With these cryptic words, she whispered a series of numbers into my ear.

"Why are you telling me this?" I asked.

"Because when you've seen everything I have, playing games is the only fun left. Besides, I am so very tired of carrying this burden."

Before I could respond, an object darted out of the tree line from the corner of my eye. A monstrously loud ripping noise filled the air, accompanied by the clicks of five guns. Men shouted at me as I covered my head with my hands.

Once I was sure the sky wasn't going to fall straight down on me, I lifted my head to find a disheveled Robert standing in front of me. A tempest of emotions came alive in his eyes. His brow was furrowed, and his lip was curled in a sneer. Blood was splattered across his face like raindrops. My eyes traveled down to his hands. He was clutching some sort of dense object. He dropped it to the floor.

I looked past him to find Abrams slumped forward. A strand of salvia dripped out of her mouth down into the dirt ground. Like a spider web that had lost its spider. It went down to where her heart lay.

Robert had ripped her heart straight out of her chest.

I covered my mouth with my hands. I wasn't sure if I did so to keep from screaming or stop from throwing up. My father pressed his gun into Robert's chest.

Robert slowly, gently reached up and pushed the gun away. "You aren't going to shoot me, Charlie. Don't you remember when you broke me out? What you whispered into my ear?"

My father lowered his gun. "I promised you that one day you could kill those responsible."

"But why? Why?" I asked.

"She let Emma die," Robert answered, his voice taking on a tone I had only heard once before—a tone of utter helplessness. I had heard it the day Emma died. He offered no other explanation. Somehow, those four words were enough.

I turned around without speaking another word. I walked away from them all, wondering if I knew anything or anyone in the world I called home. Every time I thought I understood the world, my world, it changed. Felt less mine. Nothing was as it should have been. Everything I thought I knew was wrong. Up was down. Right was left. Light was dark.

And I had no answers.

Chapter 21

Tess,

There isn't any time. Even if there was, I wouldn't be able to write much.

The pain. Thepain. ThepainThepain.

If I keep thinking of you, they'll find a way to take you away forever. They'll rip you right from my brain as if you never even existed. It's a possibility. George found me yesterday. He told me that they aren't happy with my progress. He said they had a way to completely wipe my memory. They would take from me every thought, feeling, moment I have connected to you, and there would be no way to get any of them back. He said they have been avoiding this tactic because they are afraid it will mess with my ability. But at this point, they are getting desperate.

I don't know why George warned me. Only I

think he needs me to keep my memories for some reason. He told me you were important. He said that we would need each other.

If my vision is right, you'll be here soon.

I just don't know that I'll be me. Not the me you made me promise to hold onto.

It hurts so badly.

I will hide you back away.

I don't know what comes next.

~James

Chapter 22

"How is she?" I asked.

Lockwood ran a hand over his face. I wondered if he had slept at all. Under his eyes were heavy bags and his hair was wild in a mixture of grease and life that had suddenly gotten vastly more unbearable. "She won't see me," he gruffed.

A note of anger ran between his words, and I saw that the world had finally caught him. Lockwood had been the one person I had ever known who seemed to find the best in any situation, but the man who stood by me was changed. Altered in ways that both he and I were just probably starting to understand. His face was gaunt. His body erect and unmovable. There was nothing of the carefree friend I had come to consider family.

"This is ridiculous," I muttered, pushing past him. Louisa was hurting and lashing out at the one person she didn't even realize she needed the most.

"She doesn't want to see anyone," Lockwood insisted,

following after me.

"I don't give a damn what she wants," I yelled over my shoulder. I walked into the makeshift tent made out of tarp and burlap salvaged from the destroyed community. Shortly after talking with Abrams, I had been informed that my father had Louisa moved into his temporary headquarters.

My sister had a blanket thrown over her head as she lay on the ground. I nudged her with my foot. "I told everyone to leave me alone!" she yelled, her voice cracking.

"Being alone doesn't help anyone," I said. I took a seat on the ground next to her and pulled the blanket off her head.

Louisa reached up and shielded her eyes from the rays of sun that snuck through the tent. "What do you want?" she mumbled.

"I don't want anything. I just want to sit with you. We both do," I replied, looking back at Lockwood, who lingered by the entrance.

"The baby's gone. You can stop pretending you care," she said, yanking the blanket from my hand and throwing it back over her head.

"Maybe we should just let her be," Lockwood suggested.

The sound of his voice caused a surge of anger to rise up in me. Maybe I deserved this treatment from her, payment for sins of the past, but he didn't. I snatched the blanket from her and tossed it out of reach.

Louisa sat up and stared daggers at me. Her cheeks were covered in rapidly falling tears. "Look, the baby's gone," she repeated. "It's over. I'm not going to die. I'm not—" Her words were taken over by sobs. She fell into my arms and cried into my shoulder.

I reached up and ran my hand through her hair.

"I know it's probably for the best. I know I wasn't ready to be a mother, and I probably won't ever be one, but it was still a life," she choked out. "I'm so tired of death, Tess. I'm just so tired."

"We all are," I replied. "We all are."

Louisa lifted her head and sniffled. She looked past me to Lockwood. "Oh, Lock, I'm so sorry. I've been so hateful."

Lockwood rushed to her side and placed a hand on her cheek. His eyes welled with tears. "You don't have to go through this alone. As long as I'm alive, you'll never have to go through anything alone again."

"But that's just it, isn't it? How long until you die, too?" she cried out.

"Nobody can know that, so let's just focus on now."

Louisa reluctantly nodded and shifted so she could embrace Lockwood. I wrapped my arms around my waist. They suddenly felt empty. The kind of empty that filled the pit of your stomach with lead. I stood and patted him on the shoulder. I left the tent knowing that the previous day's events would leave them both scarred, but as long as they had each other, they wouldn't be broken.

With Lockwood with Louisa and Henry somewhere with Stephanie, I was left alone. I walked through the woods, nodding and greeting the survivors along the way. So many people huddled in groups that I didn't belong to. I wrapped my arms around myself and walked deeper, away from the members of the community.

Once I was sure no one would see me, I crumpled to the ground. I would allow myself this. Only this. The pain moved from deep within my chest, clawing its way up my throat.

I'm so tired of death.

Five words. Five words were all it took to let it free. I pressed my face into my hands, grabbed at my hair, and yanked it hard. I cried and wailed, sobbed and screamed until there was nothing left of me. Nothing left of the girl who was afraid. Nothing left of the girl who waited for death to find her.

When the crying was over, I lay down on the dirt ground. The ground that lived way before my time and would continue long after I was dead. I wondered what secret it had learned to survive so long.

"I've been looking for you."

I lifted myself up and rested my weight on my elbows.

"You all right?" my father asked, his voice tight.

I reached up and touched my face, swollen and puffy from crying. I nodded. "I am now."

My father walked over and crouched in front of me. "I was wondering if you could help me out with something. It won't be easy, and I can't guarantee that it will be safe. But you're the only person I can trust will do the right thing in the end. You're my blood. Part of me. And that counts for something." He reached for my hand.

For a second, it was as if the father of my childhood had returned, but I had seen this performance too many times to give myself over to it without trepidation. If there was anything I learned, it was that I would have to play the role of daughter to get anywhere with him, and I wanted to know what he was planning next.

I sat up and let my father take my hand in his. I didn't feel anything when he touched me. I had numbed that part of myself. Not forever—I would never be *that* girl again. Just temporarily. I had to if I was going to do what came next. "What is it you need me to do?"

My father had done monstrous things, searching out ends that justified his dark and twisted means, but I needed to get to the council's headquarters. My father had told me over and over that he planned on taking down the council, which meant he was heading into the very heart of the beast. Abrams had mentioned a fail-safe. I wasn't entirely sure what it all meant, but if my father wanted it, I had to get to it first. I didn't trust him. Not anymore.

I had no home left. And even the temporary safety the community had afforded us did not stop Sharon or Eric from losing their lives. There were no guarantees in this world. I couldn't promise time, and so I wasn't going to wait for the universe to bring James back to me. I was going to get him back myself.

Besides, George was waiting for me. Before taking James, he had revealed to us his gift—to read the secrets of others. If George wanted me to hear something, I was damn ready to listen.

My father reached forward and wiped a bit of dirt off my face. He took a deep breath and stared off into the distance. When his eyes found mine, they held a confidence that seemed foreign in these woods. "I need you to help me bring down the council."

It took me a minute to find my voice. "How can I do that?" I asked. "I'm just some girl."

"Isn't that what the council has been afraid of all this time?" he asked with a wry smile.

I thought back to all the propaganda videos that spoke about our wantonness, and our ability to rule men, muddle their minds so they couldn't think straight. I thought about the words of Abrams—how her own father had feared her, and how that fear had created a monster. The council did fear us.

And it was about time I gave them a good reason to.

. . .

"Let me get this straight. You want us to just let ourselves get caught? Does anyone else think this is a bit crazy?"

A few others murmured in agreement with Henry. Apparently, he was past the point of trying to impress my father. Of course, Henry had been invited to the meeting, so my father apparently didn't need to be impressed.

Like me, my father wanted Henry involved in his plan. Also included in his secret meeting were Stephanie and two of my father's younger male solders, Thomas and Daniel

"Charlie knows what he's doing," Stephanie told Henry, breaking her stance to do so. At the sight of her small breach in protocol, my father clucked his tongue. Stephanie lowered her head.

"Tell that to Sharon," Henry said.

It took everything in me not to agree with him. Nothing about my father's plan back at the community would qualify as smart. There was no way of knowing how many people his bombs were responsible for killing. But I gritted my teeth and bore it. If I wanted inside the council's headquarters, if I wanted to see James, I would have to play my part. Besides, I believed Abrams had given me the code to the fail-safe— not that I knew what that meant—so I had something to protect myself with. Why else mention a series of numbers *and* the fail-safe? They had to be connected.

While sending me to the heart of the council itself seemed insane, I remembered what Abrams had told me. I didn't trust the council *or* my father, so if something was going to go down, something that would affect the world and everyone I loved, then I wasn't just going to sit back and wait for it to happen.

I would never do that again.

"You're alive, aren't you?" my father argued. "So I guess my plan wasn't too terrible. Now, unless you don't want to be on this team, I suggest you shut your mouth."

Henry, always quick to react, opened his mouth to speak. His eyes met mine, though, and I shook my head. He would have to understand that when it came to war, my father would always sacrifice the individual for the group.

The innocent, good people of the world could die as long as the naturals lived on.

"You will leave in a week. You'll take nothing with you. Thomas, here, will lead you back to the outskirts of your old compound. When caught, you'll tell them you met these three Isolationists from the community. You won't have to lie about much. Tell them what happened here. Tell them you ran."

"And when we're caught? What then?" Henry asked.

"You'll do what you're told and wait for further instructions."

"That's it? That's all you want us to do? Let them take us and do God knows what and wait?" I asked in disbelief.

My father took a step toward me. "You'll be safe. You're valuable to them. I have a contact on the inside. He will approach you and Stephanie once he knows it's safe. You'll work within the council headquarters themselves because of the three marks."

I reached up and touched the marks on the back of my neck. I was finally going to see what getting those three marks meant.

"Once our man finds you, you both will help him in securing information," my father continued.

"The man who sent me James's letters?" I asked.

"No, a different man," my father replied quickly. Too quickly. He was being evasive, but I wouldn't let him know I was onto his game.

"If you already have a man on the inside, why do you need us?" I asked.

"Because as women, you will be allowed into places he won't. There is a map I need you to locate, a map of the council's headquarters. There are rooms and labs that only the highest of officials know about, and we need that information."

"How do we find this map?" Stephanie asked.

"I've worked it out with my man that you will be assigned to the highest-ranking families. While in their service, I need you to spy, snoop, anything you can to find it. They won't think you're capable of treachery."

"Why do we need this map?" I asked.

"I can't tell you yet. Not till we have it in our hands. Look, I know I'm not giving you very much, but the less you know, the less you'll have to lie about if they somehow discover you."

"What about us?" Henry asked.

"You immerse yourself in the new life. Watch over Stephanie and Tess. And when we attack, you'll be there to help us fight," my father answered.

I glanced at Henry, who was staring at Stephanie. "I can

do that," he said firmly.

My father walked over to the burning campfire that lit up the night sky. He reached down and pulled out the heated iron. He walked toward Stephanie. "I'm sorry we have to do it this way, but if you don't have the three marks, they'll just send you to a compound."

"I understand, sir." Stephanie bent to her knees and robotically pulled her long hair to the side. I watched as Henry clenched his jaw. Stephanie grunted as the third mark was seared into her skin. A lone tear slid down her cheek, but still she did not cry out.

Unable to stand it any longer, Henry stalked to Stephanie's side and took her hand in his. Despite the obvious break in order, she made no objections.

When my father had dismissed us, I made my way to Stephanie. Henry whispered into her ear words of comfort and brushed the hair from her neck, touching her as if she would break. She shook her head and managed a small laugh when she saw me. "You would think he's never seen a girl branded before."

"You all right?" I asked.

Stephanie nodded. "Hurts like hell, but I'll heal. Or, rather, scar."

I shrugged. "It's not so bad. At least it's now a two-member club."

We were two girls ready for battle.

Chapter 23

"You do know you don't have to sneak around, right? I'm okay with you and Stephanie," I told Henry as we went to work on setting up the camp.

Henry froze and his mouth dropped open. Once he realized I had noted his reaction, he popped his mouth closed and went back to work building the campfire. "I have no idea what you're talking about."

"So I didn't see you holding her hand last night at dinner when you thought no one was looking?"

Henry blushed. "I...I was just asking if she was okay."

I threw my head back and laughed. "Oh my God! If you can't admit it to your best friend, how are you ever going to tell her?"

"We're back to being best friends, then?" he asked, his voice growing serious.

I dropped the tarp I had been holding and walked over to him. I took his hand into mine. "We've always been best friends, Henry."

He squeezed my hand. "I guess we have. Even when we're both pretending to hate each other."

"Even then," I said quietly.

Henry squeezed my hand once more and then went back to work. "So, it doesn't make you jealous? Not even a little?" he joked.

"You're unreal." I laughed. "So, you going to tell her?"

"I don't know. We're in the middle of a war. It doesn't exactly feel like the best time," he said, throwing a stick at me.

"Oh, Henry. Don't be a dumb-ass. There is no better time." I poked him in the ribs with the twig for good measure.

Later that night, as Henry snuck Stephanie off to talk to her alone, I pulled out a book Robert had given me before I left the camp. Our parting had been marked with strangeness. I never took my brother-in-law to be an avid reader. But as he mumbled final tips and combat instructions, he placed a copy of William Shakespeare's *Twelfth Night* into my hands. He said nothing of the book or why he gave it to me. He simply told me he found it on Eric before he was buried, and he thought I should have it.

I pulled the book from my satchel and leaned closer to the glowing fire to borrow some of its light. We would be reaching my old compound in the morning, and while I should have been sleeping, I knew I wouldn't be able to.

When I opened the book, my breath caught in my throat. Etched onto the title page was a name: *William McNair*. Below it was a hand-sketched drawing of a wild shipwreck. The sea had tossed the vessel right into a reef. Below it, he'd hastily drawn a beach and on the land stood a girl. Despite the violent sea behind her, the girl looked happy.

I remembered how McNair talked of the sea. And I wondered if he would have been as happy as the girl in the picture, weathered any storm, to find such a piece of land. Land untouched by our troubles.

I skimmed a couple of pages of the book and came across an underlined passage. It was an exchange between a captain and a shipwrecked girl named Viola. The heroine wondered what she would do in this new and unfamiliar land, and the captain told her it was a miracle she was saved.

It had been so long since any one of us had seen a miracle.

Feeling the ghost of McNair throughout the pages of the book, I snuggled down against the ground and pulled a blanket over my shoulders. I'd rather fight sleep than fight a dead man's unfulfilled hopes and dreams. I had too many of those myself.

Somehow sleep found me. I only woke once when Henry and Stephanie returned to the campsite. They held hands as they walked, and I watched as Henry placed a gentle kiss on her cheek. He was different with her than he was with me, and I wondered if it was because he sensed the fire in her was stronger than his. That he would be the one to calm it.

Did we draw people to ourselves to fill in our missing parts, or did we seek out those missing parts ourselves?

• • •

The next morning, as we trudged closer and closer to the place Henry and I called home for so many years, Stephanie and my best friend tried unsuccessfully to keep their hands off each other. That didn't mean she wasn't focused entirely on the task at hand. Their touches were small and quick. A gentle hair tug. A playful kick in the heel here and there. Looking at the two of them, I realized Henry had found his partner in war. Something I had never wanted to be. Something he had searched out in Julia Norris, the girl who had helped him murder the incubating chosen ones back at Templeton. He had wanted a warrior, someone committed to the cause as much as he was, but I wasn't that girl. I would choose love over war any day.

But maybe in Stephanie he had found both. I couldn't help but smile as I walked behind them. Lost in my own musings, I barely noticed when everyone stopped. Thomas, one of the men my father assigned to our group, held up his hand and scrunched his nose. "Do you smell that?"

I sniffed. A pungent and familiar odor crept up my nose and traveled down to my stomach, where it painfully churned. Stephanie and Henry stopped whispering to each other and tried to identify the stench as well.

My eyes darted to Henry's. "I know what that is," I said. Without wasting another second, I bolted toward where the compound stood. It couldn't have been half a mile from our current location. My heart beat hard against my chest and not just from running.

If I was right...

I couldn't be right.

"Tess! Wait!" Henry yelled. I could hear the others running after me, but I didn't slow down. What was the worst that could happen? We would get caught? That was all part of the plan anyway.

I skidded to a stop and Henry crashed into me from

behind. We both toppled to the ground. "Holy shit," Stephanie breathed.

Home was a strange concept to most naturals. Forced to leave the shantytowns that we grew up in, we had nothing but cement walls and communal living quarters for most of our lives. A place to wait for the end—but never a home. But as we stared at what was left of the compound, I realized the building was more than a collection of walls—it was the people who lived inside. A people destroyed.

Henry and I lifted our heads to find the compound burned to the ground. Piled high in front were bodies upon bodies. Everyone we knew. Everyone we shared meals with and passed in the hall. Everyone the council promised to protect.

Eradicated.

I vomited into the dirt. Stephanie fell next to me and pulled my hair back, saving what wasn't already soiled the first time from my second round of throwing up.

"God damn them!" Henry screamed into the sky. I reached up a shaky hand and clutched onto his shirt, attempting to hold him in place. Hold him together. He pushed my hand away and brought himself to his feet. "Damn them," he sobbed. He paced back and forth, pulling at tufts of his hair.

"What do you think happened?" Thomas asked our fifth traveling companion, a solider named Daniel.

"Charlie said this sort of thing's been happening," Stephanie said. "The war isn't going so well, so they've been getting rid of the compounds. That way they can use the chosen ones to focus on the front. What do they need naturals for anymore?" She ran her free hand up and down my back.

I wiped my mouth with my sleeve and sat on my

backside, pulling my knees to my chest. "Henry and I came across another compound like this one before. Everyone had been taken out and shot, and then they burned it to the ground. Didn't want to leave anything that the Isolationists could salvage. But I never thought it would happen here."

Henry rounded on me. "Then you're naïve."

"Calm down," Stephanie pleaded with him.

"Calm down? That's our whole species' problem. We've just been sitting back and letting this happen. Over and over again we let them get the best of us. We should have —"

Stephanie got to her feet and walked over to Henry, placing both of her hands on his face. She pressed her forehead against his. "We're going to get them. I swear it. We'll make every last one of them pay."

"Going to make us pay? How do you plan on doing that?"

I whipped my head around to find three chosen ones surrounding us. They were the tools of the council, the weapons of the men responsible for the destruction of my people. The one who asked us the question was carelessly throwing a stick from one hand to the other.

"You sons of bitches!" Henry screamed, and without warning or thought, fueled by the fire that always burned inside of him, he ran straight at them.

The chosen one flicked his wrist and it was over. The small, seemingly harmless twig struck Henry right in the neck. Blood spewed from him like water from a fountain. His eyes bulged as he crumpled to the ground.

"Nooooooooooooooo!" It ripped from me like my soul was tearing with it. I had lied to James when I said he had all of my soul. I stupidly thought that Henry's lie had forever destroyed his claim to a small part of it. But when he lied about James being in the community, it hadn't ruined what took years to build—our connection. Instead, I had been right those early days back in the compound when James had once asked me what my definition of the soul was, and I told him a soul has many different aspects.

My words drifted back to me. *There are people who can fill a part of you, make it stronger. The part of my soul that longed to be carefree, the part that didn't know fear of disappointment, that was the part of my soul that Henry belonged to. He took it with him.*

Part of me would die with him, and I would always, forever, be undone.

Stephanie instinctively reached for her gun, but before she could lift it, a chosen one held her by the neck off the ground. In the blink of an eye, the chosen one who speared Henry was crouched in front of me. He reached up and placed a finger on my lips.

I wanted to bite it off. My eyes darted to Henry. He lay shaking on the dirt floor, his body jerking and moving like some uncoordinated dance. I rocked back and forth gently to try and control the lightning storm that raged inside of me. I looked up at Stephanie, who remained stoic, and I attempted to channel her.

The third chosen one stood behind Thomas and Daniel, who both held their hands up in surrender. That had been the mission, after all.

"Look what we have here," the one holding Stephanie purred. He yanked her hair to the side. "This one has three marks. A fresh one at that! What could you have done to earn that last one so recently? How naughty were you?" he teased.

"I struck one of you bastards right in front of his friends. He thought he had the right to put his hands on me. I guess he didn't like it when I marked up his pretty little face," Stephanie boasted without hesitation. If she was still reeling from Henry's death, she was hiding it well. She was a pro. Striking a chosen one would earn a girl a one-way ticket to doom. I wondered if this was something she had practiced with my father.

The chosen one in front of me narrowed his eyes. "Do you have three pretty little marks, too?"

I swallowed down the bile that sat rotting in my throat and nodded.

"Isn't that lovely? Looks like we get to keep you two," he said with a smile. He stood up and held out his hand to me. I jutted my chin away from his touch. "Let's not start out like this. Hmm?" he replied, pushing his hand back into my face.

I clenched my jaw and grabbed his hand. When he pulled me up, I turned my head to look back at Henry. He wasn't moving anymore. I blinked away the tears that pooled in my eyes.

"Friend of yours?" the chosen one asked.

I pressed my lips together and looked away. I wouldn't put up a fight, but that didn't mean I had to give him everything he wanted. His eyes darkened and he slapped me hard across the face. I fell forward.

The time between crashes of lightning and thunder was getting shorter and shorter. Soon, I wouldn't be able to stop hell from breaking loose. Mission or no mission.

"I asked if he was your friend," the chosen one snarled.

I nodded, unable to stop a lone tear from trailing down my face. "Tell me, what are you two girls doing out here?"

"We ran," Stephanie answered. "From the compound a few weeks back. We didn't want to know what happens after we got the third mark. These men are Isolationists. They were supposed to help us escape, but she got sick, and so we had to wait her illness out."

I was caught off guard by how easily her lies came. I cleared my throat. "When we saw the smoke, we thought we might be able to find something in the wreckage. Something to help us survive."

"Well, I'm afraid you're going to find out what happens after all," he said with a causal shrug. He looked up at his two compatriots. "Kill them." In a synchronized series of movements, Thomas's and Daniel's necks were snapped.

I gasped.

"What?" the man asked, looking at me as if I was the crazy one. "We always kill the men. What do we need them for?"

As the three chosen ones led Stephanie and me to our new destiny, only one thought kept me going: my father knew this was going to happen. He knew Henry, Thomas, and Daniel would be killed.

Henry.

I would make it through this.

If only for him.

Chapter 24

I leaned my head back against the wall and tried to slow my breathing. I was sucking in too much air, and I didn't know how much longer I would be locked in the closet. It was the third time this week that I had been forced into the cramped room and bolted inside. The last time I had passed out from lack of oxygen.

I was being punished for my sins.

After the incident in the woods, our captors, Stephanie, and I had traveled by foot for a week to a safe point belonging to the council's network of outposts and training facilities. Of course, these places were quickly becoming abandoned and obsolete. The council no longer had the manpower to run the establishments, so they moved their armies closer to the headquarters themselves. There, we were joined by other female prisoners taken from the compounds and training centers destroyed in what the chosen ones were calling the Great Reckoning.

The Great Reckoning. I didn't ask what it meant. It remained a series of words for me. The only meaning they held was created by the council, and I had stopped caring long ago what they wanted me to believe.

Even the war that seemed to be brewing out of control felt unimportant to me. What did I know of Eastern and Western except what was told to me through the council? A distorted and dirty filter that attempted to shape my world in whatever fashion it desired. This wasn't a war I was part of; I was merely collateral damage. This was a war between two giants who used science as their weapons. And I was just trying to survive.

Surviving meant living in the council headquarters themselves, the heart of evil. If I were going to find that beach McNair dreamed of, I'd uncover the map there.

The chosen ones were proud of the council's headquarters and boasted of its beauty almost as if I should feel honored to be imprisoned within its walls. Built in what was once called Nevada, the headquarters, like the chosen ones who protected it, was a work of art that left one breathless. The chosen one who had killed Henry explained that it was copied from a building that once existed in England. This hardly came as a surprise, as much of the council's prescribed buildings, clothing, and etiquette harkened back to ideas of English propriety. They had always tried to recapture the spirit of that great empire.

But they should have known that all empires fall.

Somerleyton Hall was the name of the original building the headquarters was copied from. When Stephanie and I came upon it, after a week of walking and several days in a council transport, we both gasped. We couldn't help it.

Surrounded by formal gardens and mazes built from hedges, the vast greenery glared against the harsh tans and golds of the desert that surrounded it. Worlds that weren't meant to live together. When I had dared to bend down and touch the grass, marveling at its ability to exist in such a place, I discovered it was fake. Learning this truth did little to diminish the splendor.

Creating something artificial wasn't an entirely new practice for the council. Their scientists were called creators, after all. They simply had to think of what they wanted, and then it would come into existence. Or it would be forced to.

Stephanie and I were informed the building was constructed in a mixture of Tudor and Jacobean designs. Those terms meant nothing to us. All I could know was what I saw—a mixture of brick and granite. Crèmes melting into reds. Domes and spires that reached for the sky. Flowers that crawled up from the ground and danced with the brick, weaving and twisting over columns and railings.

Inside, the grandeur of Templeton was taken to the extreme. Gold and silver gleamed and sparkled like the sun and stars themselves were at war. Marble floors were covered with rugs with the most interesting designs and colors I had ever seen—blues, yellows, indigos, greens, and reds meshed and melded together in perfect, dizzying harmony.

So much color for an organization that infused our lives with darkness. Did they think they were the only ones who got to keep the richness and beauty of the world?

When we lined up that first day to receive our orders, I had convinced myself that my time at the headquarters would be spent in a similar fashion to my time served at Templeton. I would keep hidden, cleaning and tending to the needs of the great estate that kept and trained young chosen ones.

I couldn't have been more wrong.

Terribly and utterly wrong.

I should have known from the noise.

We were forced to wait more than an hour in the grand lobby of the establishment. As we stood there, men, chosen ones and naturals alike, hustled and bustled through the halls. Their movements were always with a purpose, always anxious. Their conversations hummed like a hive of bees had taken residency inside. The pounding of soldiers' boots echoed across the halls as groups marched in order.

These men paid us little attention. We were a hodgepodge of girls ranging in age from one girl who barely made it to her teens to an older woman who must have been nearing seventy. Dirty and worn from our long travels, we all stank of sweat. But there was one girl who stood apart. Injured and hastily sewn up after the attack on her compound, a small, waifish girl named Rachel had a haphazard set of stitches that ran from under her left eye down to the top of her lips. She would be hideously scarred forever. The rest of the girls stood apart from her as if they sensed what was coming. Like her disfigurement would crawl from her face and mark theirs, and amongst the finery around them, they were already feeling self-conscious.

Was this feeling, this need to please, something the council had conditioned us into believing, or had it always existed in us girls?

Everyone except Stephanie.

She had made it her mission to stick by the girl during travel. While part of me thought she did it to avoid talking to me about the loss of Henry, Stephanie ate her meals with the girl and slept near her. The firm reserve that she'd called from within herself minutes after he was killed seemed to deplete the further we got from Henry's body. As we stood there waiting for whatever came next, Stephanie took the girl's hand in her own.

It was against protocol. We were supposed to blend in. Gather information. As I glanced at her from the corner of my eye, I was growing more certain that something broke inside of her when she watched Henry die. She had lost a sister as well...

I shifted my weight from one foot to the other. I wanted things to begin. Left with nothing to do for too long and I would remember Henry, too. The images would return of his blood spilling from him and the way he crumpled to the ground, and I didn't know how long I could repress it.

A series of bells chimed throughout the halls of the massive building and every man stopped in place. Their whole demeanor relaxed at the wretched sound. The naturals slumped and slouched their way to where we waited while the chosen ones followed behind. That was where they always stood, behind the men who had created them.

I remembered the bells that warned of the attack on the community and my teeth scraped against each other. A few girls next to me stood a little bit straighter while others tried to hide behind their hair.

A man near my father's age, dressed in a clean and finely tailored suit of tweed, walked back and forth in front of us. Inspecting us. A chosen one followed behind him and when the council member made some observation of a girl, he mumbled it to the chosen one, who jotted it down onto a clipboard. It was as if he were defining us with a simple *tsk* or cluck of his tongue. I wasn't quite sure if I wanted to hear a *tsk* or cluck when he passed by me.

When he finally stopped in front of Stephanie's new ward, Rachel, the man scowled. He slowly looked back at the chosen one who stood behind him. "What is this?"

"One of the girls brought in from the compound attacks. She had all three marks," the chosen one replied matter-of-factly.

"And who would bid on her?" the man replied.

Bid on her? As if we were something to be owned and traded to suit their needs. But hadn't that been the way they always treated us girls? I couldn't help but think of Abrams—the never-ending horror she must have felt when she realized that the two men most important to her were working to ensure the death of her gender. Sacrificing the women in order to create a new master race of superhumans. They had made her a thing, and so she destroyed the world they wanted to rebuild.

Stephanie pursed her lips. Her knuckles turned white with the force with which she clutched onto the shaking girl's hand. The inspector's eyes moved to Stephanie. "Let go of her," he demanded.

I silently begged Stephanie to do what the man said. I needed her here with me. I wasn't a solider like her, I certainly was no expert on espionage, and I was positive my father had given his most trusted compatriot information that he didn't think I needed.

Stephanie did not notice my silent pleas. She lifted her head and stared the man down. The inspector's fingers began to tap furiously against his leg. While the room was absolutely quiet with attention, there was a tension that screamed inside of my ears.

Let her go.

She's just one person.

We can save so many more.

I shuddered. The unsaid words tasted sour in my mouth, the place I would leave them to rot. I had sounded just like my father. I managed to meet Stephanie's eyes and gave her the smallest of nods. I didn't know the girl, but that didn't mean she was any less important. I didn't get to sacrifice her for anyone. That wasn't my right.

Maybe that was what Stephanie had finally realized as she watched Henry die. Maybe he meant more to her than some cause, and the council had taken him from her. She realized too late what I had learned long ago: I didn't belong to anyone. I didn't belong to any country. I didn't belong to any rebellion. I only belonged to myself. My choices and who I fought for would be entirely of my own choosing.

Stephanie brought the girl's hand to her chest. "No," she said.

The inspector narrowed his eyes. Clenching his jaw, he looked back at the chosen one. "Very well, then. We don't need them."

"Please, she was just being nice. Don't punish her for me," Rachel begged, tears streaming down her scarred, imperfect face. The chosen one pulled her by the arm, dragging Stephanie along with her. Stephanie didn't fight back. Whatever solider she had once been was gone. She had given up the last bit of it to get me here.

At first, my fears were quelled. The chosen one simply ushered the two of them off to the side as the inspector continued to go down the line. Eventually, a few others, including the elderly woman, were also placed in Stephanie's small group. Once the inspector had looked everyone over, each of us was asked to show our identification numbers—the numbers the council had long ago lasered onto my wrist.

258915

The inspector's aide pinned a piece of paper to each of our shirts, which proclaimed our number for all of the spectators to see. Men began to huddle into groups in front of us. The aide passed out green cards to each of these families. Groups of men who had lost their mothers and sisters to the illness that threatened to destroy our species. We were what were left. Replacements.

Once each group was prepared, the inspector nodded toward four burly men who waited near the small cluster of women isolated from the group. In unison, the men stepped forward in front of Stephanie, Rachel, and the other women. Each of the men placed one hand against their collarbones. Stephanie turned her head to me and gave a small smile.

And then she closed her eyes.

A wild surge of energy burst through me, and it took everything in me not to run to her and grab her free hand in mine. She still held on tightly to Rachel's hand. The chosen ones placed their palms under the women's chins, and with the cluck of the inspector's tongue, they snapped their heads back.

A girl beside me fell to the floor in a faint while others cried. I saw dark spots in front of my eyes, and I wondered if I was near passing out myself. I had seen chosen ones snap necks before. It seemed to be their specialty. But it was also some weird sort of embrace. They stood behind their victims and wrapped their arms around their necks.

This had been something different. Carried out with the least amount of human contact possible. Women murdered because they did not meet some unknown standard. Murdered because they had been found wanting.

James.

I whispered his name over and over again in my head. It was the only thing that kept me from attacking, from clawing their faces off, from joining Stephanie. James was here, and I would have to play my part to find him.

To save him.

The creators lined up before us, and then the bidding started.

I was auctioned off.

. . .

This was how I came to be in the service of the Harper family. Once they paid for me, I was taken out back behind the headquarters with Reagan, another girl who was purchased along with me. Shoved forcefully against the wall by the eldest son of the family, the younger brother grabbed a hose. Not the kind used to water plants, but the kind I had been told was carried on the back of trucks once. These trucks would rush to fires and use the traveling water source to put them out.

These trucks would have gotten a lot of use during my lifetime.

Terrance and Richard Harper, the sons of the newly inducted head of the council, turned the hoses onto us. The water burned and pounded against my skin. Regan, who was barely a teenager, stumbled to the ground and covered her head.

"Get up, your dirty, dirty girl," Richard yelled. The Harper brothers enjoyed themselves way too much.

That night, as Regan cried herself to sleep, I gingerly touched the multitude of bruises that covered my body from the painful pressure of the water. There was barely an inch of me that was left unscathed. I had been a victim. I had been hunted. But before now, I had never been property.

I was to do whatever the Harper men commanded of me. If I disobeyed, my punishment would fall to them. They had bought me, and in the eyes of the council, I didn't own myself. But, then again, to them I didn't deserve to. According to their doctrine, I was weak. Filled with such reckless wantonness that I could only corrupt, never lead. So, while the council abandoned the naturals stationed in compounds, we were forced to be the servants of the men left in the headquarters.

If only they knew the person responsible for their continued power was a woman. Was that why she did it? Some cosmically sick joke? The supreme creator a woman. It was wild.

Or did she really do it because she thought the world, and everyone in it, too dark and twisted to save? She had told me the code for the fail-safe. Whispered it into my ear gleefully. I still had no idea what any of it meant. And while the older members of the council had to know Abrams was female, these pissants had no idea.

It was no secret that soon their bloodlines would die out. That one day, the chosen ones would be the only ones left—a perfect species to carry out our civilization, a civilization molded and created by the council itself. That would be their legacy. So, these younger children, boys not smart enough to carry out their father's work, sons of man-made Gods, pranced and lived in the headquarters with no purpose.

Lives of frivolity that went unchecked.

The first time I was locked in the closet was on the third day of my servitude. I was punished because Richard had accused me of spitting in Terrance's tea when he wasn't looking. I had stood there, holding the tea tray while the boys lazily sat around the table, and watched as Richard spat into the cup. After Terrance drank from it, Richard nearly fell from the chair laughing. When the boy, who couldn't have been more than fourteen or fifteen, raised his eyebrows at me and whispered mischievously to his brother, I never would have dreamt he would accuse me of such a ridiculous action.

This petty act left me dumbfounded. I was used to seeing people who thought they were better than me take for granted the lavish lives they were given, but this overwhelming sense of mean-spirited silliness wasn't something I had ever truly experienced before.

These boys, villains who enjoyed terrorizing Regan and me, weren't so different than the naturals who lived in the compounds. Neither set of people had any true purpose guiding them through life. But I wasn't sure what made these boys so hateful. They appeared to have everything just within their reach. Thinking back on the people who shared their lives with me within the walls of the compound and the Isolationists who struggled to find freedom, I began to hate the Harpers.

Knowing full well I wouldn't be stupid enough to let his

younger brother see me spit in his tea, Terrance yanked me
by the hair and threw me into the closet. Once I was inside, I
realized all of the shelves had been removed, and there was
a deadbolt on the outside.

This space had never been used for storage.

The second time I had been locked in the closet was
because I had failed to guess that Terrance had wanted me
to set out his light blue silk shirt instead of the white one. I
was supposed to read his mind.

The unfairness of it was enough to drive me insane.
But somehow, I kept my mouth shut. *James. James. James.*
It became my daily mantra. I waited for my father's man on
the inside to reach me. Any time an errand sent me outside
of the Harper family quarters, I held my head up, hoping
someone would recognize me. But the days turned into a
week and I had no sign of my father's man.

The third time I was forced into the closet was because
Terrance was bored. He called me into the family study and
demanded that I entertain him. "You must have some sort
of talent. Show me," he chirped, chucking the book he was
reading across the room. Had I not served time at Templeton,
the sight of the book would have shocked me. The council
had long ago outlawed them, but the council often picked
and chose what rules they followed.

I looked Terrance up and down. There was a part of
me that was slowly becoming infected by the nastiness
that spewed from these boys. I wanted to tease him, laugh
at his ugliness. God, or whoever created him, had certainly
given no attention to the construction of his face. Comically
wide, Terrance's teenage face was covered in acne. It was
too plump for the rest of his body. His head looked as if

someone got confused and switched it with a much bigger man's by mistake. Bushy eyebrows and gapped teeth.

I wondered why his father, one of the world's most gifted scientists and leader of the council, didn't fix him. Perhaps Harper didn't worry too much about his sons; I barely saw him around the living quarters.

Behind the greasy elder son stood a beautiful gleaming piano. There was a talent I could show him, but it wasn't one I was willing to part with. Playing it for him would feel like I was giving him all the moments connected to it—the moments when I'd still looked up to my father and the moments when I'd fallen for James.

"Stupid, useless girl. What did we even get you for?" he screamed at me.

Most of the times Terrance or Richard put me in the closet, they would let me out after a few hours. They would remind me of how I had misbehaved, and then made me promise never to make those same mistakes again.

This time felt different. As the minutes turned into hours and the hours into a whole afternoon, I wondered if they had forgotten about me. I brushed the hair out of my face, which had been matted with sweat. I felt my eyelids droop, and I knew there wasn't a lot of time before the darkness came for me again. I couldn't help but think of The Void. I was trapped once again. I reached a sluggish hand up and began to trace slash marks against the back of my hand.

Sharon.

Eric.

Louisa.

Emma.

James.

Myself.

Henry.

Stephanie.

I forced my eyes open and managed to get myself to my knees. If I had to, I would use whatever strength I had left to kick down the door. I wouldn't go out like this; I would make some sort of stand for the people I loved. With a grunt, I felt around the black void for something to help pull me up.

And then there was the brightness. It was so strong that I fell backward, knocking my head against the wall. My eyes slammed shut, trying to protect themselves from the new light battling the darkness that had successfully lulled them into submission.

In front of me stood the last person I had ever expected to come and rescue me—George.

The chosen one who had nearly ruined my life crouched in front of me and held out his arms to help me up. I gathered every bit of strength that hid within my muscles, balled up my fist, and let it fly straight for his face. My punch didn't seem to do any damage to the chosen one in front of me, but it caused me to fall straight back on my ass.

"I wouldn't suggest you do that again," George said, reprimanding me like I was a naughty little girl in the schoolroom.

I punched him again.

And when that still didn't make me feel better, I pulled back my fist once more. This time, George caught it in his hand before the hit landed. "I said stop," he growled.

"Actually you didn't," I panted. "You suggested I didn't do it again."

"See, that's the kind of attitude that gets you locked in

a closet," he said. "Now, would you like me to let you out or not?"

"Why the hell would you help me?"

"Oh, Tessie. Don't you remember our fun little meeting in the woods? I whispered that I couldn't wait for you to join me. That you'd help me. And here you are." He grinned.

I had always hated that damn grin.

"Now, how can you help me stuck in here?" he continued.

"I have no intention of helping you," I said. "I remember everything about our little meeting in the woods. I remember how you killed McNair. I remember how you returned my sister to me pregnant. I remember how you took James from me."

George placed a hand over his chest. "Are you implying I treated you unfairly? I killed that grizzly man because he was about to attack me. And if there is one thing I know you understand about this world, it's kill or be killed. In regards to your sister, I returned her, didn't I? It's not my fault she couldn't keep her hands off me."

I opened my mouth to scream every obscenity I knew at the creature in front of me, but George clamped his hand over my mouth. "And as for James? I needed him here, too."

"Where is he?"

"Closer than you think, actually. I can bring him to you. I bet you won't mind my help out of this mess now, will you?" he asked, reaching his hand down for me again.

When he touched me, his eyes widened. It was only for a second, but a shudder ran through my body. I didn't want to give him the satisfaction of seeing how much he still unnerved me. Once I was out of the closet, I sucked in as much oxygen as I could possibly get. The rush of air through my lungs caused me to feel a bit dizzy.

Once I had gained my composure, I looked up at George. "You know, Terrance wouldn't like it that you let me out of here."

"Terrance is the one who called me here, my dear," he whispered in my ear. "Seems he doesn't like the merchandise. Wants to return you. Considering that would mean your death, and the fact that you are exactly where I need you, I figured it was about time I stepped in."

"Why would Terrance call you?"

"I'm the one they call when there is something wrong with the girls. I've been assigned to finance. Sort of helpful to have a man around who can read every secret ever hidden, especially when it comes to money."

I had forgotten about George's gift. I pulled my hand from his grasp. With a simple touch, he would know everything I kept hidden inside of myself. George chuckled beside me and ushered me into the study where Terrance sat on the couch, pouting.

"This isn't going to work. You have to play the part," he leaned in and whispered to me.

I wanted to wipe the floor with the petulant ass.

"I believe this man has asked you to entertain him," George said. "I'd advise you, girl, to fulfill your duty. You must have some talent you can show him?" His eyes darted to the piano.

Once, back during our days at Templeton, George had stalked me in the piano room. He had tainted James and my sacred space. Now, it seemed like he was trying to take it from me again. I pressed my lips together, then looked down at the back of my hand, and I remembered the slash marks I had drawn over and over again while entrapped in the room of darkness.

If George had been telling the truth, then James was near. Which meant that if I wanted to see him, I had to survive, and if I wanted to survive, I had to play that piano. I had to bend to the pest of a boy's every whim. I had to bide my time and team up with one of the vilest men in all of existence.

James was worth it.

I hesitantly moved to the piano and took a seat. My hands trembled as I brought them to the keys. I took a deep breath and began to play. I played my mother's song because if I was going to be forced to share this secret side of myself, then I would play what I wanted to play.

There was a part, a small part of me, that came to life as my hands danced across the keys. It had been so long since I had touched one. I thought of my first moments alone with James, and I closed my eyes. Maybe it wouldn't be so bad. Maybe I could lose myself in these memories when I played the piano for Terrance, fool him into thinking the music belonged to him.

The sound of clapping broke my trance. When I opened my eyes, Terrance look amused. George continued to clap. No doubt, he was happy that I was playing my part.

"Did my father send you for me?" Terrance asked, looking over my head to the entrance.

I turned around and he was there.

James.

Chapter 25

At the sight of him, my face flushed. It was like the lighthouse that beckoned the ships home. I pressed a hand against my burning cheek, hoping that it wouldn't give me away. James was much better at hiding his recognition of me. In fact, he only but glanced my way.

"Yes, your father would like a word with you and your brother. He believes you took something that was not yours. He would like you to bring it with you," James said. It read as a request, but his voice carried an edge — a warning.

"I...it wasn't me. I didn't take anything. I s-swear it," Terrance stuttered. His skin looked clammy as he shot up out of his seat.

Terrance seemed scared out of his wits. Either he was deathly afraid of his father or what he took was of some worth. Inwardly, I kicked myself. If Terrance or Richard had taken something important from their father, something that could have been laying around unguarded in one of the rooms I was cleaning, and I had missed it, I would never forgive myself. I was there to spy, and I hadn't discovered a single thing yet.

"It really is none of my concern. I am merely here to collect you and your brother," James replied dully.

I bolted out of my seat, nearly knocking over the piano bench in the process. "I'll go fetch Richard." George, confidant that neither James nor Terrance could see him, raised an eyebrow at my impertinence. I had not been given permission to leave the room. I cleared my throat. "If that is all right with you, Terrance?" I bowed my head.

Terrance opened his mouth to object, but James cut him off. "I think that is a good plan. If things are as you say, Terrance, your girl here can instruct your brother to bring along the stolen map." Terrance nodded, a layer of sweat forming on his brow. I didn't wait to be told twice. I gave a small curtsey before beelining it out of the suddenly cramped and tense study. I knew I didn't have long before they would expect me back. I would have to look and look fast.

A map. My father had told me that I would be assigned to the family of a creator. Once in their service, I would need to find a map. The map would lead me to every secret room and lab in the council's headquarters. It would lead me to the fail-safe.

It all seemed too easy, but my father was no idiot; he would make sure I was placed with the creator most likely to have the map in his possession. Could this stolen map be the same one he spoke of?

Beneath the anxiousness of searching for the map lay another emotion. I tried to force down the butterflies that fluttered happily inside my stomach as I almost ran to

Terrance's room. James was here. He had seen me. I knew he would be altered by the terrible things the council did to him, but he was with me, and I knew we could overcome anything that stood between us. He wouldn't let them destroy us. Not completely. I just needed to find a way to get him alone. For now, it was enough to know he was still alive.

I knocked on the door to Terrance's room to make sure Richard wasn't in there before I barged in and began my search. The little pest enjoyed going into his brother's room and messing up the work that Regan or I did only to call us incompetent later. Satisfied that I was alone, I quickly opened and then closed the door behind me.

Terrance's skittish behavior when questioned by James proved to me that the stolen map had to have been in his room. He, no doubt, took it just because he thought he could. That was the only reason he ever seemed to do anything. But maybe it was something else, some pathetic attempt at trying to get his father's attention. I had been assigned to the Harper family for more than a week, and I had only ever seen his father during the bidding.

Searching the room felt impossible, knowing I had very little time and couldn't leave any trace of my actions. I had no training for this kind of work. I had grown up in a compound and not in my father's army. He had seen to that. Which meant that after throwing aside the blanket to look under the bed, I had to make sure it was put back into place without a single wrinkle. Every drawer I opened had to be closed, and every book I moved off the shelf had to be put back.

And the clock was ticking.

I ran my hands through my hair, spinning around in

a small circle, searching for any sign that something was out of place. And then I remembered finding *Tess of the D'Urbervilles*. It seemed like a lifetime ago that Henry and I had discovered the novel. The injured girl had hidden it under a loose floorboard. While the floors of the headquarters were made of marble tiles and not wood, I fell to my knees. I crawled around the room, running my hands over the smooth, cold surface looking for any imperfection.

After several minutes, my hand bumped against a loose tile in the corner of the room. I glance behind me to make sure I was alone, then pried the loose tile up. "Well, I'll be damned," I whispered.

I lifted the folded-up map from Terrance's hiding place, then laid it across the floor and smoothed out the wrinkles. It was a map of the former United States of America, separated into East, West, and Isolationist territories. All of the compounds held by the council were marked on the map, most of them now covered in giant red x's. These must be the compounds that had gone through The Great Reckoning.

The lightning storm inside of me flared up once more. The insatiable anger tossed and turned like the storm that separated Viola from her family in McNair's book.

There was a wave of green on the map that stemmed from the Eastern coast and spilled almost all the way to where the council itself stood. I furrowed my brow as I ran my fingers across the color that soaked almost the entire map. What could it mean?

This was how far into our land the war had come. We were losing, and we were losing badly. There was almost nothing left of the Western sector. That was why the council had abandoned the compounds and murdered the naturals who lived in them. The council headquarters was all they had left—their stronghold. When that fell to the hordes of the Eastern army, it would all cease to exist.

We were running out of time.

The map outlined the country or, at least, what was left of it. It wasn't the map my father wanted, but this was the map *I* desired. It would lead me to freedom.

I began to fold it up when the corner bent. There was a second map underneath the first one. I peeled back the top sheet to reveal a floor plan of the council's headquarters. I placed the first map of the country on the floor and held the object of my father's desire. Somewhere on this map was the fail-safe. Bringing the map closer to my face, I took it all in: meeting rooms, large banquet halls, the homes of creators, and then the places hidden to the eye—labs and control rooms located behind secret panels and camouflaged doors. How many secrets did the council have?

The doorknob to Terrance's room began to twist. I scrambled frantically to fold the floor plan map and stick it in my pocket, but I didn't have time to grab the U.S. map on the floor. When the door opened, my throat went dry. I looked up to find James staring down at me. All the tension that I held inside my body relaxed. A deep sigh shook me to my core.

It was only James.

James.

I was alone with James.

A smile danced across my face.

James narrowed his eyes and looked me up and down. Sizing me up. "What do you think you're doing?" he barked. I jumped at the tone of his voice. "I asked you a question!"

I couldn't open my mouth, couldn't speak. I didn't know how to react to this James. He snatched the map from the floor beside me, and his eyes burned with accusation. "Were you the one who took this?"

I fumbled around my brain for words, some way to make sense of what was happening. This was James. My James. The boy who showed me how to love. The boy I had given myself to. But it wasn't him at the same time. I hadn't been foolish enough to think that James wouldn't be different, but I never expected this.

James reached down with his free hand and dragged me to my feet by the collar of my uniform. He pushed his face into mine. "Answer me," he said coldly.

My eyes pricked with tears, and I had to look away. Otherwise, I would lose it entirely. They had won. The council had won. They made him into a monster. No matter what he had written in his letters, I never thought they would win. I didn't think it was possible. He was the kindest soul I had ever met.

I shook my head. "I didn't take it—I found it. I came in here to look for Richard. I didn't take it."

"Let her go," said a seemingly bored George from the doorway. "Can't you see how scared she is? She didn't take it. Besides, you know how these two imbeciles are."

"She was snooping," James growled, still holding me.

"Don't you have a creator who's waiting on you? You think he will like that you wasted so much time on this simpleton? I highly doubt it," George said. James shoved me away and I fell to the ground. Without a second glance or word, he walked out of the room.

Once he was gone, George shut the door behind him.

With the outside world locked away, I could no longer control the emotions that flowed through me. A sob broke free from where my soul, despite the world's many attempts to destroy it, still managed to live. I pressed the palms of my hands against my eyes. I couldn't stop the tears that spilled from me, but that didn't mean I had to look at George while I was doing it.

The first time James had disappeared from my life, I had attempted to give him up. I made peace, albeit a flimsy one, with the fact that I would never see him again. But then I did. He had come back into my life to save me, and even after George took him from me, I always expected him to come back. Somehow. Some way. I knew it wasn't the end of our story. I lived with that hope, even if I never spoke it aloud, every day.

I lived to find a world where we could be together.

But he had changed. James had always told me that I kept the darkness from him. The truth was we had both done that for each other. Like Jane and Mr. Rochester, the couple from the first book we had ever read in secret together. There was nothing James feared more in the world, except for maybe my own demise, than losing himself to the council.

And they had finally succeeded in taking him from me.

"You done?" George asked. I looked up to see him leaning against the door. He offered no words of comfort or sympathy, and I was thankful for it. It wouldn't have helped. Not from him. Words of kindness from the man I hated would only make the malice that oozed from James even more unbearable.

"There's something I want to show you," George said, not waiting for my answer.

"What about Terrance and Richard?" I asked, my voice strained.

"I have a feeling they'll be busy getting read the riot act for a while. But that doesn't mean we should sit around and waste time. Get up."

I pulled myself to my feet and followed behind George. That was my place after all. Creators. Chosen ones. Naturals. That was the order of things. "I saw the map," I mumbled.

George stopped dead in his tracks. "And what map was that?" he asked casually—much too casually.

I had to decide which map to give up—the one that outlined my possible freedom or the one that would give him every secret he couldn't take for himself. I didn't bring up the map by accident. I knew how George worked. He would find some way to touch me and discover what Terrance and Richard had hidden. He would never even mention it, but he would take the information all the same. This way I would bring it up. I would decide what he got to know, and I would do everything in my power to make sure he didn't place a hand on me.

But what information to give him?

I didn't trust George. Not a bit. Which meant I knew what I had to do.

I cleared my throat. "There's a map that shows the damage of the war on the land. Every battle. Every destroyed compound. Every loss and every win. All the things about the war the council doesn't bother to share with us."

"Did you understand it?" he asked as he began walking again, a note of disappointment seeping through his words.

"The war. It's here."

"It's not just about the war. It's about something bigger."

"Something bigger?"

"Yes, Tessie. It's about the end of days."

. . .

George took me down to the basement. I had to force my legs to continue moving as we delved deeper and deeper into the belly of the beast. My time spent roaming around basements had never ended well. It didn't help that I was traveling to one with the most maniacal man I had ever come across.

The enemy of my enemy—wasn't that how the saying went? Except I still wasn't sure why George hated the council. All I knew was that he seemed hell-bent on taking it down.

As we walked through the halls of the headquarters, no one even looked up at us. I understood the frenzy of the men who zoomed past us now; they were trying to stop the destruction of the world they worked so hard to create. They didn't care that a chosen one was escorting me through the halls. They had stopped caring about my kind. I was simply a toy bought to amuse those too weak to be of any use in the coming final battle. Little did they know, I was planning on fighting, too.

Much like Templeton, as we voyaged down below the surface of the headquarters, the marble and finery of the world above gave way to cold grays and violent silvers. I wrapped my arms around myself to stop the shivering.

"They have to keep it near freezing down here. Helps preserve the specimens till they are ready," George said.

"Specimens? You know I have no idea what you're

talking about, right?" I snarked. I was growing tired of his relentless word games. He enjoyed flaunting my lack of knowledge in my face.

George rolled his eyes as he slid a card though an access panel. "Soon, you'll know exactly what I'm talking about," he said, a glint of enjoyment in his eyes.

Standing before me in a room constructed of cement and steel stood dozens and dozens of incubation stations. They were the containers that housed the chosen ones until they reached maturity, their holding cells till they had been formed into the perfect solider—their minds filled with endless propaganda and subliminal messages while they slept.

"I've seen those before. Back at Templeton," I said.

"Not like this you haven't. Go on, take a closer look."

Maybe it was my imagination, but the lights above our heads flickered. I took a hesitant step toward the incubation stations. As I crept closer to the sleeping chosen ones, the hairs on the back of my neck stood up.

Lying in front of me were the monsters of the woods, replicas of the deformed chosen ones that hunted us down while traveling to the community. All of the creatures had misshapen skulls covered in unnatural ridges and bumps. Their eyes were sunken in, and in most cases, one was larger than the other. Scars cut across their faces where science had failed. They were taller than I had ever seen any natural man.

They were monsters.

"They have sped up the creation process," George said. "The East has been doing this forever. Creating a masterpiece takes time. These things don't even have fully functioning brains."

"You're talking about your own people," I reminded him.

"They're nothing like me, and I advise you never to say anything of that nature again," he warned.

"Why are you showing me these?"

"There's a control panel behind that door there," he said, pointing across the room. "The code is 45981. Enter it and you're in. Then you can dismantle all of the cords. Just like your friend Henry did. Where is my favorite natural? Not hurt, I hope."

"You want me to kill them?" I asked, shocked. I ignored his jab at Henry. There would be time to fight for his memory later. Besides, nothing George said was untrue. Even his death couldn't erase that. Now, George was asking me to become a murderer as well.

"I'm giving you the option. I'm giving you the information. You must do with it what you will." He shrugged.

"Why are you telling me this?" I asked, raising an eyebrow.

"You gave me a code. It's the least I could do. These days you'll find I'm all about a good partnership. You help me and I help you," he purred.

The code. When he had helped me out of the closet, grabbing for my hand, he must have read the code. I suppressed the urge to reach for the map hidden in my pocket. If he got it, he would have everything he needed to enact the fail-safe. And until I knew what that meant, I couldn't let it happen. I hadn't had enough time to truly study the map, which meant if he touched me, he wouldn't know where it was because I didn't know. He would just know that I had the map. I had to get away from him as quickly as possible and hide it. If only Stephanie had still been around, then I could have given it to her to hide, and then its location would be free from my mind as well.

"Come along, your boys should be heading back now. Don't want to deprive them of your services," George said, turning and walking toward the exit.

I looked back at the row of deformed soldiers and then turned to George. I had no idea what his plan was or why it involved me, but one question forced itself to the front of my mind: Was George my father's man on the inside? They seemed to be after the same thing. And he had been present at my bidding.

"George? Are you telling me this because you want to stop the end of days?"

George paused and slowly turned around to face me. "No, Tessie. I'm telling you because I want you to help me speed it along."

Chapter 26

Terrance was waiting for me outside of his family's living quarters when I returned from my adventure with George. Slumped against a wall, he held his hand gingerly to his face. I couldn't miss the swollen lump that was growing at an alarming rate underneath his eye. Upon seeing me, he drew a flask from his pocket and brought it to his mouth.

I fought back a sigh. The last thing I wanted to do was deal with a drunk. I had to find a way to keep the map from George and figure out what was going on with James.

James. My heart skipped a beat just thinking about him. The way he looked at me—that couldn't have been an act. I remembered the words in his letters. Had he truly forgotten me? Could I entirely blame him if banishing me from his memory was the only way he could survive?

"Wipe that look off your face," Terrance sneered.

I bit the inside of my cheek and looked down. I was growing tired of his antics, but George had been right—I had a part to play. I kept my head down as I moved past him, but I didn't get very far. "I didn't excuse you," he snapped.

"Is there anything you need from me, sir?" I mumbled. I had tasted freedom in the woods while living with the Isolationists, and even knowing my father was on his way to take me from this place, playing the part of enslaved servant was near impossible. I would never accept that life again.

"Is there anything you need from me, sir?" Terrance mocked. He shoved his face into mine. "What did you do with it?" he growled.

I swallowed. "With what? The map I found? I gave it to your father's chosen one."

"What did you do with the second one?" he asked darkly. "I know you have it."

I shook my head, keeping my eyes on the floor. "I don't know what you're talking about, sir. I found the map accidentally. There was a loose floorboard. I nearly tripped on it fetching your brother."

Terrance's hand jutted forward and clutched me by the front of my blouse. I could smell the alcohol wafting from his breath. "I know you have it, and I want it back!"

"Is there a problem here?"

I managed to turn my head to find James staring at us from down the hall. Terrance grimaced at the sight of him, and I couldn't help but wonder if he had been responsible for the black eye. "Don't you say a word," Terrance whispered to me.

"I asked if there was a problem," James repeated, walking toward us. Terrance trembled next to me, and I couldn't blame him. James had always been someone bred to enforce the will of others, but the power that oozed from his voice was overwhelming in its magnitude. He had power of his own.

"No problem, James. This wench here is late with my supper. She is constantly forgetting her place," Terrance said, shoving me hard against the wall. I nearly fell from the force of it. My head smarted and ached. I reached a hand up to the back of my skull, and when I pulled it away, I found blood. I wanted to claw the bastard's face off. "I'm not going to repeat myself," Terrance spat, pulling back his hand. Before he could smack me, James grabbed onto his wrist.

"I think she got the point," he said.

James had stopped Terrance from striking me. Despite the pain that radiated inside my head, a warmth spread through me. "Your father suggests you go back to looking. I'll make sure the girl fetches your supper." Terrance narrowed his eyes and looked from me to James. "I wasn't making a request," he warned.

Terrance, too afraid of James, didn't dare say anything or even look at me as he stalked back inside his living quarters. Apparently, his father knew he had stolen the blueprints of the headquarters, and he would do just about anything to get them back. The map wouldn't be safe in there, and I was wondering if I could ever be safe with Terrance. Things were moving too quickly. Everybody seemed to be in motion except for me. I needed to figure out my next step.

Lost in my thoughts, I hadn't noticed that James had been staring at me. I tried to stop the blush from creeping up my neck to my cheeks, but I couldn't help it. I had never been able to control my body when it came to James; it had always wanted him desperately. James cleared his throat and my legs nearly gave out from under me. I knew what it meant when he did that.

It meant that I was making an impression.

James turned on his heel and began moving down the hall. I sat frozen in place. I had been dismissed without a word. Whatever I thought had happened between us as he stared down at me had only been my imagination. An emptiness had threatened to consume me each time James had left my life, but somehow, this was worse. He was so close, and he didn't know I existed.

And then he stopped and I couldn't breathe. Without turning back to look at me, he reached a hand in the air and impatiently beckoned me to follow after him.

I couldn't have stayed in that spot if I wanted to. I would have followed James anywhere. No matter what version of the man I loved walked before me, he was still the man I loved.

I nearly had to run to keep up with him. When he finally stopped, he opened the door and pointed inside the room. He didn't look at me once. Not even when I moved past him, our bodies nearly touching. Every hair on my arm stood up with anticipation. So close. I had been so close.

James cleared his throat again.

He had led me to a small medical station. "Sit down," he said, his back still turned on me as he began to rifle through cabinets. His voice was empty, devoid of any emotion. No concern. No anger. I knew what it was to be the person who felt nothing, but to see James become this was the saddest thing I could imagine. I managed to plop myself up on the medical table that stood in the center of the room. Sure that James couldn't see me, I closed my eyes and took a few deep breaths.

He had warned me that he was forgetting me. That he needed to forget me. This man before me wasn't my James, and I had to watch myself.

James turned to face me holding a bottle of alcohol and gauze in his hand. He had brought me here to help me. To clean my wound. There was a part of my James still in there, after all. Tears pooled in my eyes and my lip trembled.

"Bow your head and I'll..." His voice trailed off, seeing my expression.

I sniffled and did what I was told. An eternity spread out before us. He neither spoke nor moved. With my head bent down, I wondered if James had fled.

"This is going to hurt," he finally said softly. I nodded, too afraid that if I opened my mouth I would betray myself. I would tell him everything. What he meant to me. What I meant to him. And while I knew there was a part of the man I loved still inside, I wasn't entirely sure how much of him was still that boy.

James gently pressed an alcohol-soaked cloth against my head. I hissed at the pain. "I'm sorry," he said quietly.

"It's all right," I whispered.

"I don't think he did any real damage. If you start to feel nauseous, you must let someone know. But I don't think you have a concussion."

"Thank you," I managed despite the dryness of my throat. I wanted to reach out for him so badly. He was right there. We were alone. We were together.

"Just doing my job," he replied.

"Taking care of natural girls who other men hit is your job?" I asked, my voice all breath and want.

James cleared his throat. His hand slowly moved from my wound, but he didn't pull it entirely away. I was afraid to breathe, to move at all, afraid that I would shatter whatever moment was happening between us. The tips of his fingers slowly moved through my hair. My eyes fluttered and it took everything in me not to sigh. His thumb grazed my cheek, and I couldn't help but lean into his hand.

"I'm sorry for the way Terrance treated you tonight. You didn't deserve that. He is angry at his father. A weak boy who is upset because he doesn't get enough attention, but what he fails to see is that Harper has a lot on his shoulders. He spends all his time searching for something very important to the council, a creator he desperately needs," James explained.

My eyes popped open. Searching for a creator. They were still looking for Abrams.

"So, Terrance does foolish things to try and get his attention. It's all very…human," James went on.

Human.

The way he said it: disgusted. Something wasn't right.

"Tell me, girl. You look after him. Have you stumbled across anything else the boy may have taken from his father's room? A second map, perhaps?" he asked, his thumb continuing to graze my cheek.

Something inside of me twisted and broke. I slapped James's hand away from my face. "What are you doing?" I demanded.

James stepped away from me, his hands held up in surrender. "The touching? I can tell you like it." He motioned to my reddened cheeks. "I can do it some more. I just need you to help me a little."

I wanted to throw up. James had been playing me. Trying to gain my trust so he could use me to discover the location of the second map. Little did he know, it was sitting in my pocket.

I hopped off the medical table, trying to ignore the wave of dizziness that overtook me. "Looks like you liked it yourself," I challenged. His face was flushed.

"I...I was just..." he mumbled, backing away from me.

He *had* liked it. Some part of him remembered what it was like to touch me. I stood as straight as I could. I didn't care that he was a chosen one. I didn't care that he couldn't remember our time together. I walked right up to him. "What part of it did you like? The way it felt to touch me? Or the fact that you were doing something they told you was so wrong? Or was it both?" I asked, raising an eyebrow.

James's face paled as he gulped. I reached a hand toward him, stopping just short of placing it against his chest. "I can do it some more. I just need you to help me a little," I whispered.

"Get away from me," he said.

"What is this map you're looking for? Why is it so important? If you tell me, I'll let you do it again," I promised, placing my hand against his chest. His heart pounded beneath my palm. I could feel my own heart beating to keep pace with his. "I can tell you want me to," I whispered.

James wrapped a hand around my wrist but he didn't pull me away from his chest. "I...I need you to stop doing that."

I licked my lips. Abrams had been right. Women had all sorts of power. "Is that really what you want me to do? Come on...just a few answers, and we could have so much fun."

In a quick succession of movements, James yanked on my wrist and twisted me around. He pushed my head painfully against the counter while holding my arm against my back. "You will never speak of this again to anyone. Not a word."

Before I could open my mouth to reply, James was gone.

Chapter 27

I woke up when a hand clamped over my mouth.

I grabbed my assailant's wrist, pulling with all of my might. It was too dark to see who was in my room with me. My heart screamed for someone to hear its pounding as I dug my nails into the skin of the person who held me down. Suddenly, the room was lit up.

James. A wild thought broke through my sleep-muddled mind — had he come into my room to kill me? He had lured me into the medical station in an attempt to get me to spy on his creator's son. It hadn't been about dressing my wound. But he had felt emotion when he touched me, and I wondered if he would do something to ensure he never allowed that weakness in again.

He brought a finger to his lips and nodded toward my bedroom door. I managed to lift my head and look over to the bed where Regan slept, but she was nowhere to be found. A sick thought slithered into my head: had James done something to her?

I lay my head back down on the pillow and stared up at him. James slowly lifted his hand from my mouth. He leaned over me and pressed his lips against my ear, and I tried to suppress the shudder that ran through me. It was as if my body didn't know this man before me was no longer my James, but, then again, my mind wasn't entirely sure either.

"I need you to come with me. Can you do that without screaming?"

I nodded, and James held out his hand to help me off the bed. I took it and a rush of warmth ran up my arm. The minute I was standing, he let go. My hand had never felt emptier.

I spun around when he turned away from me and grabbed the map from under my pillow, sticking it inside my nightgown. I didn't trust that Terrance or George wouldn't come looking for it. Not that I felt entirely safe having it on me walking with James either.

James led me out of the Harper family's living quarters and down a long maze of halls and corridors. He neither spoke to me nor looked at me during the entire journey. His shoulders were stiff, and he kept his hands clutched into fists by his side. He stopped in front of a door, looking right and left down the hallway to make sure no one could see us.

It reminded me of the past. Another time we snuck around. Those times where he would take his hand in mine, and we both thought the world couldn't get any better.

James ushered me inside of the room without any pretense of hospitality. Once in, he set the candle he was carrying down on a table and bolted the door locked behind him. And then he stood staring at me. Taking in every single ounce of me.

Seeing something he disliked, or even worse for him, liked, he pushed me roughly against the door. He placed both of his hands on either side of my head. Trapping me in his glare. His forehead almost touched mine. "How do I know you?" he whispered.

My chest tightened. I shook from head to toe. He could kill me. I knew how to fight, and if it came to it, I would, but James wanted to kill me.

"Did I know you from my time at Templeton?" he begged. I nodded as the tears streamed down my face. "What the hell did you do to me?"

"I saved you. We saved each other," I said, reaching forward a hand and placing it against his heart.

He jumped from my touch as if it burned his very skin. And considering what the council had done to him, maybe it had. I pushed myself off the door and walked closer to him. I refused to let them take him from me. Not now that he was so close. I couldn't let it end with death—that wasn't the story we deserved. The council had already ripped from me too many people I loved. Good people who deserved to live long and happy lives.

James and I deserved to be happy, too.

"We loved each other."

"Loved? How could one of my kind ever love something like you?"

"You're only saying that because they want you to feel that way. They made you feel that way using mind control and manipulation. But it's not how you really feel. We were together. We made each other," I argued, finding it harder and harder to keep my voice quiet. The more I talked about what the council did to us, the angrier I got. The less I cared if I woke the whole lot of them up.

I had to make James see. I just had to. And I knew I was running out of time. There was no denying it any longer— the end was coming. I didn't know what that meant for the people I cared about, but I knew we couldn't run from it any longer.

"I can prove it to you. If you just listen to me, I can prove everything," I begged, reaching my hands up to his face. Once I touched his skin, his eyes widened with a split second of recognition. It was different than the way we'd touched in the small medical room. This touch wasn't born out of hidden motives; it was born out of love. James fell to the floor, his hands clutching the sides of his head.

"It hurts. It hurts," he groaned out.

I crumpled to my knees in front of him, reaching for him but avoiding actually touching him. My hand dangled in the air, yearning for contact. "It's all in your mind. This is what the council did to you. They conditioned you to feel pain and anguish any time you thought of me. That's why you're feeling it now. Because part of you knows I'm telling the truth."

"You're lying," he said. "That's what your kind does."

"Why did you come to me tonight? If I'm not important to you then why did you feel compelled to come for me?"

James groaned, his face turning a dark shade of red. "I came because I dreamed of you. This dream…" His voice trailed off in a series of grunts and curses as he fell back, scratching at his skin, attempting to rip it straight off his bones. His eyes rolled slightly to the back of his head.

"What about the dream? What happened? Maybe if you

can tell me, we can stop this. You're stronger than what they did to you," I urged.

"In the dream…the dream…Terrance…attacked." James's fist flew up to his mouth as he bit it in an attempt to keep the pain that burst through him quiet.

I didn't know what to do. I didn't know how to help him. There was a part of me that wondered if I should have left. He would stop hurting once I was gone. I could pretend that I was just some girl and he just some boy. He could go through life without ever knowing the pain I brought him.

But what kind of life would that have been? Our love had never been easy. Never. And those difficulties made us stronger. I put myself in his shoes. If someone had forced him from me, and I knew there was a way I could get him back, I would do anything. I would walk through hell itself.

It was only then I noticed the map peeking out from the inside of his coat pocket. Despite the way he writhed and trembled on the floor, I reached in and took it. It was the map I had found in Terrance's room; the map it pained me to part with. He had kept it. He hadn't turned it in to Harper. "Why did you keep this?"

"Please just leave," he begged.

"No. The fact that you kept this proves that what I'm telling you, everything I'm telling you, is true. You don't want this life. You want the places on this map that are untouched by war, places where you could be free. That's why they wanted you to forget me and tried to kill me. We would always choose a life together, a life filled with the unknown, rather than the life the council gave us."

Suddenly, I flew across the room and landed painfully against the wall. James held me in place, a constricting hand around my neck. "I need you to stop," he said.

"The first time I kissed you…" I squeaked. James's hand tightened slightly, but he would have to kill me before I stopped fighting for him. "I asked you if you wanted to. You were so nervous. We both were. But when your lips touched mine, I thought that everything was changed. Everything I knew. Everything I would become."

James loosened his grip on my neck. He staggered away from me, his whole body trembling. "Please, Tess, stop. I don't want to hurt you."

"Tess?" Hope flared inside me. "That's the first time you've said my name tonight." I rushed to him and pressed my lips against his. He stilled, but I didn't pull away. I knew what his touch did to me, lit me up like the stars in the night sky.

James fell to the floor and began to convulse. I fell to my knees next to him, reaching for him, attempting to keep him from hurting himself. If his reaction to the kiss was this violent, I knew he felt something, too. If I just pushed a little harder, maybe I could get him to break through the walls the council made him put up. It was a gamble, but I knew, had our roles been reversed, I would want him to bet it all, too. I bent over him and began to share with him every beautiful moment we'd shared together.

The piano room.

Reading *Jane Eyre.*

Playing in the snow.

Reuniting in the small, cramped jail cell.

Losing ourselves within each other in the woods.

James's eyes closed and he didn't move. I pressed my ear over his chest to make sure he was still alive. My heart was pounding so hard against my ears, I couldn't hear his. Or at least that was why I hoped I couldn't hear his. It could very well be my heart was pounding for his quiet one, too.

Slowly, James reached a hand up and tucked a piece of hair behind my ear. A sigh shook my entire body. His eyes fluttered open. "Tess?" he asked weakly.

I nodded, blinking back tears. "You're back?"

James reached up and pulled me into his embrace, wrapping his arms around me. "Only because of you," he whispered into my ear. "I'm so—"

I turned my head and pressed my lips against his. This time he pressed back. I shifted my body so I was straddling him. "I don't want to waste any time with pointless apologies. The council doesn't get to steal any more from us."

James sat up so I was in his lap. I wrapped my legs around his waist, my nightgown riding up in the process. "I have missed you," he said, pressing his forehead against my chest, his fingers trailing up and down my exposed legs.

He tilted his head and began to kiss up and down my neck, and I thought my heart would be the one to give out. "I missed you too," I half moaned.

James took my face into his hands, gently rubbing my cheek with his thumb. "What are you doing here?"

"We'll talk about it all later. Right now, I just want us. I want you," I mumbled, bringing his lips to mine. He turned us over so I was lying on my back. He pulled his shirt over his head and tossed it across the room. My back arched under his touch, and my shoulders pulled up off the floor. "I just want us forever," I breathed.

We were the ocean McNair spoke of. We were gentle and wild. We rushed and remade. We had the power to protect and destroy. And as we moved together on the floor of his room, losing each other under the current, I didn't need some far off land. I just needed him.

He was my anchor.

And I was his Viola.

. . .

Later, as we lay tangled in each other, James made me promise to never allow myself to be alone with Terrance. I assured him that his nightmare would remain that — a nightmare. I avoided alone time with the sleazy teen as much as I could. I also told James everything that had happened after he left. I told him of the people I lost and informed him about George's new place in my life.

"You really think your father would align with him? Then why stop you from trying to meet him?"

I sighed, casually running my fingers up and down his back. "I don't know. But he's the only man who has approached me with any sort of plan or information. That was the whole reason my father sent us here."

"Unless someone got to your father's man first."

I raised an eyebrow. "What do you mean?"

"For some reason, George wants to take the council down, right? Well, he has the ability to read the secrets of any man he touches. Say he found your father's man and discovered his plan. What would he do?"

"Kill him and take his plan for his own?"

James nodded. "Exactly. Then, he would convince you he's on your side. You would pass along to your father whatever information he wanted you to know. Thus, setting off a series of chain reactions that would accomplish his own end game. Your father and George might have the same goal, but I doubt it's for the same reasons."

I furrowed my brow. "But that still doesn't explain why he would get Louisa to lure me out of hiding. He wanted to bait me into coming here, and that was before my father even got the information he needed from Abrams."

"You know what this means, right?" James asked.

"We're going to have to talk to George," I replied.

Together. Just as he wanted it. Just as he orchestrated it.

"Great," I muttered.

Chapter 28

"Oh, your father's here?" George asked, looking wildly around him.

"You know he isn't," I gritted through my teeth.

"Then how would I be working with him?"

George, James, and I stood huddled together deep within one of the council's maze-gardens. Everyone in the headquarters was so insanely busy that the entire garden was empty. Creators and chosen ones alike practically ran from one corner of the massive building to the other, mumbling about advancing armies and strategies.

"Then why the hell bring me here, George? Why do you need me?" I asked.

"I told you what I wanted you to do. I gave you the code. I reunited you with your boyfriend. What else do you want from me?" he responded, casually plucking flowers from the vines that seeped through the hedges and chucking them to the ground.

"How about some answers?" James said.

"I really don't understand why you two are so angry. You're together. Isn't that the most important thing in your pathetic little worlds?" George sighed.

"Why do you want me to kill the incubating chosen ones?" I asked again, my voice rising. James put a hand onto my arm in an attempt to calm me, but I could tell by the clench of his jaw, he was just as fed up with George's antics as I was.

I tapped my foot. "Taking out the group of chosen ones down in the basement would only deprive the council of *that* army. It wouldn't get rid of their power. They'll still have all of the chosen ones walking around in there."

"Yes, dear," he clipped, "but it would be one less thing standing between the council and the East."

"And why would we want the eastern sector to win? Why trade one round of power-hungry dictators for another?" James asked.

"If there is one thing I can promise you, James, it's that you won't see the eastern sector come to power." George clapped his hands as if he was signaling the class to quiet down. "Now, if you want the council gone, taking out that army is the first step," he replied. He was losing his patience with us.

The feeling was mutual.

"I can't kill an entire army of chosen ones. Deformed or not, they're still human," I snapped, reaching over and taking James's hand into mine.

"It's their greatest source of power," he said, sounding exasperated by my morality. "Tell her. You have to know that I'm right, James. Keeping her safe is the most important thing in the world to you, right? Well, as long as that army sits down there sleeping, she won't be. The creators designed our kind to do their bidding. What will the council demand that damn army down there do?"

James stared at me long and hard. "Don't let him get inside your head," I said, cutting James off before he could agree with George. The man was smart enough to use our love against James, and I wouldn't let him be a pawn in his game.

"Why do you want the council destroyed anyways?" I asked.

"It's better for you if you don't know all the details. In fact, you're safer if you don't," George replied.

My father's words. Those were the exact words my father had said to me back in the community. I pulled my hand from James's grasp and shoved George with as much force as I could muster. He barely moved an inch, but his eyes narrowed slightly. I couldn't read the emotion that brewed beneath them. It was only there a second, quickly replaced with a fake mirth. His go-to charade. "What the hell were you trying to do there?" He laughed.

"I want to know everything," I yelled.

George clamped a hand over my mouth, but before he could reprimand me James smacked it away. "I'm here because apparently you have information we need, but if you touch her again, I'll rip your head off," he promised.

"I want to know how you are working with him," I demanded.

"The girl who stabbed you," he replied dully.

"Go on," I said.

"On my way to meet you, I found her. I used my gift and discovered that your father had kidnapped Abrams. Oh,

Abrams. I am sorry your friend killed him. Actually, I mean
her. Wasn't that a fun surprise when I pulled you from that
closet."

"You discovered my father's plan?" I repeated, hoping
to hurry him along. I didn't have time to listen to his own
creator-mommy issues.

"He needed you in the community, so he would have a
base to hide and question Abrams. He didn't want to take
the community by force. If we have learned anything from
living under the council's thumb, it's that power works much
better when you get the weaklings to just give it to you. Your
father's a smart man. I knew he would discover what I have
shaking the hands of all of Abrams's advisors."

"And what would that be?" James asked.

"That she never gave a fuck about us. Not chosen ones.
And certainly not naturals. She wanted to create the perfect
world. She wanted to be God. And when things didn't go her
way, she wanted someone to end it for her."

"So, how did you end up working for him?" I asked. I was
nearly rocking out of my skin. If my father had truly aligned
himself with the man who lied and seduced his daughter, I
didn't know what I would do.

What wouldn't he sacrifice for his great cause?

James ran a comforting hand up and down my back.

"Once I discovered your father had Abrams, I simply
melded his plan into mine. I had always known I would see
you again. I used your sister to lure you out of hiding, so
I could get James here back. Knowing that without him, I
wouldn't ever make it to the inner circle, and I had so many
wonderful secrets I wanted to discover," George said with a
grin, his eyes lighting up like a child who was reaching for

candy.

"My rendezvous with you and your people really had nothing to do with you when I conceived the plan. I just needed James, but when I discovered it was your father who had Abrams, everything changed. The great thing about reading people's secrets is there are so many people who have so much to protect. Things they are willing to do anything, and I mean anything, to keep hidden. I sent messages to your father. Told him I wanted a meeting."

I thought back to the last month in the community. There would have been multiple days I would go without seeing my father. It was entirely plausible that he could have held a meeting with George without my knowing.

"One handshake and I knew what he discovered from Abrams. And *her* disdain for *her* people, her glee at watching it all burn away only fueled me. When I informed your father that I knew what Abrams had told him, he had no choice but to let me in. So, we agreed that he would send you to the headquarters."

"But you just said it was never really about Tess. You had gotten to her father. What did you need her here for?" James asked.

"I needed her to get to you," he replied.

I didn't have a good feeling about any of it. I fumbled for James's hand again. He took mine in his and brought it to his lips. "Why would you need me to get to him? What's his role in this? What the hell are you and my father planning?"

"When your father and his men come, I'll need as many chosen ones on my side as I can get to help them in, so he can do what he has agreed to do. I'll need your help, James. If I don't have it, we have zero chance of succeeding. Me.

You. And the chosen one, Robert. We are the three that give the naturals hope of doing what they'll come here for."

I gulped. "And what exactly is that?"

"We're going to enact the fail-safe."

"Fail-safe?" James asked.

"I won't give you any more details on that now. So, don't waste either of our time asking. I've already told you too much. If this doesn't work, the less you can confess the better. We both know you don't handle pain too well."

I gave James's hand a squeeze, silently pleading with him to ignore George's not so subtle dig. "I understand the importance of taking out the incubating chosen ones, but why do you need me to do what you can do yourself?"

"You know what? Like I said before, do it or don't. I don't care. Either way, soon enough you'll all have to make some choices. You won't be able to just talk your way through them. War's an ugly thing. You should have realized that before you signed up," he hissed at me.

"I suggest you walk away," James warned.

George scowled and turned to head down the pathway that led back to the headquarters. "You're welcome for the reunion, by the way," he called over his shoulder.

"Oh, shit," I muttered.

"What is it?" James asked, lifting my chin up.

"Bringing you into this isn't the only reason he needed me here. He must have known from my father that Abrams whispered the fail-safe code to me. He would have gotten that when he pulled me from the closet. But just now, back when I pushed him, he would have seen that I have the map he needs. Or rather that you have it."

I had given the map to James on the night of our reunion.

"It's locked in my safe back in my room."

"A safe you need to go change the code on right now," I replied.

"Are you sure we don't want him to have the map? What if he's really trying to bring down the council? No tricks. Wouldn't that mean we would be free?" he asked, pressing a kiss on my forehead.

I sighed. Could my father and George's plan make that dream a reality?

"You know he has us exactly where he wants us, right?" I asked James. I no longer knew who was working for whom and what the endgame was. It seemed impossible that George could be on our side.

"I know," James said quietly.

I was petrified of what he had planned for us next.

· · ·

The next couple of days went by without incident. I hadn't seen George since our meeting in the garden, and James's duty as bodyguard for the elder Harper kept us from each other. He had told me that Harper didn't trust him entirely yet, so his access to information and daily routines was limited at best. Mostly, he stood watch outside doors. Neither of us wanted to risk getting caught, so we didn't attempt to see each other. We both knew George had been playing us, and we didn't want to do anything else that might put us further in danger.

At least not yet. Not till we had to. Every morning, as the sun broke through my sleep, a rush of gratitude filled my soul. I was eternally grateful for another day where the world didn't fall down around us. Another day of knowing James was still out there. Another day of knowing that he knew I was still out there, too.

So, for the time being, we had to be content within our memories.

I busied myself with fulfilling the meaningless and insulting demands of Terrance and Richard. I followed after them, building an iron shield around myself to keep their petty and unkind words from eliciting any anger. After the incident with the piano, I was sure that Terrance was more miffed than pleased that George was able to produce results where he could not. Terrance had not bothered me about the map again. James had recreated a fake one to take its place, and for the time being Terrance's father couldn't tell the difference.

Late one night, when I had finally finished cleaning the pots and pans of the four different dishes the boys demanded I make for dinner, I sluggishly walked toward my room. I was thankful for the exhaustion that claimed my body. It would make sleeping a bit easier. But as I got closer to the room I shared with Regan, I had to make one stop.

The piano.

It was the one luxury I allowed myself. I slowly creaked open the door and stepped into the study. I was never crazy enough to play; I simply touched the keys. I needed to know they still existed as well. The piano was my connection to the past, rooting me in the knowledge that some things would never be lost.

I was making a mental list of all the times I had played when a hand came down over my mouth. I grinned under the hand, remembering how James has snuck me from my room. Smiling over how we had found each other again. We had always been able to find each other. He was the only one who would think to find me there. Perhaps he felt like I did, that it was, while crazy, worth the risk.

I leaned back into his body and went still. I knew James's frame as I knew my own, and he wasn't the man standing behind me.

I reached up to try and pry the hand off, but the culprit was too strong. I screamed but it only came out muffled. The man's other arm wrapped around my waist, squeezing so tight that I found it difficult to breathe. He began to pull me backward. I tried to drag my feet, but it barely stopped him. I kicked. I let my body go limp, forcing him to carry dead weight. Nothing worked.

He pulled me further into the darkness of the room. As soon as he lifted his hand from my mouth, I screamed again as loud as I could. I didn't care if the whole chosen one army came running because that would bring James, too.

Shocked by the noise that issued from me, the man dropped me to the ground. I scrambled across the floor, praying the darkness would be my ally. I pulled the velvet drape over me and scrunched against the wall as much as I could.

A hand grabbed my ankle and yanked me across the floor from my hiding place. The man walloped me in the side of the head as a reward for my screams. Spots appeared in front of my eyes, and soon the darkness I was always running from was back.

When I came to, I was on my back. The moon reached down for me through the window like it wanted to cover me, protect me like a shield from whomever it was that wanted to hurt me.

I gingerly reached a hand to the side of my head. My fingers came back wet and bloody. With a groan, I sat up. It was only a matter of seconds before I threw up everything I had in my stomach. I wasn't going anywhere anytime soon.

"Wipe that blood off your face, girl."

Terrance.

He stood before me. Above me.

"What the hell do you want?" I asked, forcing the fear down somewhere deep inside me. Hoping, praying, that it would stay hidden. I was pretty sure my life depended on it.

"Is that how you talk to a man? Is that how you talk to your master?" he leered.

"I don't see either," I spat. Terrance opened his mouth to berate me, but I cut him off. "What are you going to do? Tell your daddy on me? I don't think he'd like how you treat your toys."

I had to keep him talking. Robert and my father had been right. There were some weapons more powerful than a gun. The longer I talked, the longer I lived. The longer I could wait for someone to find us.

Of course, a gun would have been pretty helpful in this moment, too.

"Why do you think my father got you for me? It's all pretty clear what he means for me to do with you. And I'll do so much better at the job than he did. You know how much I've despised that man? And here he bought you for me because of what you can do and didn't even tell me." Terrance laughed bitterly. "Maybe he didn't buy you for me after all. Maybe he wants you for himself."

"What are you talking about?" I asked, glancing around the room for something, anything I could use to attack him.

"But *he* told me. *He's* always telling me things. I heard about how they were going to get rid of you. The council. They were going to say you ran off into the big, bad woods. And when you never came back, they would tell your people the Isolationists got you."

What I could do. So he knew that I could give birth without dying. Bile ran up my throat, and I wanted to throw up again. Had his father purchased me to continue his line? Was I meant for him or his sons? And did that mean Regan was like me as well? Wasn't it all pointless now that the whole damn world was falling apart?

"Who told you? You said your father didn't, so who?" I asked.

"There isn't anything that goes on here that he doesn't know about," he replied, taking a step toward me.

I scrambled a few feet away from him using my elbows. The rug burned painfully against my skin. "So, what? You're here to seduce me? Doing a pretty shit job," I challenged, looking desperately toward the door.

James. He had seen this. Which meant he would know. He would come for me. I just had to stall and give him time.

"I don't need your permission," Terrance said, bending forward and grabbing one of my ankles. With a growl, he yanked me across the floor toward him. I yelped, trying in vain to claw my nails into the ground for traction.

Terrance was on top of me in a matter of seconds. His breath whipped me in the face, and I could faintly detect the smell of shine on his lips. I squirmed and thrashed, but he was so damn heavy. I curled my arms around him and clutched my hands into fists. I hit him as hard and as long as I could. Terrance reached back a hand and slapped me brutally across the face. My mouth tasted of blood.

"You think you can walk in here and not pay a price for the freedom we gave you?" he grunted.

Freedom? He, or his kind, had never even let us say the word. I screamed again. I screamed for the girl I found stabbed, bleeding out in a closet as Henry and I ran from the council. I screamed for Louisa. I screamed for Stephanie. I screamed for myself. I screamed with everything I had inside of me.

His hand clamped over my mouth, silencing me once more.

I grabbed the edge of his hand using my lower teeth and bit down hard. He cursed and pulled away. I had just enough time to scream again before he brought back his bloody hand not over my mouth, but wrapped around my throat. I moved my hands from his back to his wrist, pulling with all my might.

I could see the blackness dancing around the edges of my eyes.

It was calling for me once again.

Waiting.

Predator.

Prey.

But I couldn't let it take me, because if I did, I was pretty sure I was never coming back from it.

"You were brought here for one reason and one reason only. And it's about time you start paying up. It doesn't have to be like this, girl. It could be so much nicer," he whispered.

My vision blurred again. And then it was no longer Terrance who was holding me down but George.

You don't actually think you can refuse me, do you?

I can have whatever of yours that I want.

You're more foolish than the rest of the girls if you think you have any say in what happens to you here.

Now, now, Tessie, stop fighting and I will let you go.

George. He had been the one to tell Terrance. But why? How did this play into his plan?

Blackness clouded my vision. If I just stopped, gave up, shut down, would he let me go? I felt myself go still. I looked back up at the moon shining through the window, except the moon was no longer there. A cloud had covered it against its will. Only shadows remained, and I felt them running over my body without permission. They pulled my shirt off over my head, not bothering to apologize as my head hit the ground with a thud. They began to unbutton my skirt, tugging it off me, cursing when it got stuck on my ankles.

It would be over soon. He promised that it would. If I gave up, he promised I would be all right.

Just like the other Tess.

My namesake.

Except she wasn't all right. Not ever again.

No.

No.

No.

NO!

I screamed again and began to twist and turn my body as violently as I could. I punched the side of his head with as much strength as I could muster. Terrance's hands grabbed onto my wrists and pinned them to the ground. I lifted a knee into his groin, and he rolled over, holding onto himself and moaning.

With a grunt, I managed to get to my feet. Terrance was

quick. He was already pulling himself up on his knees. I grabbed a vase from the mantle and, whipping it back, let it slash across his face. He cried out in pain.

I had to move. Now.

I didn't know where I would go, but I started running through the hall in nothing but my cotton slip. I didn't get very far. Terrance tackled me to the ground before I got ten feet, knocking me down face-first. He grabbed a clump of my hair and shoved my forehead into the marble floor. Then he flipped me around, his knees pinning my arms. "You are a pathetic excuse for a human being," I howled, angry tears streaming down my cheeks.

Terrance leaned back and grinned. Sadistic. I turned my head to the side to escape his sloppy kiss. That was when I saw the lamp had fallen over from the hallway table during our scuffle. The second Terrance took the pressure off my arms so he could adjust himself, I snatched the lamp.

With a guttural roar, I hit him in the head. I hit him over and over and over again.

I didn't stop. Not when his body went limp. Not when he fell to the floor. I kept hitting.

It was only when his blood splattered onto my cheek that I ceased. I looked down at Terrance's face, shocked that it was no longer recognizable. I lay back and tried to catch my breath. I brought both hands to my face and sobbed.

"What did you do?" a girl's small voice squeaked.

I managed to pull my hands away from my face long enough to see Regan standing above me. The sight of her caused me to start crying all over again. How long after he was done with me would he have waited before going after her? Did she even know it was wrong what he would take from her?

When had men been told this was all right?

When had this become acceptable?

"Is he dead?" she asked, slowly backing away from the body.

"Yes, he's dead," I replied, my voice hard, certain.

"Murderer!" Regan screamed at the top of her lungs.

I was doomed.

Chapter 29

Drawn by a combination of my screams and Regan's cry, a slew of chosen ones broke down the door to the Harper living quarters. When they entered, the normally stoic chosen ones, creatures built to keep their emotions at bay, stared at me in shock.

I, a girl in nothing more than a tattered slip, had killed Terrance Harper—son of the head creator of the council itself. Grandson of Abrams. There would be no arguing my way out of it. No explaining that it was he who attacked me. The council never cared what I had to say anyway. I was a natural. Despite trying to decide every aspect of my life, they had never bothered to ask my opinion about anything. They had locked my people away, waiting for us to die, and in some cases, when their patience ran out, killed us themselves. I was surprised one of the guards didn't snap my neck right then and there.

I held my head straight as I walked to my would-be

jailers. I didn't feel ashamed of wearing nothing but my torn slip. I didn't glare at Regan, who sat simpering in the corner. I only felt pity for her. She had no idea what I had saved her from; she didn't know she could be saved from such a fate. She didn't have the people in her life that I had had. I had been blessed with people who told me it was okay to fight back.

When I had a daughter, I would make sure she knew.

That was the only time I hesitated on the long walk to the center of the council itself. A daughter. It was the first time I had ever realized that I might want a daughter one day. I might want a future that I could help make better.

But I would never see it.

There was no getting out of this.

As they shoved me into a small room with nothing but a wooden table and chair, I waited for the remorse. The guilt. But I didn't feel any of it. I placed my hand against the chair, and I remembered the start of my story, the events that led me to this very moment.

When the door opened, I didn't know who I expected, but it certainly wasn't Mr. Harper himself. The leader of the council. The father of the boy I had killed. It was odd to see him in person. I had only ever glimpsed his face in the posters that covered the walls of the compound, propaganda meant to make us feel safe when all it did was keep us trapped.

He wasn't what I expected, but, then again, Abrams hadn't been, either. Harper was old. Weathered. Worn out. His eyes nearly bloodshot. His stringy salt and pepper hair combed to the side in an attempt to convince himself it was worth salvaging. He shared the same plump cheeks and large head as his eldest son.

Harper slumped against the wall and crossed his arms. "You're the girl who killed my son?" There was no anger to be found in his voice. Just exhaustion. Everything about him screamed tiredness.

I pushed my shoulders back. "Yes, sir."

Harper chuckled. "Yes, sir?" He ran a hand though his perfectly parted hair. "He do that to your face or was that the work of the chosen ones?"

I reached up and touched my cheek. It was covered in bumps, bruises, and cuts. Until Harper mentioned them, I hadn't felt the pain. But now that he had, my face smarted and ached something fierce. "Your son did it."

Harper nodded. "That little shit."

My eyes widened. "Excuse me?"

"I never did know what to do with either of my children. My wife was always the one who took care of them. But then she died like all the other mothers. I tried to keep them busy with nannies and pretty little girls to amuse them while I worked, but they were always causing problems. I was trying to create a better world for them, and they just couldn't keep out of the way."

Pretty little girls? Naturals he plucked from their families to pacify the sons he didn't have time for. If Terrance hadn't been a real monster, we might have found we had a lot in common. Our fathers had chosen lives of service to great ideas rather than to be the parents we needed.

"Your son was under the impression you purchased me so that he could continue the line," I explained. After all, if this was my trial, I might as well testify. "When I wouldn't give myself to him, he tried to force me."

Harper wrinkled his forehead. "How did he know about

that? When I bid on you and the other girl, I did it with that in mind. But things out there are so bad, I didn't bother telling him. Not till I was sure it was a war we could win."

"*Is* it a war you can win?" I didn't worry if my question was impertinent. I didn't have a lot of time left. I wasn't going to let anyone own my voice in my final moments.

Harper squinted, staring me down as he tapped a finger against his lips. He turned his back to me and knocked three times on the wall opposite of where I sat. Suddenly, the marble transformed into glass. I sat straight up in my chair.

"We keep the observation room cloaked," Harper explained. "So none of the unauthorized can see inside." One of the cloaked rooms on the map.

I understood why. Peering through the glass, I could make out nearly a dozen chosen ones training in a larger, nearly all white room. Filled with every weapon imaginable, from knives to spears to guns, the room was an oversized gym. The things I was seeing were impossible to imagine. One man flashed into existence and then disappeared, camouflaging himself to hide in plain sight. Another chosen one touched the boy who stood next to him and took on his appearance. While yet another one pulled the paint from the wall with a simple flick of his hand, morphing the flakes of white into a solid sphere.

"When Abrams and the other men first created these things, they saw a chance to remake the world. Make it better. More honest. Us humans are messy equations. We corrupt so much. Rarely do we make a damn bit of sense. It was only a matter of time before we or something else took out the entire species. I'm sure you've been told what it was like back then. War. Famine. Homegrown terrorists popping up in every state. So, Abrams decided to create a new master race. To mold them into something greater than what we are. That's what all creators want—to see their work exceed them," Harper said, moving so he stood behind my chair, staring at the master race Abrams had designed.

"But what all creators, all people who seek to control the uncontrollable, must learn is that perfection can never be obtained. So, we create only to hate what we created. We watch as the very things we made in our very best image become everything we hate about ourselves."

"That's what Abrams meant. Robert was right. He had abandoned them," I said to myself. I gritted my teeth. I knew Abrams was a woman. I knew Abrams was, in fact, his mother, but revealing my knowledge would let Harper know that I had aligned myself with the Isolationists, destroying the story I created in the woods when the chosen ones found me. I couldn't put my father, evil or not, in danger just to make a point.

"Abrams stopped caring long ago. Even with the creation of his superhumans, he would lose. The other side created, too. And even if they hadn't, after we were gone, the chosen ones would simply turn into us. He saw that in the end. He always kept ranting and raving about a fail-safe."

"You abandoned your sons," I blurted out. I didn't know where it came from or why I said it, but once out, I couldn't stop myself from continuing. "That's where you creators went wrong. You were the most brilliant men in the whole world, and you tried to will our problems away. To cook up some solution in a lab. But the easiest solution is not always the best one. Your sons needed you, and you abandoned them. I'll never do that to my children." He had inherited this trait from his mother. She had abandoned her children, too.

"That's what all creators think."

"No, just the terrible ones," I countered.

Harper sighed. "Perhaps you're right. Not like any of it matters now. I am sorry for what my son did to you. It's odd; I almost understand what Abrams must have felt like when he created the fail-safe. It's strangely comforting to know my disappointment is no longer running around this world."

"What *is* the fail-safe?" I asked, the blood pumping too loudly in my ears.

"I really shouldn't say, but considering there is a chosen one outside this door waiting for my command to rip your limbs from your body, I might as well. You did do me a favor. The fail-safe is a way to kill all the chosen ones."

All the oxygen was sucked from the room. I staggered away from Harper, clawing at my skin. It felt too tight. My father was going to kill all the chosen ones. He was going to kill James. I pulled in air through my noise. I couldn't fall apart. Not now.

"How? How the hell does one do it?" I knew I only had seconds. Seconds to know how to destroy the fail-safe, because there was no way I was going to let anyone kill James. No way.

Suddenly, the door to the observation room banged against the wall. James. He had come for me. We would always be there to save each other.

I took a step toward him, desperate to wrap my arms around him. To make sure, absolutely sure, he was still with me.

But Harper's voice halted me. "I wouldn't suggest you do anything rash here, James. You make a move toward me, and it won't save her. They'll find you, and then they'll just kill you both."

"He's right. Just leave. You can't help me here." I needed him to survive. Even if I couldn't.

"Let us go," James said. "We're only two people. We aren't rebels. We just want to be free."

"That's just it, isn't it? You want what I could never give you. None of us have ever been free," Harper replied sadly.

And then James snapped his neck.

. . .

James slammed the door to the observation room shut, grabbing the wooden chair and bracing it against the handle to keep it closed. Once the momentary shock wore off, I rushed to James and threw myself in his arms.

"Are you all right? Tell me you're all right," James breathed into my neck, wrapping his arms tightly around me.

I brought my head back so I could look at him. Seeing my bruised and battered face, he clutched onto my arms. "I'll kill every last one of them," he growled.

"Sssh, I'm fine. Are you okay?" I asked. It was difficult to find my voice. He had just killed a man. The world I lived in made me increasingly immune to watching the death of others, but seeing the boy I loved kill, that was never something I would get used to.

James's face paled, and it was only then that I realized he was trembling. He had committed murder for me. I knew what that meant for him. He had been created to be a killer, and he had done everything he could to run from that destiny. What he had always feared about himself had come true: he had become a monster.

I reached up and took his face in my hands. "It's going to be okay. You're still you."

James shook his head. He was no longer looking at me but past me. Searching for something bright in what now felt like a dark and desperate future. "I'm not sorry I killed them," he said.

My stomach tightened. "Them?"

"Harper and the chosen one waiting outside the door. I killed them both." James had stopped shaking, his body rigid with the memories of what he had done. He swallowed. "I didn't see it, Tess. Any of it. I think they messed with my gift. Re-wired it when they tortured me. I can't see anything when it comes to you. I can't protect you from them. I heard they had taken you, and I came here. I killed them," he repeated.

"I killed someone, too. Terrance," I replied, my voice frantic. We probably only had minutes before the army of chosen ones descended on us. They would kill me on the spot, but my mind reeled thinking of the torture they would put James through before ending his life.

He had betrayed everything he was created for.

The battle between creator and created. Had it always existed?

James placed a hand under my chin and lifted my face so his eyes could dance with mine. Perhaps for the last time. "You did what you had to do, and I am glad you did."

"You did what you had to do, too," I said weakly.

James merely nodded, and I knew he would never see it that way. He had done the one thing he had promised himself he would never do. He had killed—and killed mercilessly. I stood on the tips of my toes and pressed my desperate lips against his. It took a moment before he responded, but when he did, his anxiousness matched my own.

James sighed, pressing his forehead against mine. "What kind of world does this? Makes us into these things?"

"I don't know," I said. "I wish there was a way to fix it, go back, but that's not possible."

Hadn't Abrams said these very things to me? Hadn't the world, a dark and twisted place, made her into a mirror image? She had found a way to go back and fix it—to simply let it die out.

James didn't speak or move. He simply stared at me. His eyes were darkened by the thoughts that lived inside of him. I hesitantly walked closer and pressed my lips against the scar on his chin. "We're not just this," I whispered.

His eyes began to water. "Not just this," he repeated. He took my head into his hands and kissed me softly on the forehead.

The door wailed and moaned. They had come for us.

James managed a simple smile. He leaned forward and lightly brushed his lips against mine. Despite the way my heart thrashed about my chest, every cell in my body lit up at his touch.

James walked to the door and removed the chair. His shoulders squared and his hands in fists by his sides, he readied himself for whatever would come next. He opened the door.

"There you two are! We got a damn battle going on out here, and you're in here making out."

My mouth fell open. Standing before me was Henry.

The air rushed from my lungs and my eyes grew wide. How was it possible?

"Henry!" I screamed, running to my best friend and embracing him.

"Easy there, Tess! I did get impaled with a stick in the neck." He laughed.

I untangled myself from his arms and reached up gingerly to touch the bandage at his neck. "But how? They killed Thomas and Harry. Everyone from the compound was dead. Who helped you?"

"I definitely deserve to win the friend of the year award," boasted a gun-toting Lockwood as he entered the room behind Henry.

My lips pulled into a grin at the sight of him. Lockwood hugged me. "Louisa sends her love," he said.

"Is she okay?"

"Demanding as ever but doing well."

"Being demanding is a family trait," Henry joked.

"I still don't understand. Were you following us?" I asked Lockwood.

"Yep. Seems your sister didn't trust your father either. I was an hour behind you. When I found Henry here nearly bled out, I used some of the things Sharon taught me and stitched him up. He's the biggest baby in the world, by the way."

I couldn't help but laugh. "Oh, I believe it."

"As much as I'd love to sit and watch this happy little reunion, we have a revolution to start," a third new voice said as he entered the room.

My father.

Chapter 30

"I can't believe Charlie trusts the bastard," Henry told me as I led him down to the basement where the incubating chosen ones were kept. My father had sent the two of us to guard the room, to make sure that once the council found out we had infiltrated their headquarters, they wouldn't send someone to wake them.

So far, my father's arrival, along with that of several of his soldiers, had gone undetected. George had set up a rendezvous point several miles outside of the headquarters. After putting into motion his plan to have Terrance attack me, George met with my father, using his knowledge of secrets, codes, and pathways to sneak in my father, his men, and Henry and Lockwood. I couldn't figure why George would convince Terrance to attack me…except that it had turned James into a killer. And maybe that's what he needed him to be for his plan to work. He was a genius when it came to manipulating people.

"I don't think my father trusts anybody. He just doesn't pass up an opportunity for destruction when he sees one," I replied, constantly looking back over my shoulder as we walked down the corridor to the basement.

"You're being too hard on him," Henry countered.

I stopped and spun around to face him. "He almost got you killed. He knew those chosen ones wouldn't take you to the headquarters. He used you to make the story believable."

"He used me to start the revolution. I would die for that a thousand times," he said urgently, passionately. The fire that lived inside of him was in full rage now.

I rolled my eyes. "While your pledge to die a thousand times is noble, you only die once."

"I know about what happened to Stephanie," he said quietly.

I licked my suddenly dry lips. "I'm sorr —"

"She would have wanted to die for the cause," he interrupted, blinking away the tears that pooled in his eyes. I did the only thing I could do for him in that moment; I pretended I didn't see them. I kept what I knew about Stephanie's final moments to myself. That my father's cause was no longer hers during those final days. Watching Henry die had changed something for her. She gave up her mission to save all to save one.

But Henry wasn't Stephanie. Even the news of her death didn't change his need for revenge. I could tell him how she died for something purer, something worth dying for, but he would never see it that way. That's when I realized that more than his love for her or me, he loved revenge best of all.

And I felt sorry for him.

"I don't have a key card for this," I admitted, turning my attention back to the door.

"Good thing I do." He grinned, pulling George's card from his coat pocket. Of course he did.

Once we unlocked the room, Henry surveyed his surroundings, making count of all the incubating chosen ones to ensure none had been removed from their cases. He pressed his face against one of the chambers, his reflection mixing with that of the very thing created to destroy him. "What were they thinking when they made these things?"

I shrugged. "They probably thought what every man thinks when he attempts to control the world — they're making it a better place. I don't think anyone truly intends to harm people when they go about this, destroy them for joy. I almost feel sorry for the creators," I admitted. Maybe Abrams wasn't so different from me — a girl betrayed. Maybe if she knew love, she would save the things she wanted to destroy.

"You care too much. You want to think the best of people. That's a weakness."

"You know who you sound like when you're talking like that? The damn council," I said.

Ignoring my insult, Henry walked past me and pointed to the control panel room. "Is that how I end this? George said you had the code."

I felt sick. That was why my father had sent me down here. Not to take count but to end the lives of the incubating chosen ones. George had planned this moment long ago. He knew I wouldn't kill them on my own.

He should have known I wouldn't kill them now.

"I'm not telling you anything. So if you want to kill them, you'd better go find George and tell him to give you that damn code," I spat.

Henry sighed. "I really don't want to make this more difficult than it needs to be."

He was right. This was more difficult than it needed to be. George knew me. He knew how I worked. That was part of the reason he had made my life so difficult. He knew I would fight Henry over the codes.

"He's trying to distract me. Keep me busy," I said slowly.

"What are you talking about?"

I raised a shaking hand and pointed it at my best friend. I would love him forever, but that didn't mean I wouldn't shoot him. He couldn't help my father take James from me again. "You're going to tell me what my father's doing, and you're going to tell me right this second."

Henry opened his mouth to protest when the alarm bells began to blare throughout the entirety of the headquarters. I clamped my hands over my ears to protect them from the painful noise. Henry, obsessively focused on the mission at hand, stalked over and dragged me to the control panel.

"The code. Now," he ordered.

I shook my head furiously. "I'm not giving you anything. You can go to hell," I snapped.

"We don't have time for this," Henry warned.

"You're right. We don't. George could have given you the code, but he needed you to keep me busy. He's always playing games," I muttered, walking past Henry toward the exit. Before I could get far, Henry grabbed onto my elbow.

"You can't win," I told him. "You do know that, right? Every chosen one up there now knows the building is being attacked. How the hell do you expect to beat them?"

"We don't have to beat them," he yelled over the noisy warning system. He opened his jacket to reveal a makeshift bomb attached to his chest. "We just have to slow them down."

I felt dizzy.

Lightheaded.

He used me to start the revolution. I would die for that a thousand times.

The fail-safe.

My father was going to kill the chosen ones. All of them.

I tried to yank my arm from Henry's grasp but he wouldn't let go. "You can stop fighting me. I'm not letting you leave this room. We came here for a reason. Now give me the code!"

I hated him. I hated my best friend. He had always been this person, and I was too blind to see it. Henry had been right when he said that I wanted to see the best in people.

"45981," I mumbled.

"Good. Now, hold this," Henry said, shoving his rifle into my hand. Once he turned his back to me to punch in the code, I knew what I had to do. Trust was a mighty powerful weapon in itself.

I whipped the rifle back and let it fly against the side of his head. With a grunt, he crumpled to the floor. I hadn't killed him. He'd wake up. It was something.

"Don't ever call me weak again," I shouted over his body. I wouldn't help him commit murder. I wasn't like him.

The headquarters was under lockdown. The chosen ones were alert and ready to fight. I had George and my father trying to wipe every chosen one from existence.

But it didn't matter.

I ran as fast as I could. Straight into the danger.

I had to save James.

• • •

Complete and utter chaos had erupted on the main floors of the council headquarters. I ducked my head as I ran through the mass of people that seemed to be everywhere doing everything. Like the roaches that scurried across the bathroom floor of the compound when the lights were turned on. There was a group of creators who worked together to pull free several paintings nailed to the wall. I wondered if they were trying to save the works of art for the sake of the art or steal them for themselves. Hidden amongst the clumps of men searching for a purpose were the natural girls forced into service. I watched as one girl pulled on another girl's arm who lay curled in on herself in the corner, crying and wailing that the end had come. Several chosen ones ran past me in formation while creators huddled in corners arguing over strategies and best laid plans.

I had no idea where I was going. I didn't know what the fail-safe entailed, so I didn't know what to look for. I just ran as fast as I could through the halls, hoping to see my father or George, but mostly I searched for James. My father had taken him and Robert along.

That was the part I couldn't wrap my brain around. Why would he have taken three chosen ones with him to activate the fail-safe that would kill them?

"Now, if you want the council gone, taking out that army is the first step."

George wanted to die. He wanted to ruin the council so badly that he would sacrifice his own life for it. Like Henry, he was willing to die for his revolution. My father would certainly have no qualms about killing the entire chosen one species, including his son-in-law and the boy his daughter loved, but George must have lied about what the fail-safe did to get Robert and James onboard.

As I rounded the corner, I practically collided with three chosen ones who formed a barrier in front of the offices of the inner circle. If there was a place to start looking for a fail-safe, it would be here.

One of the chosen ones grabbed me by the shoulders. "This area is off limits," he warned.

I swallowed back my fear. "I...I was just looking for Richard Harper. I was assigned to his family, and I can't find him anywhere. I need to make sure he's safe."

"He's not here. Now move along," he commanded.

If the chosen ones were still guarding the main offices, it meant that either my father's men hadn't reached them yet, or the fail-safe was located there. Or both. I mumbled an apology and turned to walk away. I would have to find a way past those men.

Suddenly, standing in front of me was a man I recognized from my father's army.

"How many times do I have to repeat myself? This area is off limits," the chosen one screamed at my father's man.

The chosen one didn't know. How would he? My eyes darted to my father's solider as he opened his jacket, revealing an intricate maze of wires. I bolted. As fast and as hard as I could. I wasn't far enough away to miss what he yelled at the chosen ones who stood before him. "You're done telling me about my limits!"

I pulled open the door closest to me, throwing myself in.

That was when the first explosion went off.

The bells were back. Ringing so loud inside my ears that each time the blasted noise rang, the sound clutched onto the vertebrates of my spine, separating and smashing them back together, paralyzing me with pain.

But I didn't have time to waste.

I pushed against the door, desperate to get out, but it didn't want to budge. I figured that debris from the soldier's makeshift bomb was blocking the way. I rammed my shoulder into it harder, but it still stayed shut. Locked. Trapped. I thought of all the times Terrance and Richard forced me into the small, cramped room as punishment. With a howl, I ran my shoulder into the door over and over again until I was quite sure it was going to fall off.

And that's when I hit the door again.

I wouldn't stop.

Not for anything.

Finally, the door gave. It wouldn't open all the way, but just enough that I could squeeze through. Once I was out, I realized that several bodies tossed over each other from the force of the blast had been why the door wouldn't open.

My father had begun his revolution, and these were its first victims.

A hazy and tar-ish smoke filled the air, making it damn hard to see. Gray-skinned men and women fumbled past me searching for release from the acrid air. I was going the opposite direction of all of them. If my father's man was instructed to blow up the guards, that meant he needed to get to what was behind those doors.

The closer I got to the scene of the crime, the denser the smoke got. Plaster and marble buckled and fell from every direction. I tried to ignore the nausea that consumed me as I walked by countless limbs torn from bodies.

I kept pushing.

A hand grabbed onto my hair and snatched me down to the ground, flipping me over to my back. I raised my arms in front of my face to protect myself. Two hands grabbed onto the front of my shirt.

"Hello, Tessie."

And karma paid me back for Henry.

George slammed my head against the floor.

Chapter 31

When I came to, George was tying my hands up with rope, fastening me to a railing used by the feeble little man who occupied the office. "Why are you doing this?" I asked groggily, grasping for consciousness.

"Because you'll get in the way."

"Of what? Eradicating your species?"

George's eyes widened slightly. "I see someone has been running their mouth. Let me guess, your other boyfriend? That pathetic little Henry."

"Harper was the one who told me. You know, the father of the boy you forced me to murder," I replied between clenched teeth.

"I really have no idea what you're talking about," he replied, in the same sickly sweet tone he had used during our time together at Templeton.

I threw my body at him, but the ropes kept me constrained. "You told him what I could do, you sick, twisted monster!

Why? Why the hell would you do that?"

"That had nothing to do with you. Why must the whole world revolve around you? You're nothing. Do you hear me? You never have been, and you never will be," he sang, tugging on my ropes to emphasize his point.

"James. You needed me to make him hate himself," I fumed.

George chuckled to himself. His laughter was filled with pride. Pride at how he played us all. "That's why I convinced your father to send you here. I needed you two to reunite. Cast that spell over him that makes him reckless. Throws out the window every damn bit of logic he has been wired to use. And just when he thinks he can have you, I'd make sure he knew he couldn't."

"It didn't matter to you if Terrance killed me or not."

George shrugged. "Probably would have been easier if he had, but things worked out well anyways. You killed him, and James murdered two people to foolishly try and save you. And better yet, he enjoyed it. Innocent, holier than thou James. And what it must have been like for him to know his saintly Tess smashed a man's head in till he was barely recognizable."

What kind of world does this? Makes us into these things? James's words haunted me.

I yanked liked a madwoman against the ropes that bound me. George continued to laugh. As he stood up, satisfied there was no way I could get out of the ropes, he patted me on the head. "It's been fun, Tessie."

"Why?" I asked. "I don't understand it. Why would you want to die?" George froze at the door. I could still hear the muffled screams and groans of the injured on the other side.

"I don't know anyone who loves himself more than you do."

George turned around and walked to where I sat imprisoned. He crouched down so his eyes were level with mine. "That's the way they made me. To think I was superior. It's the idea that became both my mother and my father. And then when I shook their hands, found out they didn't even care, knew I was only a means to an end, that they could kill me with a series of numbers and pushing a button, I made my decision. I would take their army from them. I would let the eastern sector invade. I would prove to them that in the end, I was God.

"And your boyfriend is going to help me do it. I knew once I pushed him to the edge, made him see that in order for you to be safe, he had to let his kind die out, he'd help me," George said.

"I'm safest when I'm with him. We keep each other safe," I yelled.

"As long as he lives, the rest live. He'd rather watch a whole species die to give you the smallest hope of finding peace. In fact, he was the one who told me where the fail-safe was. He memorized the map you gave him. I didn't even need to take the secret from him."

"Your child died," I spat out. I needed something, anything to keep him in that room with me.

"Good. I wouldn't want it to grow up in this world anyway. Would you?"

• • •

As soon as George was gone, I thrashed and pulled against my ropes. Sweat covered every inch of my body, and my muscles screamed in agony. I yelled for help as long as I could. I kicked at the door, and when that didn't work, I swung my feet around the small office, knocking anything I could off the walls. Trying to make as much noise as possible.

After a half hour, I lay my head against the railing. I was panting. My legs and arms trembled so hard that my teeth chattered. I closed my eyes and thought of James. All the things I would say to him to not let George enact the fail-safe.

All the ways I loved him.

All the ways he loved me.

How that love was worth living for.

"Tess!"

Someone was screaming my name outside of the door.

"I'm in here! Please! Help me!" I begged.

When the door opened, I had never been more thankful to see anyone in my life. "Lockwood! Thank God! Friend of the year award for sure." I laughed, near delirious.

"Yeah, I'll remind you of that the next time we get into a fight," he replied, bending down to untie me. Once free, he lifted me to the ground. I nearly fell right back down. My whole body was sore from trying to fight against the ropes.

Once I steadied myself, I explained to Lockwood everything that George had told me. "Then what are we waiting for? Let's go save your boyfriend," he replied, punching me playfully in the arm. I nearly fell on my ass again. "Sorry," he said sheepishly, offering his hand for support.

George had been wrong. I *was* a force to be reckoned with. I had a weapon he couldn't comprehend.

A friend.

Chapter 32

Lockwood held up his rifle as we climbed over the debris that blocked the entrance to where the fail-safe was kept. "You really think James and Robert will just let them end their kind?" he asked me as he slowly moved the gun from left to right and back again.

"I think either they don't fully comprehend what the fail-safe does, or, yes, they'll let him," I replied, a coldness slipping down my throat to the very center of my soul.

"But why?"

"Think of everything they've seen, Lockwood. Everything their kind has been responsible for."

"Yeah, but the council was responsible for that. Not them."

"But how does one take down the council?" A chill was spreading from my center to the tips of my fingers and toes. "You show someone enough darkness, and they either become consumed by it or do anything to bring back the light."

Abrams. That was what Abrams had taught me.

James would do anything to keep me safe. I just had to locate the fail-safe and destroy it before he had the chance.

"I think we're here."

I nodded and placed a finger over my lips. We stealthily moved down the hallway to where a door stood open. I could tell by the numerous arms, legs, and various carnage strewn across the floor that we had come to the right place.

Lockwood counted down from three. As he mouthed each of the numbers, my heart beat a little faster. Once the countdown was done, he whipped his rifle around the corner. When he held up the all-clear sign, we both moved deeper into the room. The lights flickered above our head to reveal a seemingly bare white room.

"Damn it. I think we're in the wrong place," Lockwood said.

I walked to the wall and placed my hand against its surface. Three times. Harper had knocked on the wall three times to reveal the training chosen ones. A seemingly simple hiding trick. So simple no one would guess it. I lifted my hand and knocked it against the wall three times.

The marble crackled and changed under my touch, revealing a huge glass window and a door. Inside the observation room was a series of machines I had only ever heard about. It looked like a violent symphony of lights and buttons, flashing me code I didn't know how to break.

Four men stood in front of what I had been told was called a computer. My father. George. Robert. James. I ran for the door only to find it locked when I reached for it. I pounded on it frantically, but none of the men turned to look at me.

"It's soundproof," Henry said from behind me. So he had made it through the chaos.

I immediately snatched Lockwood's gun from his shoulder and pointed it directly at Henry. A large gash cut across the side of his head and blood trickled down his neck.

"Open. It," I demanded. My hand clutched so tightly around the rifle that my knuckles turned white.

"You'll have to shoot me," he challenged, moving deeper into the room.

I didn't hesitate. I remembered what Eric had told me. Remember my stance. Steady my aim. Focus. I emptied a bullet right into his leg. Henry dropped to the floor, screaming in agony. I shifted the gun so it was pointed straight at his head. "Open. It," I repeated.

"Tess! You can't be serious. What are you doing? He's your friend," Lockwood said.

"No. He isn't," I choked out. I narrowed my eyes at Henry. "You have three seconds. One. Two—"

"I don't know how to. I swear. They didn't tell me that much," he yelled, holding his palms up in surrender. Lockwood scrambled over to him, placing his hands over Henry's wound to stop the bleeding.

"What did he tell you?" I hissed.

"Abrams. He put a device in every chosen one ever created. He told the creators it was for tracking, like the one they put in us. Each device is connected to that system in there. Once they enter the code, the device implanted in the chosen ones will release a toxin. At first they'll feel lightheaded. Then, it will slowly paralyze them. Finally, it will stop their hearts."

I staggered away from Henry. I spun around on my heels and pointed the rifle straight at the glass. I pulled back the trigger and shot. I had to get their attention.

But whatever the glass was made of stopped the bullet from penetrating; it ricocheted off and lodged in the wall above my head.

"Let's...not try that again," Lockwood said shakily.

I stumbled over to the window and pressed my forehead against the glass. I reached up and touched my fingers to it, and I prayed. I never really knew if I believed in God. Wasn't he just another creator who abandoned his people? Made them think they were special only for them to realize how expendable they really were?

But I prayed to him in that moment.

Let him turn around.

Let him turn around.

Let him turn around.

My father bent forward and typed something onto the keyboard. Then he stepped away from the system and turned his back on the chosen ones who were taking their destinies into their own hands. He turned and saw me. I banged with all my might against the window. I screamed and yelled for him to let me in, but he just sat there and stared at me. He glanced at the door once. Only once. He gave me just enough hope to show me that he could just as easily rip it from me. Then, he bowed his head and turned away.

My chest heaved. I felt so much emotion I thought it might cause me to explode, taking down the window with me.

Let him turn around.

I continued to pray.

Let him turn around.

I stared daggers into his back, and then he started to shift. It was a slight movement at first. He reached up and scratched the back of his neck. It was enough to make my whole world freeze.

Let him turn around.

Then his fingers twitched by his side.

Let him turn around.

His head turned slightly to the left. And then he was staring right at me. He rushed to the window. Sobs shook my entire body. He smiled through the tears that streamed down his own face. He reached up and placed his hand against mine through the glass. Despite the barrier between us, I could feel him. Every touch he had ever given me rushed through my body.

I would get to keep him.

This wasn't the end.

But then I realized he hadn't made a move to the door. I started to pound on the window again. "You don't have to do this. We can make it. We can fix it," I screamed. I knew he couldn't hear me, just as I knew the promises I made were empty. I didn't know how to fix this world.

Suddenly, James jumped. He turned to face the men behind him. I followed his eyes to where George lay seizing on the ground. Blood pooled under him. The gun in my father's hand was still smoking.

My father had shot George right in the chest. I couldn't hear what he yelled over George's twitching body, but reading his lips, it seemed to be something along the lines of: *this is for my daughters.*

Apparently, my father did care. Just not in the way I needed him to.

George wouldn't get to decide his ending after all. He had become the thing he feared most—powerless.

My eyes darted to James. My father's action would be

the final proof that he needed. Another reminder of what his kind did to mine. He could only see the bad. I could only see the good. Neither one of us entirely right. Neither one of us entirely wrong.

Robert turned around and nodded toward me. A wordless good-bye. I knew that he was thinking of his promise to Emma. He had vowed to keep her sisters safe, and this was the best way he knew to accomplish it. If he took away the council's army, their power would be gone. We could run without being chased. We could search for freedom. The naturals would have a chance. Even if it was the smallest of chances.

I continued to pound on the glass until my knuckles bled. Robert said something to James, who nodded in response. It was going to happen. James walked back over to the glass and pressed his forehead against mine. Or at least as much as he could with our two worlds separated.

Please live for us. We're worth living for, I mouthed.

I love you, he mouthed back.

His eyelids began to flutter. He buckled slightly as the toxin spread its way throughout his system. Despite falling to his knees, he kept his hand firmly pressed against mine. For as long as he could. When the poison made him fall completely back, I looked down at him. My eyes didn't leave his. I blinked away the tears, furious that they temporarily took his image from me.

"I love you," I cried out as his body slowly stilled.

And as he stared up at me, the light gone from his eyes, a smile on his face, I realized that to him, there was something worth dying for.

Us.

Epilogue

It had been a year since all of the chosen ones from the western sector had ceased to exist. Soon after the destruction of the chosen one army, news spread of the rebellion. The eastern sector was on its way to attack the lands where my people once lived, and the men of the council, fearing for their lives, knowing they had no chance, ran. Cowards.

They chosen ones of the west were only memories now. Except most of them would not be remembered. No mothers. No fathers. No loved ones. That was the way the creators wanted it.

So many gone and forgotten.

Not Robert.

Never James.

They lived inside my mind, my heart, my soul every single day. I understood why they did what they did. They felt like they didn't belong. Science had messed with things they never should have meddled with. By pushing that button, Robert and James were taking the power from the people who abused it. The people who controlled them.

Sacrifice.

It didn't dull the pain that throbbed inside of me. The pain of an unknown future. There was no way of knowing if I would have had a future had they not enacted the fail-safe. The council would have limped on as long as they could have. Hell, maybe they would have found a way to fight off the eastern sector.

That's what haunts me most—the possibilities.

I never would have made the same choices that Robert and James had made that day. I wouldn't have sacrificed the few for the whole. Maybe that made me selfish. I didn't know. I just knew that they didn't do it out of malice, or even hate of their own people; they did it because they hoped.

That didn't make looking at my father any easier. After he managed to get Lockwood, Henry, and me back to the community's temporary camp, I let myself get lost in the crowd of lost people. No home. No government. No place to go.

We had nothing to do but wait for the Eastern army to come for us.

Days turned into weeks. Weeks into months. Months into a year. And still, they did not come for us. Rumors floated around that word of our uprising spread to their people. Civil war erupted. Now that those in chains knew it was possible to break free, they were fighting.

Henry left when he heard these whispers. He needed a war to fight. I wondered what he would do when they found their fail-safe. How would he fill his empty life then?

I hadn't talk to him since the day I shot him. Not once.

I spent most of my time with Louisa and Lockwood. It brought me a certain measure of peace to know they found happiness within each other. It was good to know that despite all things, happiness could still exist. We would still have to worry about her future if she ever decided to try for children. There were still answers to be found.

It's what kept me going.

It was only three months ago that I found the map. Searching for a book in Lockwood's tent, I came across McNair's copy of *Twelfth Night*. I thought I had lost it back when Stephanie and I were taken. Lockwood explained that he found it when he came across Henry wounded in the woods.

As I flipped through the play, I became more and more engrossed in the story. It was a comedy, and I couldn't help but wonder if James would have found the comedy of errors as amusing as I did. That was another way he continued to live for me as well. I constantly found myself wondering how he would feel about things, reminding myself that James died because he believed that by doing so I would go on feeling them.

I wouldn't ever stop feeling again. You couldn't feel the joy of life without the pain, and the joy was overwhelming. I heard it in the laughter of Sharon's children. I saw it in the way Louisa and Lockwood looked at each other. I saw it in my own daughter's eyes. The mismatched eyes she shared with her father.

I didn't know what the future held for baby Jane. Would she possess superhuman powers like her father or would she be "natural," like me? Only time would tell. And for once, not knowing was something beautiful. Either way, I knew she would be loved.

I had wondered if miracles still existed, and I had gotten my proof. Not in the way I begged for, but things never tended to go by plan.

When the map fell out of the book, I hardly knew what I was looking at. Scrawled across the top was a note:

Tess,

I hope that one day you are brave enough to seek out a brand new world.

~Robert

I ran to Lockwood's tent and showed it to him immediately. "Is this real? Could this be an actual place?"

Lockwood ran a hand across his chin as he stared down at the map. "I mean, it's one of the latest versions I've seen. See how the border crosses here," he said, pointing down. "That was only after a battle that happened last year."

"So, this place could be outside of eastern control? It could be a place to start over?" I asked, a lightness I hadn't felt in a long time glowing inside of me.

There would be no guarantees. We could travel to this new land and there could be a whole system of people there waiting to enslave us with their strict laws and customs. It could be a barren wasteland. There was no way of knowing. All we knew was that it was a place Robert had circled. A place he dreamed of us going.

A place to start again.

As we gathered our group of explorers, a hodgepodge of men and women with a variety of skills we felt necessary for starting a new settlement, I made the arrangements the best I could. The list was extensive. We would have to find a boat. We would have to gather enough supplies to survive the voyage. Which meant that we would have to travel into occupied lands.

Only thirty people from the community agreed to go. I didn't blame them. It was a gamble, a risk. But it was better than waiting around. The group included Sharon's children and Lockwood and Louisa.

As we loaded the wagons and hoisted our bags over our shoulders, my father stood directly in my path. "You're going to need a steady hand on your trip. You could find nothing but wild men where you're going."

"I have everything I need," I replied.

"Let me go with you, Tess. Let me help you protect these people. Protect your girl."

I crossed my arms on my chest. "I don't like your way of protecting people."

"You don't like how, but you like that I do. Look—"

"Enough!" Everyone stopped and stared at the voice that boomed louder than anyone could ever imagine. "I have had enough of you," Louisa continued. "You made a choice when you walked away from our family. Maybe you did it because you convinced yourself you were making the world a safer place for your children. But I don't give a damn. You left, and there are consequences for that."

I had never been more proud of Louisa than in that moment. I stalked past my father, not caring that I knocked my shoulder into his.

"Tess—"

I spun around. "I'm done with you," I replied, staring up at my creator. "You want war. It's all you know. It's about time we try peace. I'll fight if I have to." I looked over the people who were following me into the unknown. "But I won't search it out. We're looking for a new world, and that world has no place in it for you. So, if you open your mouth one more time, I promise it will be the last time you do so."

My father raised his eyebrows. Disbelief and amusement flickered in his eyes.

With a snap of my fingers, ten guns pointed directly toward him.

That was the last time I ever saw my father.

. . .

I don't know what happens next. I don't know that I'm making the right choice. I just know that the thing that made the last year of my life nearly unbearable is the thing that drives me now:

Possibility.

Acknowledgments

It's hard to sum up an entire journey in a few, sparse words, but I will give it a try. Of course, I must thank the entire Entangled family. It has been my pleasure to take this first voyage into writing with each and every one of you. I can only hope that one day our journey will continue. Special thanks to the lovely Stacy for being such a great captain!

To my students…you threatened my life if I did certain things in my book. While I now live in fear, I am continuously grateful for the excitement you show for reading.

To the readers…read on! Thank you for allowing me into your world and venturing into mine.

About the Author

Tiffany Truitt received her MA in literature from Old Dominion University. Her debut series, the Lost Souls trilogy, is a searing look at what it means to be other and how we define humanity. Visit her online at www.tiffanytruitt. wordpress.com

CPSIA information can be obtained at www.ICGtesting.com
Printed in the USA
LVOW09s1558200215

427733LV00017B/558/P